THE DS HAMMO

FALLEN ANGEL

MAGGIE WILSON

THE DS HAMMOND INVESTIGATIONS

FALLEN ANGEL

MAGGIE WILSON

HandE Publishers Ltd

HandE Publishers Ltd

First Edition

First Published by HandE Publishers Ltd in the United Kingdom 2010.
Epping Film Studios, Brickfield Business Centre,
Thornwood High Road, Epping, Essex, CM16 6TH

ISBN 978-1-906873-32-5
A CIP catalogue record for this book is available from
The British Library

Copyright © Maggie Wilson 2010
Cover design by Ruth Mahoney
Typeset by Ruth Mahoney
Edited by Kayleigh Hart, Natalie-Jane Revell and Sarah Millward
Story Editor: Justine Maynard

Printed and bound in England
by CPI Bookmarque, Croydon, Surrey

www.maggiewilsonbooks.co.uk

For Mum and Dad,
with Love

ACKNOWLEDGEMENTS

My thanks to everyone who believed in me as a new author and for your support and guidance throughout the entire process leading to publication.

I have had so much support and encouragement from friends and family throughout my journey to see 'Fallen Angel' published, my thanks to you all.

Here's to doing it all over again with my second book!

1

As Detective Sergeant Charlie Hammond entered ward 73 the proverbial hospital aroma hit him. A clinical, familiar antiseptic fragrance that he wasn't at all comfortable with. It was unnerving; forcing him to relive the times he visited Westwood General throughout the days when his wife Valerie was dying. Although he tried to put those events to the back of his mind each stride he took along the eerily still corridor felt heavier and heavier.

He reached the sister's office feeling uncomfortably clammy, nothing she had told them yesterday had been of any value to their investigation and he wasn't in the mood for more softhearted excuses.

Sister Cate Carter didn't seem to have any reservations about any of her staff or any cause to suspect any of them - she also wasn't in the mood for a pedantic detective to start throwing his weight around and pulling answers out of the air.

Charlie felt as though he was choking on the scent of death. An odour that made his stomach heave and his throat gag involuntarily. Why did he have to be the one leading this investigation? Right now a stint in traffic would suit him just fine.

The high-pitched buzzing sound of the nurse call system, the clatter of crockery and the sound of doors banging as the tea trolley entered the ward behind him caused him to unsteady his gait a little. Regaining his stride, he knocked on Cate's office door. The sound of his rapping echoed in his head aggravating and intensifying his already thumping headache.

Charlie met with a very haggard looking Cate coming out of her office just as he was about to open the door himself.

'I take it you've not slept well either then?' Charlie asked as he came face to face with an exhausted looking Cate.

'Slept? You really expect me to get any rest when I am facing investigations about my patients dying. My staff are all suspects in your mind and you wonder if I have had any rest?' she snapped, her face reddening as she spoke.

'You seem ruffled by the possible outcome?' he said calmly, secretly admiring her frankness.

'Find out what the hell is going on here so that we can all return to normal.' She shot a scowl at him.

'Normal? I don't know what that is Sister Carter. Do

you?' he asked matter of factly.

'And I suppose I am a suspect too in all this?'

'Sister we...'

She cut him off. 'If this is going to take some time, sit yourself down and I will go and get some coffee. At least something here can remain civilised,' she said, and without allowing him time to reply, she made a speedy exit to the door.

She glanced back at him fleetingly and caught him watching her as she left the room. She became slightly unnerved by the experience, or it equally could have been him making her feel that way.

'Was it the suit he wore as a uniform or the man inside making her feel on edge?' she thought, not sure if she liked him or loathed him at that moment. Anyway, what did it matter if she liked him or not? He was destroying her and her team with his mere presence.

Cate returned a few minutes later with two mugs of coffee and a couple of sugar sachets, she put them down on the corner of her desk. 'Here, now I am listening.'

'Thank you,' he said, smiling with appreciation as he went on, 'we have four unexplained deaths. We are treating this as a murder investigation. We will leave no stone unturned until we get whoever is doing this. We are going to put someone behind bars for a bloody long time. Forever wouldn't be long enough,' he muttered.

Cate could feel the anxiety build up around him; it was as though his core was burning up. Suddenly shock and realisation about the situation hit her and she physically stopped in her tracks, the feeling she endured at that split moment in time was surreal.

'You really are serious that it is one of my staff that is responsible for these aren't you?' she said unsteadily. She clung to her warm coffee cup looking for security and comfort. 'Not due to a drug error then?' she added.

'With four dead patients it is looking unlikely, especially as they seem to have been administered drugs from different places.'

Cate's thoughts were to argue the case that it couldn't be any of her staff, how could any of them be responsible for deaths of patients in their care, in her care! Yet, Charlie stating it outright so matter of factly like he had, hit her like a brick in the face.

'I'd like to kill them myself if I find out one of them did this,' she thought a little too loud.

'If the suspect is amongst your staff, they will know that their game is up. In cases like this they often slip up and expose themselves to the investigation. They are looking for praise and glory for their achievements, for the attention and infamous status that they have created for themselves,' he said with such confidence.

'Whatever you say, Detective.' Cate tried to take the

nervous sarcasm out of the tone of her voice but knew she had failed, she was feeling very outranked by the detective and very insecure. Where were the managers? Usually the place was crawling with them. She sure could do with their backup if they could shift themselves out of their offices to come and see her. *'They were probably too engrossed in meetings about meetings and issuing statements to the press. How dare they leave me to deal with all this myself?'* she thought, her palms getting sweatier by the minute.

'We are treating the deaths of these patients as murder! You understand that? Everyone at this stage is a suspect,' said a very harsh looking lady detective, who had just burst into Cate's office.

'We have just been through all of that!' Charlie said, staring intently at her as he spoke each word precisely. He watched for her reaction and waited unwearyingly for her response. He was in no real hurry, yet she just glared at him, a glare that clearly said, *'everyone is a suspect!'*

'This is DC Vicky Trent, Sister, she is my senior officer on the case.'

Cate felt nausea rising within her as the butterflies in her stomach gathered and rushed about, confusing the clarity of her thoughts. 'Hello,' she managed, feeling an instant mutual dislike between them.

This was a meeting Cate had never envisaged herself having at any stage in her career. Two detectives in her presence was bad enough, but this woman was just making things seem a whole lot worse. She felt as though she was about to take a grilling from them - she suddenly felt very alone and vulnerable, which for reasons out of her control made her feel guilty, made her feel as though she should be confessing to the crime herself. She also had a horrendous feeling that she had failed in her duty of care to patients and staff, yet she hadn't done anything wrong. *'Had she?'* she thought, *'I've not seen any of my staff doing anything wrong.'* Her head was spinning; she was trying to concentrate on the questions being asked but the thoughts were just confusing matters, she was beginning to feel exhausted.

Momentarily the room fell silent. 'Sister Carter?' DS Charlie Hammond enquired, shattering the silence and slicing tension in the room with his words.

He broke into her train of thought, maybe that was his intention, stop her thinking about what she was going to say.

She looked up towards him, attempting to avert her gaze from him directly, yet appear attentive. She begged her inner calm to kick in and enable her to construct a coherent reply. She just didn't know what she was supposed to say. Should she immediately jump to the defence of herself and her staff? She wondered if this was what he expected her to do, or would this merely confirm his suspicions. Still pondering his expectations, she found herself once again interrupted by the sound of DS Hammond's enquiring tones. Words just were not coming to her.

'Let me enlighten you,' he continued. 'Four patients on your ward have died - two last week and two this week. These were unnecessary deaths and should have been prevented.' He uttered his words slowly and deliberately, continuing to scrutinise her reactions.

Charlie's initial feeling was that she seemed to be genuinely surprised by his announcements, he doubted that the Sister had any significant involvement with these deaths, but experience had taught him caution and he reserved his judgement for the moment.

'Sorry, Detective, but... I just don't get this,' she mumbled. Cate found herself staring at the bare wall in her office, it offered her no solace or inspiration, and it simply compounded her current feelings of emptiness and isolation.

'What don't you get Sister Carter? That you and your staff should be looking after your patients and preventing their deaths?' Vicky Trent added.

'Oh come on. You are twisting my words now,' Cate said as anger and frustration rose within her bypassing her initial feelings of nausea. Spinning the dial on the fob watch that was pinned on the left breast pocket of her deep navy coloured uniform dress, she inhaled sharply and paused for a second before continuing. 'What I am saying is, how can you be sure it is murder?'

'These patients were all healthy, and cleared as fit for surgery; they should have been discharged home within days of their operations. There is no obvious reason for their demise. The matter has been referred to us for investigation,' Charlie said, quickly interrupting Vicky's second planned attack on Cate.

'I can't comment on that Detective, I would need their notes to confirm what you are saying. Why has no one come to me on the ward to investigate this? None of the consultants have raised concerns to me. That, I would certainly have expected.' Cate glanced over towards where he was sitting, she found herself pondering on the reality of his presence and if she would have ever met him in another circumstance, shopping or something trivial like that?

'The information that we have suggests that foul play may be involved with these unnecessary deaths. That would lead me, us,' he looked towards Vicky, 'to suspect members of staff on the ward. You have to agree with that Sister?' Charlie said, shooting a long hard stare directly towards Cate, his eyebrows raised and his deep brown eyes sparkling with anticipation.

'Hang on here.' Cate was getting irritated by their presence, she looked directly at him, preparing to launch a verbal attack. *'Sod him,'* she thought, though she desperately wanted to show them the door she somehow resisted, quickly remembering they were detectives and it would not be the brightest move she could choose to make. 'Detective, I can assure you that there are no members of my team that would intentionally cause harm to their patients,' Cate said shifting uncomfortably in her chair, trying to straighten her posture. For the first time she found herself sitting squarely opposite him, upright, addressing him purposefully.

'Are you really sure of that Sister?' he raised both eyebrows simultaneously as he directed his gaze towards her.

'Of course I am. I was involved with the recruitment of each and every member of my ward team and work with them on a daily basis. I repeat my words Detective, not one of them would intentionally cause harm to their patients.' She was beginning to lose patience with him, he had offered her no evidence to support these allegations.

'Unfortunately Sister that doesn't take away the fact that four of your patients have died and we will be commencing informal interviews on the ward to speak with the staff,' he replied.

'That includes you of course!' Vicky added.

'Of course Detective!' her cynical tone was catching up with her thoughts. 'But are you actually suggesting that you think I had something to do with this then?' Cate said sternly to her.

'Do you?' Vicky retorted quickly. 'Is there something you

want to add to help us with our enquiries at this moment?'

She really was irritating her now. *Who on earth did she think she was barging in on her, making allegations against her and her team?* 'If you want to continue this conversation Detective, I will ring my managers to come down. I will not continue this charade without someone else being present to hear what I am saying to you.' Without a thought Cate folded her arms in a reaction to her current predicament.

'No need, we won't keep you now,' Charlie said, turning towards the door. 'You will be hearing from us Sister Carter, don't get too used to us not being here, will you?'

Cate sat in her office motionless with her head in her hands, trying to make sense of Detective Hammond's revelations. Surely if there was any doubt with regard to the death of a patient, staff would have been involved and policies followed. She wondered why she had not been party to any of this.

The reality of the situation was beginning to dawn on her. Were they saying that she was somehow involved in their deaths? Was that why she hadn't been consulted? Was that why she hadn't heard any concerns being raised?

Paranoia was setting in rapidly; she just couldn't seem to make sense of any of it as she saw her entire career flash before her eyes; seeing the end of her career, yet seeing no end for herself. She really could not get her head around what was happening. Cate felt so alone, so confused and really felt quite sick to the stomach, there had to be a logical solution - something that they had missed.

2

Cate's mind was all over the place, jumping from one daft thought to another, from one psychopathic and deranged nurse to another, recalling the stories she had read about these monsters. She didn't know whether to sit, stand, or pace about, she really didn't know what to do with herself and certainly didn't want to speak to any of her staff at the moment. With her office in darkness, they would assume she had gone home so wouldn't be disturbing her. When the time was right, she would slip away and retreat home to digest today's events and try to make some sense of it all.

* * * * *

Cate was relieved to be at home, she felt both physically and emotionally exhausted, she was confused to bursting point with conflicting thoughts running wild in her head. As she drew up in front of her red brick Victorian terraced house and parked her little black Mini Cooper in her driveway, she smiled as she saw her two beloved Persian cats peeping out from behind the cream calico lounge curtains. Probably the first smile of her tortuous day. She hesitated at her front door for a moment, taking in a deep breath to consume the freshness of the evening air, trying to draw in some tranquillity amongst all the madness currently surrounding her.

She had worked many years in nursing to get where she was today as the Sister in charge of ward 73, a mixed surgical/orthopaedic ward, yet somehow in the space of a few hours she felt that it was all being taken away from her. That's how she saw it anyway. It really wasn't her fault, but as the Sister, she was the senior nurse in charge of the ward. She was accountable for the nursing practice on her ward twenty-four hours a day. Twenty-four hours a day meant just that. If she was on a day off, she was still accountable and responsible for the actions of her staff.

She was very hot on ensuring her staff attended their study days and were up to date with the latest clinical practice. Their staff files too were up to date, she was meticulous in that field. There was no way she would have employed someone who would be less than professional. She wondered if she had missed something, had her judgment been impaired during any of their interviews? Tiny seeds of doubt were creeping in, sown by the two detectives. She had followed up each and every one of their references, verified their criminal record checks and selected the successful candidates herself. No, there was no way she could have let some sick-minded professional slip through the net - but what if she had? She was obviously not thinking straight. No nurse could do this on purpose to their patients, could they?

It had happened before though, a situation she never envisaged being part of herself. Nurses had been found to be giving lethal doses of prescription medications to patients that they were not prescribed to. Nurses, that fortunately for her profession were few and far between, but none the less had been very real and working alongside staff who would never have had the thought that one of their colleagues could do such a thing.

There was Carrie Roberts; she had only just finished her training when she was caught giving intravenous medication to a patient. Stupid girl, she hadn't even undergone her IV drug training, so when seen to be administering the drug was immediately challenged by her colleagues. When they checked the patient's drug chart they found that the patient wasn't even prescribed any IV drugs!

The dose of insulin she was attempting to give the patient would have been lethal and an almost instantaneous death would have occurred.

Carrie had said that she simply wanted to see if she really could put the patient out of her misery. She had allegedly heard the patient say that she wanted it all to be over.

'*What right did she have to act upon this though?*' thought Cate.

She felt ashamed to even be thinking that one of her staff could be like David Waters. He was the worst of them all. She had read about several nurses who were in psychiatric units or prisons after causing the deaths of their patients, intentionally.

She had to pull herself together, there had to be another explanation because she knew her staff inside out and none of them were capable of emulating him. Deep down she knew that she had to believe this; otherwise, the consequences were unimaginable.

All four of her patients had been admitted for routine surgery, none of them were emergencies and none were expected to encounter complications. Routine admissions with expected routine uneventful recovery - all dead. She concluded that the detective might just have a point, however much she didn't want to believe this thought.

She had a funny feeling that they were going to find something that she really was not going to like.

One of their patients had died in the theatre on the operating table, two post surgery in the recovery room and the fourth on the ward a few hours after their return from theatre recovery.

She would have to see if she could get hold of their case notes herself to read the surgical notes and see what had happened, see if they were all jumping to conclusions before the facts were available to them, but she doubted she would be able to, they would probably be in the hands of the detectives. Yet if that were so, why would the hospital have contacted the police? They must have some basis for that call.

Fact was, it had happened and was the existent thought in Cate's head, someone like David Waters could have happened again, and on her ward. The detectives must be thinking this too. She could not give them the answers they sought, except for remaining adamant that her staff weren't responsible.

David was one of the profession's sickest members. None of them would contemplate a repetition of his work, what he thought to be caring turned out to be his view and not that of any other members of the vocation.

He really was a law unto himself, until it lead him to being a subject of the real law.

*****

Detective Sergeant Charlie Hammond and Detective

Constable Vicky Trent sat together at opposite ends of the Detective Inspector's desk, having just returned from their visit to Westwood General Hospital and their unannounced meeting with Sister Cate Carter.

The air was still and falsely calm, giving them the illusion of space in which to think and plan their investigation. The only notable fragrance was emerging from the two steaming mugs of cappuccino sitting cooling in the middle of Chalmers' desk.

Detective Inspector Chalmers was out of the station and they needed somewhere to brainstorm before the team briefing later that afternoon. They had to get a plan of action for their investigation straight, before Chalmers caught up with them on his return and started to demand answers. His desk was always eerily clear, none of them could quite comprehend his obsession for having it so neat and tidy, but at least it gave them the space they needed for the time being.

Charlie was taking the lead on the investigation, standing at just over 6 foot 4 tall, he was often seen as being intimidating in his stance; taking root to the spot when talking and waiting for a response, while appearing expressionless. Those who didn't know Charlie were often ill at ease with his definite closed body language. As he waited for responses from those he was addressing his arms would always be folded across his chest, his glare intense and almost menacing. It was though, merely his way of unsettling people and testing them and their reactions. He proudly received the intended reactions, on almost all occasions.

At 38 years old, Charlie had been a widower since his wife Valerie died of cancer three years previously. His life had been without substance from the day he lost her, the world as he knew it had collapsed around him. Single since her death, he had thrown himself into his work to keep himself going and get through life. He was a chips and caffeine guy who lived for his work, he allowed himself to do nothing else but let his work rule his life. Looking after himself was certainly not high on his list of priorities.

Vicky, on the other hand, was almost the opposite of Charlie. A petite, 5 foot 2, 35 year old, slender built 'slip of a girl' as Charlie called her. She had though earned Charlie's respect in that her build didn't match her attitude, but he didn't tell her that too often. He listened to her ideas and followed her leads when her gut instinct kicked in, she reminded him of his late wife, she had good instincts too.

Vicky had a soft spot for Charlie, that was her downfall. Sometimes she had to try hard to be one hundred percent professional, she had caught herself deep in thought about him on occasion, staring into space during briefings and such like... She could not afford for him to know how she felt, it would change the dynamics of their working relationship to a level that wouldn't be practical. She knew he hadn't dated since his wife died. It was well known around the station, and so was her affection for him - it was also painfully obvious that he didn't look after himself, didn't eat properly and had eased himself into the role of workaholic too easily. It was as if nothing else mattered to him anymore. He always threw himself into a case, like a Rottweiler with a fresh bone and didn't resurface until it came to a conclusion.

Vicky was though a great believer in keeping work and romance very separate and would not allow herself to waver on this however she felt.

'Something's got to give here,' Vicky said, breaking the eerie silence as she chewed on the end of her pen. 'What is really going on down there? Someone has to know who is responsible for the deaths on ward 73!' she said in a questioning manner that was evidently aimed at Charlie.

'Cate, Sister Carter, didn't appear to know anything; she genuinely seemed shocked when we suggested it could be one of the staff,' Charlie said in her defence, almost forgiving in his tone. 'We don't even have the full post mortem results yet. There could have been a dodgy batch of drugs or something. Maybe there were factors we have overlooked that affected the patients' responses to the anaesthetic?' he continued.

'Ah, but they had all been seen by the anaesthetist and declared fit for surgery, doesn't that tell you they should still be alive?' Vicky said, following his statement with a curiously icy stare.

'We have to find the common link here before we start thinking that there could be a killer on the wards,' Charlie added.

Vicky looked pensively at him, 'You were flirting with her.'

'Flirting?' he smirked. 'Sister Carter is a suspect! I don't flirt!'

'I have just had a thought. Do you remember David Waters?' Vicky added, not wanting to digest any more thoughts of Sister Carter.

Charlie turned to face her, his eyebrows raised; he loosened his tie and undid his top button. He looked puzzled. 'Who?'

'David Waters. He was a nurse who trained in the Midlands and moved to The South Coast, about two years ago if I remember correctly. He was responsible for the deaths of seven patients, or at least that's all they could get him for. Unofficial estimates say there were many more, up to twenty-five, but not all the suspicious deaths could be officially linked to him. He tripped himself up in the end, that's how they found him, these sick people can't go on for long without arousing suspicion, sooner or later they either get so cocky with their achievements they slip up and expose themselves or they start to brag about their results, their successes as they see them.' Vicky continued, 'Also, remember Samuel Gates? He was a have-a-go hero, thinking he could end the pain and suffering of end stage cancer sufferers on an oncology ward. He said he wanted to put them out of their misery and pain so took it into his own hands, injected drugs into his victims. Fortunately, he was stopped after three successes. Track marks from the needle insertion point got that sick son of a bitch. Linked him to all three victims as he was the only member of staff on duty when all the deaths occurred.'

'He got three life sentences at Hartwell Prison,' Charlie added. 'I remember him, nothing less than he deserved. Thought he had the right to play God, taking the decision of life or death into his own hands. Thought that would justify his actions. Anyway you seem to know a lot about all this,' Charlie said looking on intently.

'Part of my research dissertation in university,' she said matter of factly. 'So surely you can see why I want you to look into this seriously before we go down that route. What if we really do have another health professional engineering the deaths of their patients? I just don't think that we should rule it out, bloody hell if Chalmers gets a whiff of this he will have Westwood shut down,' she stated abruptly.

'Ok, Vicky get someone on to the David Waters files would you. Get Harry Webster involved. See what he can come up with for us. Maybe there is something in it that can give us some insight into what could be going on here. Maybe there's a psychiatric report that could give us some background in to what kind of person we should be looking for, personality-wise and psychologically. If we do have another sick nurse,' he paused taking an anxious breath, 'we cannot waste a second in getting them behind bars. We have to take this line of enquiry seriously - every second we ponder is one more second towards another victim.'

The mood in the office turned frosty, as the reality as to what they all could be facing suddenly became real.

'I need a team on this case; I need a team on that ward!' Charlie promptly ordered. 'I'll give Sister Carter a ring and get her to set up a meeting with her staff,' he added. 'I will go and meet her before they arrive and discuss how to approach the meeting. They have to know what concerns are present and that we are going to interview each one of them. They don't need to know that they could be suspects, but it may just lay some seeds.'

'Including Carter, I hope?' Vicky added, the frosty atmosphere was beginning to affect her mood, she trusted no one!

Charlie didn't have to answer, his stare was good

enough for now! 'Family and friends, patients and ALL,' he emphasised, 'staff will be under suspicion until we find whoever is doing this.'

3

David was getting increasingly frustrated by the patient in bed four. He would not use her name - that would make it too personal.

All that mattered about her in bed four was that she was being a constant nuisance to him and disturbing the rest of the patients. He really didn't appreciate her waking the entire ward, the staff would all be running up and down calming the others if she succeeded with that.

Well, tonight, he had had just about enough of her shouting out to him and the rest of the staff. She was constantly trying to climb out of her bed over the bed rails that were there for the very purpose of stopping her getting out of the bed in the first place.

Bed four was soon to be available, staff nurse David Waters had already made that decision.

He sauntered up to the notes trolley, David hurried for no one, and pulled out her file of medical notes. Bed four wasn't one of his allocated patients so he had to check if she was resuscitation or not. Quickly flicking through the case notes, he saw what he was looking for. In bold red letters, signed by the consultant, was DNR - do not resuscitate in the event of a cardiac arrest.

Well, he thought, let's put little old bed four to the test and put us and her out of misery.

He had always wanted to try this. Now was his chance. He'd spent years researching all the possibilities of what he was about to do and how to achieve it. He could not afford any mistakes. Bed four was suffering with alcohol related dementia and had been drinking herself in and out of hospital beds for years and David was sure that she wouldn't be missed.

Carly shouted out to David, catching him on his way back down the ward, to ask if he could re-cannulate Sarah for her. As a second year student nurse, Carly had not yet been taught and assessed in the procedure for cannulation and needed a colleague who had been.

'Sarah?' he enquired.

'Bed four.'

'Consider it done.' He smiled, so very easy he thought. Carly had just handed him his first real opportunity on a plate.

The venous cannula needed to be inserted into one of the veins in her arm or wrist. Bed four needed it for the administration of intravenous fluids, her drip. If needed she could also be given medications through it but he knew that would never happen. She would not be around long enough for that.

David halted his thought realising he'd almost laughed out loud at that one.

He had been given the opportunity and he was going to take it. Walking over to the back of the nurse's station, he reached into a row of clear plastic boxes to gather what he needed - a five ml syringe, a needle, a vial of saline, a cannula in its sterile packet, a cotton wool ball and a clear sticky dressing. He slowly, yet with chilling calmness, placed them in a small foil tray. This was a procedure that he was overly familiar with and it needed no thought in order to gather the equipment. His eyes fixed on the syringe as he attached the small needle to its tip and began to draw up the saline from the vial. Calling to Debbie, he asked her to check the flush, the commonly used term for the saline that would be used to flush the cannula, and check that it had been inserted correctly.

'Saline, five mls, expires two thousand and nine,' said David as he spun round the little plastic vial for her to see.

'Yes, fine, saline, five mls, no problems,' she repeated as she continued walking down the ward.

Two seconds later David was on his way to bed four. He started to feel clammy and uneasy with his thoughts; he knew he had to be successful the first time. He'd been waiting for this moment, he was sure that he could beat the system and here he was facing his first opportunity. His excitement was growing at this prospect, a sense of arrogance welled up inside him. He had planned this moment for many years of his life and now he was ready, he had no idea why today, he just knew that the chance had presented itself and there was no turning back.

David held her hand firmer and smiled a sarcastic grin towards the noisy person in bed four, as he inserted the cannula into the vein in the back of her hand. Quickly grabbing the plastic covering, he applied it over the cannula like a transparent plaster to secure it.

He then proceeded to flush it to check that it was working by unscrewing the bung on the end of the cannula and attaching the tip of the five ml syringe to it. He depressed the plunger on the syringe and the fluid flowed effortlessly into her vein. It was in position, the fluid passed straight into her vein and didn't bubble up and collect under the surface of her skin. He wrapped a thin bandage around her hand and wrist so that she could not grab at it easily and pull it out.

In that brief moment he found a new power and courage to end life, to end the struggle of the patients he saw suffering, but more importantly, to end the suffering that they caused the staff by constantly bothering them when they were doing their jobs and trying to look after all the other patients who were just as demanding.

He hadn't just used the flush that Debbie had checked with him. Behind the curtains of bed four and from the safety of his pocket, David had produced an identical five ml syringe filled with another clear fluid, Insulin. He had carried one every day for a fortnight, refreshing and replacing it with a clean, newly prepared one each time he was on shift. He had been waiting for the right time and the right patient - this was his 'right' moment. He knew that, and grinned to himself. The self-importance that he felt was celestial and his contentment was disturbing.

The benefit to him was that he would have left no needle mark. The drug had been administered via the cannula straight into her vein. He had left nothing to arouse suspicion or draw attention to the possibility of foul play, simple, far too simple, he thought as he stood over bed four.

He was pleased with his work; he pondered a moment, asking himself why he hadn't actually got around to doing this before. He liked to achieve something during his shift, whether it was learning something new, performing a newly learnt skill or being praised by his patients for his gracious bedside manner and the devoted care that he gave them, and today was no exception.

He had achieved something new, something that gave him an overwhelming sense of power over the patients that were dependent upon him.

As for the syringe that he had used containing the Insulin, he would merely walk away from her bed with it lying empty on the little silver tray. All as per normal practice, simple he thought, grinning inanely to himself. The other syringe that he had used for the saline flush, he had safely tucked away back in his pocket to dispose of later, just in case someone queried why he had two 5 ml syringes with him. He didn't want to allow the slightest mistake to ruin his moment.

The exhilaration he felt was supreme, his dominance emanating from the ecstasy of his fulfilment. *'Choices,'* he thought, *'it's all about choices, the right patient, the right drugs, the right bin, and the right time to do it.'* He began to grin again, this time overtly - bed four would no longer be bothering him, would not be shouting down the ward and trying to climb out over the sides, would no longer be a nuisance to herself or others. The ward would be peaceful again and the other patients could sleep, maybe then, the staff could finally take their breaks. 'Maybe now I can sleep!' he sighed.

David was anxious to know the results of his labour, he had chosen a fast acting insulin, 'Actrapid'. He knew that this particular insulin acted within thirty to sixty minutes and its action lasted up to five hours. Soon they would all know. Excitement grew within him; the prospect of achieving his lifetime ambition was rapidly approaching.

What would they know though? That an old lady suffering with alcohol induced dementia that was not for resuscitation had died, and the noise on the ward of her calling out, climbing out of bed and annoying him would have stopped?

Yes, that's all anyone would know. All they needed to know. This one was his baby and his alone.

'Bring it on,' he thought as he turned to Debbie and informed her he was off out the back door of the ward for a quick fag. He felt he had earned it. He was part of the caring profession and here he was caring for the ones that the others just ignored. He cared enough to put them out of their misery.

However, he also cared enough about his registration and continuing his profession to ensure that if someone had suspicions at any time he would make sure that the finger of guilt would point at one of his colleagues.

He would work that out later though, if or when he found another victim. He would have to lay a trap leading suspicion to another. After all, one he would get away with but if he was going to do more, he would have to set someone else up. Just for the fun of it.

Nothing could go wrong with bed four. He knew that. She would die pain-free without a resuscitation attempt and not be a candidate for a post mortem. Her death would be put down to alcohol related dementia. He was so sure of himself. Choosing his patients carefully was essential. He oozed dispassionate composure that even took him by surprise.

He had to check they were DNR so they were expected to die and not be subjected to a resuscitation attempt. He had to ensure there was no post mortem to be done on his victims, that way he could pick another soon.

He felt such exhilaration at his work with bed four. Felt such a release with the power he had in his hands, yet he hadn't had to lay a finger on her, not really.

David returned from his five minutes of fresh air and he joined the others at the desk of the nurse's station. Carly patted David on the shoulder, 'All that shouting and climbing out of bed from bed four has taken its toll, a drink is just what I need today, hey, speaking of which, she's been a bit quiet over there hasn't she?'

'Don't knock it,' said Debbie, 'I for one am glad she has settled down, I better go and see if she is ok though, it's always a bit ominous when they shout all shift then stop!'

As Debbie slowly approached bed four she paused alongside her patient who had stopped shouting, and instead was calm and motionless.

Debbie instantly knew something was wrong. She noticed beads of sweat on her forehead and hands, her face had a waxy hue. Out of the corner of her eye she could only just catch sight of David looking intently in her direction. She put one hand lightly on the side of Sarah's neck, checking for a carotid pulse. She could feel nothing. Her neck was barely warm, moist to the touch and slightly clammy. She quickly moved her hand away, gasping and taking an involuntary step backwards. David moved closer to support her stagger. She didn't need a second opinion to know that her patient was dead, but was glad not to have found her alone.

4

David's home life was as organised as his work life. Everything in his little studio flat was neat, tidy, and desperately structured. He had his clothes neatly folded on shelves, all perfectly ironed and all arranged in colour order.

Not a thing was out of place. Books all lined up in size order, his paperwork ready in a tray to pay this month's bills, food in his cupboards lined up all facing forward.

Too orderly and spotless to a point well beyond obsession, an atmospheric sterility only David could be comfortable with. He never invited anyone to his home, if he arranged to meet anyone it would be in the pub or downtown in a café or bar - never in his home, that was for his eyes only. He resented anyone having the chance to criticize him and his home; it was just as he liked it.

At 6 foot 2, he towered over his female colleagues. His gentle manner gave reassurance in his compassion and care for his patients. He was an introverted character at work, he didn't really give anything away about himself or his home life, and they all assumed he was gay. A neatly presented, gentle, unobtrusive guy, working as a nurse who gave no mention of a wife or girlfriend and they jumped to the conclusion he was gay. He didn't allow time in his life to get close to anyone or think about his sexuality, his research into all things pharmaceutical was his life and the only priority he allowed himself. He concealed his true character to all, his public displays of sensitivity enticed all he encountered, many were spellbound by his charms, although he always kept them at a distance.

He was always neatly groomed, clean-shaven, had his dark brown wavy hair cut every six weeks and ironed his uniforms himself. He wasn't the handsomest of fellows, his nose was pointy and emphasized by his glasses, his ears stuck out too far and his neck was scrawny. He was far too thin for his height, and although always immaculately presented and polite, he would never be an Adonis and he knew it. Maybe that was why he devoted himself to his research.

He had struggled with his nurse training, there were not many male nurses when he started out, and he felt he took a lot of dissension from his female colleagues about this. He struggled with the assignments, though the drugs and their reactions and contraindications were a passion of his. He had a growing collection of pharmacological books for his reference at home, and his personal bible was his BNF.

The BNF, British National Formulary, *the* book of drugs, actions, reactions, contraindications and side effects all in one handy volume, became his best friend! His collection at home over the years had become vast and David's working life developed around his passion. He had spent all his working life at the same hospital he trained at. He had moved wards but had never considered leaving the hospital. He had grown a dislike towards his fellow staff, he hated being nice, being nurse David, he longed for greater things and he was waiting for the time to be right when he would teach them all who he was and what exactly he was capable of.

Two of the girls he had trained with, Fiona and Tammy, also worked on his ward, ward 33, a 32 bedded mixed medical admissions unit on the ground floor of the hospital, adjacent to the accident and emergency department. They had always shown a superior manner towards David and thought they were better than him; well that's how it came across to him. Not any more, he was going to use his power and they would take the fall. He got on well with most of his colleagues professionally and occasionally met up for a drink with them, when it suited him. After his achievement with little miss bed 4, going for a drink with them suited him just fine, he was in a celebratory mode, even if no one else had appreciated this, he certainly had. Ha!

David had got away with killing bed 4. He had proved to himself that he could get away with murder, so how about proving that someone could be framed for murder! He could make it so that either Fiona or Tammy were poisoning their patients, but which one?

He was going to enjoy this, bed four was his first, yet since that one he had successfully killed three more in just the same way. None of them had been in critical conditions but all were not to be resuscitated so there had been no chance of a post mortem and equally no chance of suspicion being pointed in any direction.

Now he had to up his game and play a setup game. He wouldn't dispose of the syringes this time; he would keep them to plant on the others. Maybe he could slip the syringes into the pockets of their coats or pop them into their handbags. He knew he could get away with that as their bags were in the staff room lockers. No locks on the lockers merely a key coded door to get into the staff room.

Yet David had been so obsessed with his plans that he had slipped. This had shocked him so much that he had attempted to defraud the police into thinking he was mentally unstable so that he could spend his time in a secure unit instead of a prison. He knew he wouldn't be able to cope with prison, life would be unbearable, but a psychiatric unit where he could watch telly and make out he was daft would do him just fine until he convinced them he was ok for discharge. He would then get on with a new life somewhere else and try his hand at something new.

He had no idea what but his chips were up with nursing. He'd lost his registration number to practise when the cops had got him, had been hauled up in front of the disciplinary court and had told them that he did it because he could and would do it again when he had the chance.

Those patients were better off now away from their sickness and the boring existence he assumed that they'd lived. He had managed to plant a syringe in Tammy's bag but hadn't remembered that his fingerprints would have been all over it, not hers.

What an idiot. What a stupid mistake for him to have made. If he hadn't told the others that night that the patient in bed 15 would be better off in the next world maybe things would have been different. The person in bed 15 was verbally abusive and wanted to discharge himself, nothing that the staff said or did would calm this guy down. David had sidled up to the guy's bedside and lowered his voice to him and commented that he would be better off dead, and if didn't stop shouting and being verbally abusive it would be a lot sooner than he anticipated.

That comment had reduced him to silence and a long hard stare was given in David's direction, who saw to it that it was sooner rather than later. When giving him his IV

Pabrinex that evening he flushed the cannula he was going to attach the drip to with insulin. Five mls of insulin, this was enough intake for a diabetic for a month.

He made sure he carried a syringe of insulin with him every shift, since bed 4. He just never knew when he was going to need it, and if anyone noticed the stocks of insulin going down in the fridge it wouldn't matter as it was never used the day he took it.

David had taken the IV Pabrinex, a strong vitamin supplement, and a drip line. He had attached it to the bio connector in the patient's cannula, turned the drip on and walked away. As David did so, the guy pulled out the drip and cannula from his arm, and ran out of the ward shouting abuse in each and every direction.

Tammy had called security to help get the patient back, but it takes a few minutes for them to get to the ward. The patient didn't get further than the corridor before he was found dead by a porter.

In the commotion David slipped away and put the empty five ml syringe in Tammy's bag.

That was a mistake. He had made loads of mistakes that time. The patient in bed 15 had not been declared not for resuscitation, he was 44 years old and had many years left in front of him to live, dependent on the level at which he continued to consume alcohol that was. David was the last member of staff to attend to him and had just administered his IV drugs.

When the post mortem showed lethal levels of insulin in his body David was the first to be hauled in for questioning. It was then that he asked if there was any evidence against him in particular. Of course there was, the syringe had been found by the cops who searched the ward for evidence. There was only one set of prints on the syringe they found in Tammy's bag and they weren't hers. It took forensics days to come back with the results and clear her name.

Tammy had to suffer the humiliation of police questioning, being detained in a cell overnight and being thought of as a murderer by her colleagues and her patients.

David hadn't worn his gloves when attending to the patient in bed 15, so cocksure of himself that he had overlooked one basic health and safety issue. The cops had him banged to rights before he could convince them he was too mad for prison.

David never returned to a life in the real world, the life he had promised himself he would once again have. He ended his days in Manson Prison, in the infirmary. He had complained of stomach pains to get himself admitted to the hospital wing. He had conned the nurse there into going and getting him some painkillers and then he stole insulin, a syringe and a needle from the store room when her back was turned.

When she came back, he requested to go to the bathroom

for a shower saying it may ease his stomach pains in the warm water. Once in the shower, he proceeded to inject himself with a lethal dose of the insulin. He knew even when he was found she would have to get help to get him out the shower before resuscitating him and also knew that by that time, it would be too late and he would be dead. By the time the nurse checked up on him it was too late to revive him but an attempt had to be made, even though they all knew it was too late to save him. The syringe and empty insulin vial were lying at his side giving them a clear indication of the overdose he had given himself.

He finished himself off with the dignity he afforded his victims, none.

5

Cate loved Molly and Harry, they were her life, along with ward 73 and Irene, her trusted housekeeper. Living by herself, Cate never actually felt that she was alone, with her two adorable feline buddies at her side. They were always there to welcome her, and always pleased to see her. They raised her mood in an instant however hard or stressful her day had been. She could depend on them to be there for her unconditionally and provide her with the company she secretly so desperately craved.

Today certainly was the exception, the stress she was feeling was unbearable. How could she, Sister Cate Carter, have possibly employed someone who turned out to be killing their patients?

If this was the case, how on earth had this happened? How could she have been duped by someone? Before tonight, she had been sure that she was a good judge of character. Now she was not so sure. She was totally doubting herself and questioning her judgement ability.

Molly and Harry, true to form, were at the front door by the time Cate reached it and put her key in the lock. A pile of letters sat on her inner mat, they were still there because Irene hadn't been in today.

Irene ran Cate's home and Cate ran the ward. That's how life had panned out for Cate after throwing herself into her work for the past few years. She wasn't stopping to think about getting herself a personal life, she really wasn't ready to take that chance. Cate had learnt to be content with a single life, her music and her extensive collection of books, preferring to share her evenings with a bottle of red wine and a captivating novel.

At 32 she knew that she should really be out enjoying herself and socialising. She had chosen to give frivolous socialising and dating a wide berth since Gareth - who she had caught one night in bed with their neighbour. Cate hadn't even given him a chance to speak before shouting him out of her house, she just didn't want to hear anything he had to say. He tried the usual bouquets of flowers, calling her constantly, rash declarations of love and more flowers. Cate was not the forgiving type and Gareth was history, along with her aspirations of a love life.

Cate plonked herself on the cream leather corner sofa and sank into its voluptuous luxury. She threw her feet up and awaited Molly and Harry who were both close behind her. She kept their nails clipped so that there was never any chance of damage to her prized furnishings and sure enough up they jumped to join her for their evening cuddles.

After a few minutes fussing her feline friends, Cate made herself a mug of tea and returned to the temporary sanctuary of the sofa to try to sift through the events of the day. She had to think how to make sense of it all. Reaching for the stereo remote she flicked on the radio and searched through a few channels until one took her fancy. She was in dire need of some soothing background music, hoping that this would enable her mind to clear itself of its confusion, even if it was only a temporary solution.

The tranquillity of her personal sanctuary was quickly disturbed by a harsh ringing tone, the two cats immediately leapt from her lap, disgruntled at the unwelcome disturbance of the phone ringing. It was DS Charlie Hammond who, for the second time that day, was responsible for interrupting her. The voice on the other end of the phone was asking her to call a meeting, so all staff could be officially informed of the investigation into clinical practice on their ward.

'10.30 am sharp!' he advised her, all members of her team were to be there for his address. He offered her no choice, no conversational interaction and no discussion in the matter.

She couldn't even begin to think how she was going to explain things to them. They would be questioning each other, and most of all her. Cate's integrity and professional ability would be withdrawn and any respect they had for her, she felt would vanish in an instant. After all, she was accountable for the actions of her staff; she just never anticipated being this accountable.

She now had an emergency staff meeting to prepare for, and it was already early evening. Not only had she to think about what she was going to tell her staff, how exactly she could phrase everything, but had to contact each and every one of them to request their attendance. She knew she needed to rest but her mind was all over the place and she just couldn't settle.

*****

Cate realised she must have dozed off when she woke at 5 am with a pain in her left shoulder, her papers and notes strewn all over. At first she thought that she must have fallen asleep for just an hour or two at most, but then she realised the time. Her two cats were curled up on her feet. Her head felt like it was going to burst, but she was going to have to get herself showered and ready to face another day. She was due on shift at 7.30 am and wanted to be early just in case her *favourite* detectives put in a dawn appearance to take her by surprise. She really didn't want to give them any leeway for further accusations or criticism of her, her ward or her staff.

Cate had made many calls that evening whilst still sitting in her darkened lounge, she'd put a little table lamp on, at the corner of the sofa, generating just sufficient light for her to read her list of staff phone numbers and focus on the digits of the phone dial.

It certainly hadn't made her feel very good having to ring her entire team and insist that they attend a meeting especially as she hadn't given any one of them an adequate reason for doing so.

In front of her, Cate had the photocopies of the staff duty rota for the past month. DS Hammond had requested that she let them have these copies first thing in the morning. Cate had already ascertained that there was no pattern of staff on shift and deaths of patients. If DS Hammond thought he could find a link, then good luck to him.

The trust that she'd built up with her team was fading by the second. *Trust? What the hell was trust?* Whatever it was, she had a great lack of it tonight she thought. DS Charlie Hammond had seen to that.

This was the stuff of nightmares. Even in her worst nightmare she wouldn't have come across such an absurd situation as she found herself in tonight. Four unexplained deaths on her ward and the finger of suspicion pointing at her and her staff by the police!

Whatever next?

She knew that when DS Hammond turned up at their ward meeting, his appearance would definitely upset her team's stability. It was just the unimaginable, rapidly turning in to reality.

6

Staff Nurse Sally Mears had found herself a lovely modern two bedroomed flat about five minutes' walk from the hospital. In a block of six, her haven was on the first floor with a clear view over the city, through an enormous picture window at the end of her lounge room. Maybe the rent was a little higher than she would have liked to pay but she really did love it. It was somewhere she could call home and hide away safely.

She felt that the benefit of being so close to work and not having to spend time travelling to and fro from Westwood General Hospital outweighed the high rent. The walk to work would be enjoyable, as long as it wasn't raining, it would give her time to unwind after a busy shift as she strolled home, embracing the freedom of the fresh air around her. Sally loved her job as staff nurse on ward 73 and was optimistic for her future career progression at Westwood General. In her mind this was a long term career move for her. She desperately needed this stability in her life.

To cover the rent comfortably, she would need to have a new flat mate. Marie had gone travelling for a few months and left her in need of alternative company at home. Sally knew that Marie would return, but in the meantime, she really had to find someone else to share with her. It wasn't just the issue of the rent; she just wouldn't cope living alone, thanks to her learned dependency on Marie. The two of them had been inseparable. Recently Sally had felt that Marie had become increasingly domineering towards her. They had spent all their leisure time together - neither seeking nor seemingly requiring other friends to interrupt their sometimes stifling and incestuously close bond.

Sally needed some personal space, just for a while, to explore life on her own. Just to see what it would be like, though in actuality she really couldn't cope without Marie. They both realised they were far too reliant on each other as they had shared a flat since leaving home.

This was the first time Sally was going to have to experience living without her, daunting, but she knew it had to be done. They were far too dependent upon each other and needed to start leading their separate lives.

The staff notice boards in the hospital were always full of adverts for this and that, flat shares, cars for sale and of course, the obligatory study days and lectures. Sally had advertised for a flat mate by posting an ad on the boards and on the first day that she had put the advert up Lorraine had rung her.

Lorraine Harris was about to start on ward 73, as their new staff nurse. They immediately hit it off, chatting away during Lorraine's initial phone call to her enquiring about the flat.

Sally knew that Lorraine's presence for the few months that Marie was away would be great as she wasn't looking to replace Marie - she could never do that, though the extra money would help pay her rent, give her some company and a drinking buddy until Marie returned from her travels.

Sally thought that Lorraine appeared down-to-earth, she was an imperfect size fourteen and her hips were disproportionate to the shape and size of the rest of her body. Sally thought her facial features were pretty, her high cheek bones especially. She had long dark brown hair, which curled naturally to aid her femininity.

Sally on the other hand was rather flat chested and boyish in her features. She always had her highlighted blonde hair tied up in a ponytail, and she liked her skin to appear sunkissed. The latter cost her regular time at the beauty salon with sunbeds but she was fanatical about the upkeep of her tan. Sally loved nothing more than to spend a morning at the salon relaxing whilst being thoroughly spoilt with her beauty treatments.

Sally and Lorraine got on famously, like sisters in fact, and that pleased Sally enormously. She missed Marie, and if having Lorraine around helped her get through the time without her, then that could only be of benefit to her. Maybe they would all be able to stay in the flat together once Marie returned; only time would tell how that one would work out. If indeed Sally and Marie wanted to live together again after both had experienced changes in their lives.

Lorraine needed somewhere she could call home and immediately felt comfortable with Sally, she too wanted or rather needed a mate as well as someone to share a flat with. She had left her family and friends several hundred miles away to take up the offer of this post on ward 73, Lorraine needed somewhere she felt safe for her first experience after leaving home. To feel secure and loved was essential to her and making this move was her way of attempting to fill the emptiness that she had felt inside for the past few years.

The only concern that popped into her head was the issue of them working together as well as living together. If the two of them worked at this surely they could avoid turning this into an issue. They would have to learn that they had to leave professional issues behind at work and make it a rule not to discuss them at home.

Lorraine's room was the smaller of the two bedrooms but still had ample room for a double bed and everything that she would need. Lorraine had moved into Sally's first floor flat only three weeks after Sally had moved in herself, bringing with her a few personal belongings. Essentials consisting of a few family photos, a big cuddly teddy bear and her clothes were the only traces of her previous life that she brought with her. New things could be bought along the way as she created herself a new life.

Sally had already stamped her somewhat crazy personality around their home, having scoured the charity shops for suitable furniture and accessories. She wasn't flush with money so being frugal was her main concern. The result was a quite eclectic presentation of multi-coloured throws, cushions of all textures, colours and sizes, and candles. Sally felt that a homely atmosphere, such as the one that she had created, was required so that she could lounge and relax mesmerised by the colours shapes and lights flickering from candles all around her.

Lorraine empathised with Sally as to how she missed Marie, after all she was on her own too, without the familiar faces from home to keep her spirits up. She had chosen it to be this way. In fact to Lorraine, it seemed that they had both chosen to live their lives for a while without the surroundings of familiarity.

The two of them instantly became very comfortable in each other's company.

7

'Can you be bothered with cooking tonight?' asked Sally.

'No more than you, by the sound of it,' Lorraine giggled. 'Fancy a take out?' she added as she settled sprawled out on their ever-suffering sofa.

'Exactly what I was thinking, Chinese? A nice relaxing and chilled out evening is just what we need.'

'You mean we need an excuse?' Both girls laughed at Sally's comment.

They had worked the early shift so had finished work at 3.15 pm. It had been a busy shift for them, two of their staff were off sick and the two replacement health care assistants sent from the nurse bank hadn't worked on 73 before. On days like this it felt as though you spent hours of the shift explaining what the routine was and where things were kept, instead of getting on with your own work. They were both shattered and the thought of a Chinese, a bottle of wine and their feet up watching a film together was heaven.

Things hadn't been quite right at work the past few days, four of their patients died in the last two weeks and so far no one had heard anything about the post mortem results. The morale there was sinking faster than they could believe. It was always distressing when there were deaths, something Sally felt she would never get used to. She felt the pain of the families every time she found herself in this situation and was still searching for a successful coping mechanism.

As both girls settled down to enjoy their evening of peace and quiet it was sharply interrupted by the noise of the landline ringing. The aroma of satay spices was only just beginning to fill the air, neither had had a chance to fully appreciate this before the unscheduled interruption.

Reaching over to the table, Sally was the nearest, she picked up the phone. 'Hi?' she answered.

'Sally, Sister Carter here!' Immediately Sally thought it odd that Cate introduced herself in that formal manner. Stunned by the announcement Sally didn't have time to reply before Cate continued. She waved across towards Lorraine in an attempt to catch her attention. She was sporting a bemused expression and mouthing the word 'Cate'.

'I'm calling a meeting tomorrow at 10.30 am - you and Lorraine both need to attend.'

'What's up Cate?' Sally asked, concerned that something

horrible was about to unfold.

'All members of the ward team are required to attend - 10.30 Sally, can you make sure Lorraine gets the message,' Cate said, matter of factly.

'Of course I'll tell her. She's here now.'

'10.30!' stated Cate sharply.

'Yes, of course!' With that the line went dead. Sally was left holding the phone wondering what had just happened.

From the tone of Sally's voice talking on the phone Lorraine knew something wasn't as it should be. Sally had been pulling faces at Lorraine during the brief conversation she had had with Cate.

Turning to Lorraine, Sally said, 'I really don't get what's just happened there. Cate wants us, well the whole team, to go to a ward meeting tomorrow at 10.30.'

'Bit short notice isn't it?' said Lorraine.

'I don't think short notice comes into it - Cate didn't sound right at all, quite official in fact, no, I'd go as far to say, very official, called herself Sister Carter. Now when did you ever hear Cate do that?'

'What? Like we are in trouble for something?'

'No, all she said was that the whole team was required to be there. More like she had some sort of announcement to make.'

'Maybe she's leaving or something?'

'Nah, she wouldn't demand our attendance at short

notice for that surely, bummer, I was going to go into town in the morning too.'

'Could be something to do with those two she was having a meeting with this morning?'

'What meeting?'

'Chloe saw two people, a man and a woman going into her office, stayed there for about an hour from what she said. Looked quite official she said, had the look of coppers.'

'No idea, I didn't see anyone', she paused, 'Coppers? Couldn't be. Well, I haven't heard anything. How about we go into town after the meeting? Have lunch and make a real day of it, shouldn't be too long at the meeting should we?'

'We'll know soon enough what she has got to say.'

'Put the film back on, forget Sister Carter, and let's not let work spoil our evening. There's nothing worse than cold Chinese!' they giggled in unison.

*****

The nights seemed longer when the voices were prominent, and the headaches were getting more frequent too. 'Why have the voices come back?'

'Our Fallen Angel, not theirs, it isn't such a bad title to give you, is it?'

'Fallen Angel, I like it!'

'At least the police were listening, their attention has been

captured. We like it too, it suits you, the voices are happy!'

'I have to listen to them, I have to find out what it is they want? It's like being in a crowded pub, sometimes it is hard to differentiate the voices to separate who is talking and which one to listen to. The posh lady, I like her, she is nicer than the man who speaks. Sometimes the voices all have something to say, some instruction or sometimes they get angry - I don't like it when they get angry!'

'You are no good unless you do as we tell you. You cannot work alone; you need us to lead you.'

'I need to sleep; they need to let me sleep.'

'Follow what we say. You are the one who has to do this. You will make mistakes if you try to do it your way. You have to listen to us, don't feel guilty, it's not your fault. We are your guides, we know how this is to be done. We have to get rid of these people. We need you to prepare. You must listen to what we tell you. Do not try and shut us out. You cannot manage alone. You have to listen to what we are telling you, dear angel.'

'Go away! Go away! Go away,' the muffled voice sounded into the pillow.

* * * * *

Cate just wasn't coping with the finger of suspicion pointing at her ward. She had always separated her work from her home life and now it was all merging into one. She tried to keep her problems at work where they belonged, now this was proving impossible.

Although she had been at home, she felt as though she hadn't left the ward. Did she really think that the problems would have gone this morning? Clearly, they were meeting her head on and only just beginning.

Her mind was still all over the place, she just couldn't think straight, however hard she tried. Usually so organised and level-headed, Cate didn't quite know how to cope with the turmoil she had fallen into. Coffee was her number one priority, something had to keep her alert this morning.

She was looking at her staff in a different light; her mind was accusing each and every one of them in turn. She thought she knew most of them well and was sure that not one of them was capable of, or sick enough, to contemplate murdering their patients.

She positioned herself on a stool at the nurse's station, in the middle of the ward, making it look like she was doing some necessary paperwork. This way she felt that she could scan round and watch them all as they went about their shift.

Though why on earth she felt she had to pretend to do something, she really didn't know. She was already trying to justify the situation on the ward and her newly chosen role in undercover surveillance.

Scanning around she identified where her staff were and

who they were dealing with at that precise moment. Most of the patients were still in bed, one or two she had noted going off in the direction of the bathrooms. She felt uneasy, unnerved, as if she was being disloyal to them. Maybe it was one of them who were being disloyal to her? She just didn't know anymore. She felt as though the patients were watching her, watching them and her staff, everything was growing out of proportion for her.

She really was making a poor job of even looking at the pages that lay in front of her, as she scanned around the ward. She had them all under scrutiny, did she really believe by watching them she was going to witness malpractice? She certainly hoped she wouldn't. Surely no one would be that stupid? She watched them relentlessly anyway. What if they realised she was watching them so intently, she couldn't alert them to the situation, Detective Hammond had made that clear enough to her.

There were three other trained members of staff on the early shift, Tim Simpson, a staff nurse who she had employed two months previous, though he was known to the hospital having come from another ward. Chloe Taylor, who was on her surgical rotation to consolidate her first year being qualified and had been with them there for six months, and Mark Harrington who was one of her most experienced nurses.

Clean-shaven, well groomed and professional in all his

dealings, Mark, without doubt, was heading for the top of the nursing profession. He had been qualified six years and had been working on ward 73 for the past two.

Cate trusted all her staff, she had to, or at least until yesterday she did, she previously had no reason to distrust any of them. The seeds of doubt had been sown in her mind and she found herself unable to shake them from her thoughts.

She looked at the staff names on her off-duty list and found herself doubting each and every one of her once trusted team. Was it Lorraine? Tim? Sally? Cate knew them all didn't she? Left them in charge of the ward and put her faith in them, never once doubting their competence or integrity. She always ensured an adequate skill mix so that the newly qualified staff had the back up of more senior members, or worked the shift with herself. So what had gone wrong here? Here she was now asking herself which one of her staff, her friends in fact, it was who intentionally murdered their patients? It was a very surreal experience. Her view from the nurses' station allowed her to see four patients to her right and six to her left, further beds and side rooms were not within her visual path.

Cate watched Mark and Chloe as they were doing the drug round. They were at the bed in front of her line of view, unaware of her close inspection. Chloe was reading out the prescription charts, getting out the appropriate drugs and Mark was checking her every move. It was standard procedure for a newly qualified nurse to be supervised during drug administration. Surely Chloe would not have had an opportunity to make a mistake. She would be the only member of staff who had to get every drug checked before giving it. The other qualified staff would read the prescription charts, get the required tablets and give them to the correct patient. All their patients wore identification bands and they were required to check them prior to administering the drugs.

For a mistake to have been made at such a grave level it would have had to have been one staff member who made a drug error and had tried to cover it up. Worse still if two staff had checked a drug and a mistake had been made then the two of them would have had to agree to cover up a mistake. Cate refused to believe that this would happen. Anyone making a drug error had to document it, complete an incident report form and have a doctor examine the patient. The patient could be allergic to the drug given in error or react severely to it, it could interact with other medications or prove fatal.

She got up to walk about the ward, she would make out she was checking the patients' charts, visit each patient in turn and greet them, nothing unusual there, she thought. Their charts were kept in files at the end of their beds. She approached the first bed she came to, opposite the nurses' station. Julie Marsdale, 45 years old, admitted for removal of pins and plates in her left leg.

She greeted Julie with the sincerest smile she could muster. Cate picked up her charts and began flicking through the pages, drug chart, wound chart, fluid balance record. Oh gosh, why weren't they completed correctly? Would they never learn!

Mark was two beds down with the drug trolley, she called across to him, 'Come here please, Mark.' He walked purposefully towards her.

'Yes, Sister?' He raised his eyebrows as he replied in surprise at the curtness shown in her voice towards him.

'Mark, can you please ensure that your fluid charts are up to date. Julie's chart has not had anything filled in on it today at all. Where is the record of her drip fluid, her intake and her output? Nothing is completed. You are responsible for this, you and Chloe. Get it sorted!' she snapped.

'Yes Cate.'

'Sister Carter,' she retorted.

'Yes Sister Carter,' he sported a quizzical look as he replied. It wasn't usual for Cate to snap in that manner.

Clinical practice was about to be scrutinised and her staff weren't even achieving basic chart completion.

Mark was shocked at Cate; she wasn't usually so forthright in front of the patients. Julie looked across at him, as if to ask what was up with the Sister. He turned and returned to where Chloe was waiting for him with the drug trolley.

'What's up with her?'

'Goodness knows, just make sure that all the charts are filled in and up to date will you, and we better keep out of her way this morning. Something has got to her today. Maybe it is something to do with this staff meeting?'

Cate continued to walk around the ward saying hello to her patients and chatting to some of them. She hoped she was exuding an air of professional confidence in her purposeful steps. Deep down she knew she was failing desperately with this.

Her intention was to keep watching Chloe, Tim and Mark in their duties. She knew she wasn't going to see them overtly murder their patients, but being out on the ward, visible, seemed to be the best way that she could think of to cope.

Cate's head continued to pound with the day's events and the interrogation the day before. She struggled without success to concentrate her thoughts and keep them in some semblance of order.

Old emotions were resurfacing and Cate didn't like it. Emotions she thought she had pushed far back into the depths of her mind and locked away had returned. Previously successfully dormant within her they were rapidly surfacing. Cate thought about the child that never was. What else could she have done? She was nineteen for goodness sake.

She had got pregnant by a junior doctor at the end of her first year as a student nurse. She wasn't in a position to bring up a child and was sure that he wouldn't want to know. Jack was career-orientated; Cate knew that, she also knew he wouldn't want to support a student nurse that he had just got up the duff.

Her only choice was an abortion. It was the most traumatic thing she had ever had to face, and had faced it alone having decided not to tell Jack anything about being pregnant. The emotion she was feeling now had disturbed her equilibrium, rattled her senses and brought this all back to the surface years later.

She had fleeting thoughts about seeing a psychologist to help her deal with what was happening on the ward, to help her deal with the feelings that were resurfacing. Worries about the cops finding out and then thinking that she was the killer nurse stopped the tracks of her thought process. She had to manage this on her own, in her own way, as she always did. Alone.

They would be looking for an unstable character and she would be handing herself on a plate to them so she thought better of seeking help. She had to do something though or she would go mad! Nothing seemed to be making sense to her anymore.

Somehow she had to keep herself together simultaneously

working out how to keep her team cohesive. She would not allow Detective Hammond and his cronies to ruin the career that she had spent years building up.

8

As Cate entered the patients' dayroom at the bottom of her ward, she was faced with two dozen familiar faces glaring at her. She watched as they shifted their stares from Charlie, to her, then back to Charlie again. It was obvious that few of them realised what was happening or who Charlie Hammond actually was.

'Damn,' she thought. '*They are going to be devastated in a few minutes time when they are all in the loop of what's been going on. My whole team is going to fall apart. Each and every one of them will know that they are suspects in the alleged murder of their patients. The fallout is going to be almost unworkable,*' that she was sure of.

DS Charlie Hammond rose and stood before them, arms folded and began to pace back and forth in front of them as he spoke. Cate's team listened to Charlie in silence. She watched their faces as the reality of it all sunk in, she also noted the two other detectives who also seemed to examine their every move. She had to accept that it could be one of them and they were probably too looking back at her wondering the same thing. Her palms were sweaty and her legs needed to fidget but she was trying her hardest to suppress this urge.

'Sister,' Charlie said addressing her, but she was so wrapped up in her own thoughts she didn't hear him.

'Sister Cate Carter?' he said again, this time the detective to her left gave her a shove.

Cate flinched as he prodded her, just in time to hear Charlie call her name again. Nervously she rose from her seat, and anxiously scanned around the room. She saw many sets of peering eyes all fixed on her, perplexed, all waiting for her to make her move. She chose to be informative but brief so as to hand the floor back to DS Hammond as soon as possible. She took a deep breath and to her surprise the words came out in a confident and skilfully formed manner. 'We all have a significance of purpose with the detectives in their investigation. We must help them in any way we can so we can find out what is happening. It is our duty to protect our patients and in the meantime I ask you all to continue in this professional manner. I ask each and every one of you to co-operate with Detective Hammond and any of his colleagues that come to the ward during this difficult time for us all.'

Cate then sat herself back down before any of them had

a chance to speak and Charlie rose again to address the staff by advising them that he would be calling each and every one of them for interview with him or one of his colleagues.

'The first members of staff that I need to interview are Chloe Taylor and Mark Harrington. I need you two to stay behind after the meeting and I will see you in that order. The rest of you will all be notified of the time that you are to come for interview. The initial interviews will be held in the office on the ward.' He paused, drawing his breath, taking in the silence of the room. 'These are informal interviews, so please do not feel threatened by us, we need only to establish the movements of all staff at the times of the deaths.' He sounded official but his last words lifted the atmosphere in the room, although it remained silent, it was deafening with thoughts from them all.

Chloe and Mark glanced at each other almost without motion or speech - only their eyes stirred. From the expressions on their faces each knew exactly how the other was feeling. It was almost a sense of guilt at being the ones to be questioned first. Silently they took note of the looks on the rest of their colleagues' faces. Most of them looked scared at the prospect of police interviews, at the thought of them being suspects. The terror was evident yet silent. They weren't ordinary suspects or witnesses. They were suspects for murder of their patients. Chloe was feeling like she was guilty by just having been on shift the day Betty died, yet she knew that she had died in theatre. *'How on earth could they think that I had anything to do with her death if I wasn't there?'* she thought.

* * * * *

Lorraine and Sally had listened to Charlie with intense silence, along with their colleagues. As they reached the ward door on their way out, Sally was the first to speak, feeling it was now safe to talk without being overheard by any members of the police force.

'I can't really get my head around this Loz. One minute I am working on a surgical ward, minding my own business, the next I am going to be questioned by the police, a detective no less, about the possibility of our patients being murdered. I wasn't even on shift when any of them died, were you?'

'No, I wonder who was.' Unsure if it was wise to be talking about this in the corridor, Lorraine kept her response short, just in case the walls really did have ears.

Tim caught up with them. 'What do you think?'

'What do I think?' Sally stated quizzically. 'What I think is, they have got it all wrong. How can one of us be responsible for these deaths?'

'My thoughts entirely. Can't wait to get home and tell my wife that I am going to be grilled by the cops! This one is going to take some explaining to the patients when they get a hold of what is going on, or should I say what they are suggesting is going on.'

'Don't you find it all intriguing? If I wasn't on, and you and Sally were off too then that leaves Chloe, Mark and Cate for the early shift then doesn't it. The others were on nights. That will be why they are the first in I expect. How on earth can they be expected to be accountable for Betty's death when she didn't actually die on the ward? I expect they will see me later on when I am on shift, but goodness knows what their logic is here though.' Lorraine was speaking with a rush of excitement in her tone.

'Shit, no wonder Cate is looking so stressed, and what was with that detective guy? Did you see the way he was eyeing her up as we left the room?' Tim chipped in.

'Don't be silly. That's a typical bloke comment! How can you think of things like that when the guy was talking about murder?' Sally huffed. 'Give one of us a ring if you have your interview before us, won't you? Let us know what happens. That way we can be prepared for the grilling ourselves.'

'Likewise!' Tim quickly added.

'Of course, and if we hear anything we will let you know, we have all got to stick together now.'

With that the trio parted. Tim made for the hospital car park. Lorraine and Sally headed for the main exit at the top of the corridor.

*****

Mark certainly didn't relish the task of explaining to Liam, his partner, the events that he had encountered on the ward. Liam worked as a staff nurse on the paediatric unit at Westwood and Mark was unsure if the gossips would already have reached there yet.

How was he going to begin to explain? In essence events sounded so simple, but already everyone was gossiping, sniping, and both secretly and openly blaming each other.

He found himself wondering why the detectives were interviewing on the wards and why not at the station. The mere mention of speaking to the staff had set them off, one against the other. There was a distinct frost in the air with no sign of a thaw to break through.

Together for two years now, Mark was sure that Liam would be in no doubt of his lack of involvement in any suspicious deaths, he was confident of that at least.

Association with the stigma of being a staff nurse on the ward where detectives had been brought in would be enough to unnerve him and provoke questioning from him, he really wasn't up for that tonight, he wanted to put a lid on the whole shift.

He was questioning his future, if indeed there was a

future for him on ward 73 he mused. Tomorrow he quite expected to turn up for his shift and find the ward closed down.

Turning his back on the ward and heading along the main corridor, bustling with the afternoon's visitors, Mark could feel the relief at being on his way out of there.

Two detectives was all it took to turn his formerly amiable colleagues into bitching gossips, only too ready to blame their colleagues.

Who was on shift, who looked after the patient that day, who was the one looking after them post surgery? He was sick of it already, where was the trust the team had worked so hard to build up? It appeared to have vanished in a puff of smoke, deep into the records of a certain detective's little black notebook.

He felt that it illustrated how fragile and shallow many of his colleagues were and how quick they were to suggest who it was they thought could have made mistakes that caused the deaths of their patients. How he wished he wasn't part of any of it. *'Circumstance,'* he thought, bloody circumstance had got him in the midst of a police investigation, and he was not at all comfortable with it.

His head was banging - it felt like it was splitting from ear to ear, bursting with the accumulated tension of his tortuous day. He craved a bottle of chilled water and two aspirin.

The sight and smell of the daylight and the afternoon blooms went some way to lifting his spirits as he exited the main doors and headed for the bus stop that would take him away from all this and to the sanctuary of home. Mark had never been so relieved to see the end of a shift, he just wished he could see the back of the headache he had too.

He felt the vibration from his mobile in his tunic pocket; he glanced to see if he could identify his caller. Liam. He wasn't ready for a full rundown of the day's events, he was probably just checking he was on his way home, praying that he'd not already succumbed to the gossips and whatever version of the story that had reached paediatrics.

'Hiya - just getting the bus.' He was saving his words for later, content with a semi-curt reply at present.

'Great, you are on your way then.'

'I'll be home in about fifteen minutes,' Mark said and ended the call, hoping Liam would just assume that he had lost signal. At least he would understand the stress that today had brought and comprehend the implications for the staff on ward 73. One advantage of them being in the same profession, when one had a bad day, there was usually no need to elaborate as the other knew exactly what a bad shift on the ward could be like. Today was the exception though, he was worried that Liam might face pressure on his ward from the gossips trying to prize information from him about what he knew.

Mark didn't want Liam involved, realising that essentially he already was, by association!

His return home filled him with dread. He wanted to leave Westwood behind him, along with the unwelcome nightmare scenario it was bringing him. Although what he hadn't envisaged, was that Liam had already been interviewed by the police that afternoon and what he actually found was a very distressed man that needed comfort.

9

Charlie Hammond began his interviews on ward 73 with DC Harry Webster who had joined him after the meeting with the ward staff and was to take notes from the interviews. Not the brightest star in Charlie's eyes but a sufficient colleague for the task in hand. He would have preferred Vicky to have been with him but knew that he really needed her back at the station to continue researching for him. He certainly trusted her better to do that than Webster.

He had taken over Cate's office and asked her to take out any paperwork that she may need during the course of her shift so that she didn't have to disturb him at any time. Her office was his domain for as long as he required it. He had a long day ahead of him, and maybe a long night. He would have to speak to the staff coming in on the night shift too. He picked up the phone on Cate's desk and dialled through to the nurses' station on the ward.

'Ward 73, Sister, can I help you,' the voice answered.

'Cate, can you come through to the office for a moment please?'

'On my way.' What else could she have said, he was in charge now.

As she approached her office door, for one moment Cate wondered if she should be knocking before going in. What a thought, it was her office after all but presently taken over by the cops. She paused as she raised her hand to knock. No, that was not going to happen. She put her hand on the handle and pushed the door.

'Ah Cate, sit down would you.' Charlie motioned to Cate to sit in the chair he had been using for the others he had been interviewing. 'I need to set up the interviews for the night staff, so could you ring the staff who are due in tonight and get them to come in at staggered times commencing an hour before their shift begins. The station is going to be sending another couple of detectives down here to help with these interviews. Can you organise another couple of offices for them to use?'

'Ok, I will have a look and see who is on tonight, ring them and give you a list of who is on and when they are coming in. There might be an office you can use on ward 72. I will let you know.'

'I also need to start calling in the rest of the team, the

ones that are on tomorrow I will see in the morning but for anyone who is not on today, tonight, or tomorrow morning I will need you to liaise with my officers so they can contact them for staggered interviews commencing mid morning tomorrow,' he stated.

'No problem. Anything else?' She wondered why she had said that, having no intention of pandering to him or his colleagues.

'Not for now, I'll let you know when there is.'

Cate was decidedly unimpressed as she left her office under the control of DS Hammond.

* * * * *

Chloe was the first that he interviewed, primarily because she was one of three members of qualified staff on duty the morning Betty Adams had died. Although Betty had died in the orthopaedic theatre, she was admitted to ward 73 the night before and taken to theatre from the ward. Even though she hadn't actually died on their ward she was their patient and the responsibility of the ward staff as well as the theatre team.

Charlie's initial thoughts were that none of the staff on the ward could have been responsible for her death as she had died in the operating theatre. He would have to get someone down to the theatres and interview the staff there too. He would ring the station and get that organised after he had completed one or two of the interviews, he thought.

Chloe was shaking when she entered Cate's office, hesitating at the doorway, scared of what she was to face on entering.

'Come in, take a seat.'

'Can Cate come in with me, I, um, I need someone with me please, I don't really know what is going on here,' fear evident in her voice.

'I am afraid that Sister Carter cannot, but I can have a woman officer sit with you if you would like?' he said, indicating to Webster to call an officer and escort.

'He meant no harm by it, and she will be fine,' Webster said to a very stunned Cate. 'You cannot at this stage hear her interview, however informal it is Sister!'

Back in the room Charlie introduced his colleague Detective Webster.

'This is not a formal interview, although further questioning may be required at a later date, but you will be advised if we need to talk to you again. You are free to go at any time; you are not under arrest or caution. Do you understand Chloe?'

'Yes,' she said, and although she was physically shaking the woman officer sitting beside her was giving her a momentary form of comfort. *'She has a warm smile,'* she thought.

'I am going to start by asking you what happened on the morning of the second of April, 2008 regarding the care of Mrs Betty Adams. First I need you to confirm your full name please, for my records.'

'Ok.'

'Your full name?'

'Oh sorry, it's Chloe Ann Taylor,' she answered as her head slumped forward and her eyes focused on the floor. She had no direct eye contact with Charlie or Webster.

'What is your role on the ward Ms Taylor?'

'I am a staff nurse,' she paused to catch her breath. 'I have recently qualified so I am still under supervision here, consolidating my training.'

Charlie paused with his questioning trying to work out her state of mind. 'I have here a copy of the check list for Betty Adams that was completed before she went down to surgery. It has your name and signature on it as well as that of Mark Harrington. Is that correct?'

Charlie passed the sheet of paper across the desk to Chloe. She took a long look at it. She put her hand on the paper and drew it further towards her.

'Yes, that is my signature, Mark has countersigned it. As I said I am newly qualified so I get everything I do checked, for my own peace of mind as well.'

'Do you remember doing her checks?'

'Yes and no. I do remember signing the form and checking her but not the specifics of the checks. That morning we had a full theatre list, so I checked several patients for theatre. I do remember that there was nothing out of the ordinary. If there was, I would have noted it down on the sheet,' Chloe said as she pointed to a space on the bottom of the sheet for comments and at a column at the right hand side of the page for notes to be included with the checks. 'The checks were satisfactory, see,' again she pointed at the sheet. 'There is a list here of what was checked, blood pressure and so on, all within normal levels. The staff in the theatre would go through that check list again when she was taken down for her surgery. So she was checked by me and Mark on the ward as well as by them. We always do these double checks, in case the wrong patient gets taken down to the theatre.'

'Could they have been given the wrong sheets?'

'Err!' she hesitated, 'I guess that could happen, but no! NO!' she screeched.

'Did you notice anything different about her, or anything that was a cause for concern?'

'Of course not. One thing I have learnt is that everything and anything has to be written down. If I notice something that is not right or I don't understand I would first tell the senior nurse on duty on the ward, then tell the doctor, if that was necessary.'

'So nothing bothered you with her, nothing out of the

ordinary?'

'No.'

'Did you see anyone attend Betty Adams that morning other than the staff on duty on your ward, someone you didn't recognise, perhaps?'

'No. Well only the porter who came to take her to theatre. That was the only other staff member. I didn't recognise him; I don't know all the porters yet.'

'What about Hannah Brown? You did her pre-operative check list as well didn't you?'

'Yes,' Chloe's heart sank. She was beginning to feel that at any moment he was going to ask her outright if she killed Betty. All she would be able to manage to say to him at that point would be a one word answer – 'no!' She was trying to hold herself together, act professionally and tell the truth. It was proving difficult, with the thought that the detective in front of her may believe she had murdered her patients. Her head was beginning to feel clouded and heavy. The office was stuffy and she could have done with the window open but dared not ask if she could open it. She just wanted to get the questions over and get out of there. She really did feel uncomfortable being questioned. She was giving him the answers to all his questions so why on earth didn't he stop and allow this nightmare to be over.

Charlie again passed Chloe a photocopy of the check list that she had signed. This time for another patient, Hannah

Brown. 'Can you verify that this is your signature?'

'Yes,' Chloe sighed, she inadvertently attracted Webster's attention who merely shot her a bemused look, raising an eyebrow.

'Who countersigned this check list for you?' Charlie asked, yet before Chloe had a chance to answer him, he noticed the signature was Cate's.

'Sister Carter did the checks for Mrs Brown with me. Her signature is next to mine, see?' Chloe pointed to the two signatures at the bottom of the theatre check list. 'Our names are printed after where we signed, see!' she said pointing out the signatures.

'Was there anything that you thought was wrong with Mrs Brown? Were all her checks satisfactory enabling her to be taken down to the theatre?'

'Of course. I wouldn't have ticked the list and signed it if I thought something was wrong. That is the point of checking isn't it? To identify any risks or reasons the patient can't go for their surgery. Anyway as I said, Sister Carter countersigned the checks. She went through the questions with me so if there was anything I missed out she would have picked up on it herself. That's why I have the second trained nurse with me at the moment. You asked me all this with Betty, my answers are the same.'

'Of course,' he said as a matter of fact. 'Anything that you can reflect on, there might be something that you think is insignificant but it may help us, let us know,' he added, handing her his business card.

Chloe nodded. 'I will. Is that it, can I go now?' she stated eagerly.

'Of course. Thank you. I will let you know if we need to speak to you again,' he said.

She looked down at the official business card and took a deep breath. She could hardly get her head around what was happening. Today had started out as any other, she had come to work to complete her shift and found herself being interviewed by the police. *How much worse could it get, she mused.*

Chloe turned and smiled at the officer, who rose from her chair to leave with her.

Each member of staff that was interviewed was told by Detective Sergeant Hammond not to discuss what they said in the interviews with their colleagues. If they thought of something else they wanted to report they were given Charlie's direct line to speak to him or one of two named officers taking his calls. There was to be no discussion about the deaths on the ward, that way there was no chance of any of their patients overhearing any gossip. Their patients had to be protected. He had a feeling they would find out sooner than they wanted them to anyway. Leaks of this kind always happened, this situation was no different, the gossips would be rife in no time. Unfortunately he was under no illusions about this.

As Chloe reached the tea room where Cate was waiting for her, she broke down in tears. 'That was so scary. He made me feel like I was the one who missed something. Like I had done something wrong,' she stated purposefully.

'I know Chloe but you can only say what you know or saw, I am sure you did very well. They have to ask everyone questions, horrible questions, just so they can find out exactly what happened!' Cate reassured her.

'He didn't really ask me anything. I thought he was going to ask me if I did it. I would have died if he'd asked me that! Me murdering patients, damn I have only just qualified, hardly likely to risk my registration after all that hard work am I?'

'I'm sure it won't come to all of that Chloe,' Cate said, 'Although it certainly seems that someone is possibly risking their registration, that is if it is a qualified nurse doing this!'

'This is so terrifying Cate; I never thought I would be involved in something like this. They did tell us in university about the nurses that have been imprisoned for the murder of patients but I really didn't think I would ever come across anything like this in my working life. It's just a story when you get told in lectures. It just doesn't seem real. I don't know if I really want to be a nurse if something like this can happen and put us all in the frame for murder. I merely thought they were trying to frighten us telling us about situations like this, you know, make us more aware.'

'I know Chloe; it's not something I ever thought I would be involved in during my career either. Once they have done their investigations then we can get ourselves back to normal, put all this behind us. For the time being we have to be vigilant and reassure our patients that they are safe with us. Which, I might add, is going to be virtually impossible seeing as they haven't caught their culprit. I just hope that they are wrong with all this and it turns out that it was a drug error or expired drugs or something that gives us a logical explanation. I just don't know how we would cope if it turns out it is one of our staff.'

Cate looked exhausted, she turned to face Chloe, 'Off you go pet, go home and try to forget all of this for the moment. I doubt the police will have any more questions for you. Enjoy your days off and come back refreshed. Try not to let things worry you. I am sure that the detectives will have uncovered the truth surrounding the events of these deaths by then.'

'I will Cate, thanks.' With those words Chloe was gone. She didn't want to hang around much longer in case she was called back for more questioning. An experience she certainly didn't want to repeat at any time.

Chloe took herself off home, wondering if she really did want to come back to the ward at all after her days off. She was reluctant to come back to work if one of her colleagues was killing their patients. It just seemed far too much of a responsibility. Three years at university and she was ready to quit. Nothing Cate had said to her gave her any reassurance. She just didn't feel safe on the ward.

What if she lost her nursing registration by association? Or if she was set up by one of her colleagues to shift the blame, make it look like she was somehow involved? It really wasn't worth taking that chance.

She would just have to spend her days off re-evaluating her career options. A part of her felt that if she didn't return to the ward she would be seen as guilty but her heart was telling her to get out of nursing totally if this was what she was going to face. She had absolutely no idea how to cope with what was happening around her. She saw the obvious option, and that was to walk away and make sure she was not involved in it any further. Yet her thoughts were apprehensive as she loved her job.

Her thoughts just wouldn't leave her, in fact her mother could hear her daughter's sobs only too clearly, she didn't have to stand outside her bedroom spying on her, the sound of her distress was ringing through the house. She hardly dared disturb her for fear of her daughter's reasons. Chloe was clearly distraught, her anxiety clear. Her mother could leave her no longer; she had to go to her daughter.

When Chloe had returned from her shift at work that afternoon she had told her mother to leave her alone and Madeline had not seen her since, but she had listened, for what seemed like ages, to her crying.

Tentatively she knocked on the bedroom door, then repeated the action realising that her sound would not have been heard.

As she expected there was no reply, she entered without waiting any longer for a reply. Her beautiful daughter was curled up on her bed, almost completely foetal in position, sobbing uncontrollably into her pillow.

Madeline sat on the edge of the bed alongside her daughter, words would just not come to her. She cuddled into Chloe, hoping that soon she would be ready to talk about what was causing her distress. To see Chloe like this was almost too much for her to bear. Nothing could be this bad that they couldn't sort it out together.

'The cops mum, they think we killed them.' Her sobs continued, her words just audible. 'Of course we didn't.'

'Chloe you are not making any sense.'

'Maybe I did kill them. Maybe I did, I just don't know.'

'Kill someone dear? Of course you haven't killed anyone.'

'They are dead though. Mum you've got to help me.'

'Chloe, who is dead? What has happened at work?'

Oh, how dim really was her mother, was she not listening

to a word she was saying?

'The patients are dead. The cops think one of us did it. What if I made a mistake and someone died because of what I have done?'

'Are you saying that the police have spoken to you?' Madeline asked, hardly daring anticipate her daughter's answer.

'A detective,' she sobbed. 'A stupid detective asked me questions.'

'But no one has actually said that you have anything to do with these patients dying?' she needed to get things straight in her mind. 'You should have let me know and I would have been with you, at your side through all this.'

'They think one of the staff is responsible. I can't go back there. Don't make me go back. I don't want to be a nurse anymore. I can't take it if it is going to be like this, I really can't. Oh yes, ring my mum and bring her to work because the cops want to talk to me. How bad would that look!'

'But Chloe, you have just qualified, you are on the first rung of your career. Things are bound to be hard to start with whilst you are still learning.'

'Learning? Are you mad? The patients are dead. What if a mistake I made caused this.'

'Have you made a mistake that you know of Chloe?'

'No. But that doesn't mean I didn't make one.'

'Come on love, you need to calm yourself. When you feel

able, talk me through exactly what has happened. We will go through it together and sort this out. You can't be coming home in distress like this, it just isn't right.'

'Dead patients aren't right either mum,' she replied as she buried her head deeper into the false comfort of her pillow.

'You have to go back Chloe. If you don't go back there, surely it is going to look like you are guilty of something, and we can't have that dear.'

'Mum, I already spoke to the ward sister. I told her that I don't want to be part of it.'

'But you are part of the ward, up until today you said that you were settling down just fine.'

'Well now it's different. I can't be a nurse if they are going to think that I could have killed a patient. How sick is that?' Tears were building in her eyes, the sobbing returned, she just couldn't bear the situation she found herself in.

Madeline Taylor just didn't know what to say to her only daughter, she merely held her, trying to convince herself that she was being of at least some comfort.

10

Cate found herself the next member of staff to be interviewed. Although why he had changed the order of the staff interviews she really didn't know. She'd had a brief experience of Charlie Hammond's questioning techniques earlier, when he first arrived with his colleague Vicky Trent. She knew she was going to face a harrowing time herself as the ward sister accountable for practice on her ward. She wondered why he was requesting to see her again at this stage in his enquiries.

'Sister Carter, do come in.' His face was deadpan, serious, and vacant of the rugged charm that she had noticed earlier.

'Thank you.' She tried to keep herself detached from him and the whole situation. She tried faking a smile as she entered, unsure if she had actually achieved it.

'Take a seat as you are not under arrest and are not being questioned under caution.'

Cate wasn't really listening to his speech, *'this is my office, who do you think you are? Take a seat? Listen to me? Blah, blah blah,'* she thought, though she knew she had to play the submissive role or she would draw attention to herself for all the wrong reasons.

'I understand.' Cate immediately felt intimidated, out of control and threatened. His manner was achieving its aim and putting her at a great degree of unease. She attempted to remain in charge of herself and hoped she appeared convincing in this. Again unsure of her ability to achieve this. If she couldn't convince herself she was composed and totally in charge she certainly wasn't going to convince the detective in front of her. She concentrated on her body language and her posture, she leaned forward to listen as he spoke.

'Sister Carter,' Charlie had slipped back in to his professional role with ease. She was no longer 'Cate' as he had previously been calling her. She began to feel the discomfort that Chloe felt earlier this morning; she desperately tried to appear as though she was calm and collected.

'As the ward sister, you are accountable for the clinical practice on ward 73, is that correct?'

'Yes, that is correct Detective.'

'Do you have any concerns regarding any of your staff and their practice?'

'No, I don't have any concerns regarding this, if I did I

would have acted on it sooner, and in the correct manner too.' As soon as she spoke she realised she shouldn't have said that. She hoped he wouldn't think she was being sarcastic. It was just the way her words came out.

'I would hope so Sister!' he replied coldly.

'Sorry, I meant to say I would act on a suspicion I had about a member of staff on my ward. Presently I have no concerns.'

His harshness instantly made her nerves kick in for some reason she didn't expect him to be so cold towards her.

'You will realise that we have been brought in at an early stage to investigate the unexpected deaths of the patients on the ward. In view of previous situations in other hospitals, where a member of staff was found to have interfered with medications and given drugs to intentionally cause harm, we cannot afford to wait for post mortem reports and risk further deaths. Right now we have to assume it is a member of staff who is causing the deaths, until we can prove otherwise.'

'I understand. My foremost concern too, is the safety of my patients.'

'Were you on duty when any of the patients died?' He looked at his copy of the staff duty rota as she began her reply.

'Yes, I was on duty, I mainly work seven-five during the week to cover the ward for the ward rounds and support the staff. I was on duty when Betty Adams and Hannah Brown were taken from the ward down to the theatre for their surgery. As you are already aware, I countersigned the theatre check list for Staff Nurse Taylor,' she said, looking down at the theatre charts Charlie had in front of him.

'Did you have direct contact with the patients?' he questioned.

'I observed the theatre check list being completed, other than that I didn't perform any clinical care for them.'

'You didn't administer any of the medications?'

'Not as far as I can remember. I may have put up a bag of infusion fluid. To verify that I would need to have a look at the fluid prescription charts to see if I signed for any of their fluids.'

'You didn't give any intravenous drugs?'

'Not that I remember, again, I would have to check the drug prescription charts to verify this, one way or the other.'

'You don't remember if you gave patients' drugs?'

'No, Detective, I don't. We have a high turnover of patients here, sometimes I help the staff with their drug administration, if they are busy with poorly or dependent patients for instance. I don't do the medication rounds as a matter of routine. I would usually be accompanying the doctors on their daily rounds of the ward when the medications are being done.'

'First thing in the morning?'

'Usually, yes. The doctors come to see the patients before they commence their theatre list, or before they run their clinics. Each patient is re-assessed by them usually on the round between eight-nine am.'

'What about the doctors, I presume they give the patients' injections and things?'

'Not as a rule. It is the nursing staff who administer what they have prescribed. There is the odd occasion that a doctor will give some intravenous medication, but it isn't standard practice. Any injections or antibiotics to be given will be drawn up and given by the nurses.'

'Do all members of staff on the ward have access to the drugs?'

'No, the qualified staff hold the drug keys. They never give them to the other members of staff.'

'Not even the doctors?' Charlie was beginning to think that this investigation would be more difficult than he'd initially imagined!

'Not as a rule. There may be occasions when a doctor asks for the keys to go and get a particular drug, but this is not standard practice. They would not be questioned if they asked for them though.'

'There is one big bunch of keys for the drug trolley and cupboards in the clinical room. There is a separate bunch with two keys on it that are for the controlled drug cupboard only. They are held by the senior staff nurse who is in charge of the ward, or me,' she said defiantly, 'and obviously, if they need access to controlled drugs, morphine etc, there would be two members of staff present when the cupboard is unlocked as all drugs in there require two signatures for their administration. Also the pharmacist for the ward will have the keys and access to all the drug cupboards and drug trolley. They come to the ward to check the stock levels and check our ordering.'

'So you hand over the keys to them? Or does someone go with them?'

'No they have access in their own right. There are two or three pharmacy technicians that come to the ward so we are familiar with them. Also they carry an ID badge,' Cate pointed to her own badge that was clipped to her lower tunic pocket. 'If one of us didn't recognise them we would always ask to check their ID.' He enjoyed listening to her speaking, she always sounded so precise in her speech. *'Signs of a confident, strong and professional woman,'* he thought, and he liked that in her, more than he liked his ever increasing list.

'Has there been any sign of missing drugs on the ward recently?'

'No. If I had cause to suspect this I would have acted on my suspicions and investigated it. Any situations like this are always recorded as a clinical incident.'

'I would like to think that, but I do still have to ask you about this.'

'*Of course I would investigate if I thought drugs were going missing. Is he really thinking that I am incompetent, or is he on my side?*' she thought, she was hoping for the latter to be true.

'Would you, as the ward sister, notice if drugs went missing?'

Another stupid question she thought. Cate sighed before she dignified him with a reply.

'Yes and any of my staff that had concerns would come to me about this anyway and I would investigate any allegations made,' she answered with a heavy sigh.

'What was that for?'

She looked across at him, 'Truth is, not immediately. Oh gosh, this makes things seem a whole lot worse doesn't it?'

'Not necessarily, we just have to be sure we are covering all the right angles. So how would you recognise that drugs were missing?'

'*What an idiot, the cupboards would be empty wouldn't they; the stocks would be noticeably low.*' Fortunately she stopped herself from saying this out loud and answered instead with a more practical answer. 'Well, we regularly order drugs and a record of what we order and receive is kept on the ward. There is a box file especially for these records. If there was cause for concern these records could be checked to see what had been ordered.'

'Is there a daily record of drugs that are used by patients?'

Cate gave him an empty look.

'Something that will match the stock sheets?' he said coyly, thinking he had just said something totally stupid!

'Oh, yes, of course there is!' she reassured him.

'Right. So you have absolutely no concerns about missing drugs on the ward?' He was looking directly at her, was this a technique he had learnt over the years or was she now being paranoid?

Who did he think she was? Did he think her so unprofessional she wouldn't act on missing drugs? Or was he trying to trip her up? She had to raise her guard with him, before he managed to twist her thoughts as well as her words but this time he was right.

'No I don't,' she replied calmly after some further reflection.

'What about the morphine in the controlled drug cupboard?'

'What about it?'

'Would you notice if that was missing?'

'Of course. That would be much easier to detect. Those drugs are counted each time they are administered. The number of tablets is recorded in a book, when someone is given a tablet their name and dose amount is recorded. This record is signed by two qualified nurses. The same staff both go to the patient and check the patient and drug prescription chart before the drug is given. They do not sign for the administration of the drug until the patient has taken it.'

'So they cannot go missing?'

'No. If they did we would pick up on it. The drugs in the controlled drug cupboard are checked at the beginning of each shift, day and night. Any discrepancy is instantly picked up and would be the responsibility of the staff on duty for the shift that they went missing. That would narrow it down to one of three or four staff. No one would contemplate stealing these drugs because they know that they would be caught during their shift.'

'What if they hid the drugs?'

'That would be stupid wouldn't it? As I said, if they go missing on your shift, you are held accountable.'

'Right.' Questions seemed to be continual from him, he was allowing her no time to breathe or think about her answers. She realised that was obviously his intention.

'What about other wards, do you ever have to borrow drugs from them?'

'Unfortunately, yes we do have to sometimes. There will always be an occasion when you don't have a particular medication. For example, if we have a new patient admitted who doesn't bring in their own tablets, and we don't stock those particular tablets, then we would ring around the other wards to see if we can locate somewhere that stocks them.'

'Who then goes and gets the tablets from the other ward? Any member of staff?'

Cate hesitated, 'Actually yes, more often it is the case that it is the health care assistants that go to collect them.'

'Why not a qualified nurse? Surely if they are the only staff that have access to drug cupboards they should be going to collect the drugs if you are borrowing from another ward?'

'Yes, what you say is correct. But, in practice it would usually be the health care assistant that goes to collect them. But not if it is a controlled drug. The qualified staff may not be able to leave the ward. We have to have a minimum of two qualified on the ward at all times, one can't just go off elsewhere.'

'Why?'

'Why can't they leave the ward?' Cate questioned.

'Yes,' replied DS Hammond.

'Because they are too busy, or the patients are too poorly and we need them on the ward. It's not often practical for them to be off the ward, as I said, we have to have a minimum of two qualified nurses on the ward at all times. At busier times there are more qualified staff on duty, at these times one will often be accompanying a patient to or from theatre.'

'And is it practical for the heath care staff to be collecting drugs?'

'Yes, I believe it is. Detective, we have to put our trust in our staff.'

'But what happens when that trust is misplaced Sister?' he stated sternly, 'you said accompanying to theatre?'

'What? Erm, yes I did didn't I!' she was confusing herself now.

'Was Betty accompanied to theatre?'

'No, I don't believe so!'

'Can you be so sure?'

Oh why wouldn't this guy just give it a rest? She had answered his damned question adequately. What did he want from her, blood? She looked directly into his gaze, 'Of course.'

'Four of your patients have died.' He shot her a scowl, simultaneously raising his eyebrows.

Cate shot him a scowl back. 'I am only too aware of that Detective.'

'Do you have any concerns that a member of staff could be stealing drugs?'

'No. Not at all!'

'What about the health assistants? Do they never give drugs then?'

'No. Never.' She felt as though he wasn't really listening to what she was saying.

'Not even when the staff nurses are busy?'

'As I said. They do not give drugs under any circumstances. They are not trained to do so.'

'Right.' Charlie got up from his chair and paced about

the office for a moment; he had his head down and appeared to be extremely pensive. Cate was glad of a minute or two to catch her breath, and indeed her thoughts. She was beginning to think that her present ordeal would never end. She realised now why Chloe had been so upset.

Charlie turned to Cate, and momentarily didn't speak. She wondered what he was thinking and what he was going to ask her about next. He appeared to have lost his train of thought.

'That is all for now. I may need to speak to you again later.' He signalled towards her to go, waving his hand in the direction of the office door.

Unsure of what cut her interview short, Cate merely rose from the chair, opened the door and left. She didn't turn to look at him on her way out. If she had done so she would have seen him watching her every move as she left the room.

11

Cate returned to the ward and looked through glazed eyes around her. She still had patients that were post surgery to look after and they were her priority, not Detective Hammond and his tinpot theories.

She also had staff to support and had to retain some form of teamwork and cohesion on the ward. She was the one they were looking to, to hold the team together. She was certainly resolute in her belief that she could at least attempt to achieve this.

Despite what Detective Sergeant Hammond thought of her and her management skills she had a team to lead, and that was exactly what she intended to do. Somehow.

Once this was all over they had to continue as a team, or at least she hoped they would. She had to support them and be there for them until such time as all this was resolved.

Charlie continued to interview all the members of staff

that were on duty that shift, including the domestic team.

He allocated fifteen minutes interview time for each of them, although some came out rather quicker than others, but having been in that chair herself she couldn't make her mind up if it was a good sign or not. He had palmed off many of the later interviews for the night staff to his colleagues.

After Cate's interview he had disappeared off the ward, she thought for about an hour, no it was sixty-two minutes, not that she was watching the clock.

He rang the station and asked Vicky to organise a team to go to the theatre and recovery room to interview the staff there as well as getting someone to question the porters. The list of staff they needed to question just seemed to be getting longer, and so far not one of them had anything to say that was of any help to him.

The day seemed very long to Charlie, between interviews he took himself out of the office and walked around the ward. Despite the rising nausea from the antiseptic smell of the ward, he made his presence felt. The importance of surveying the staff at work outweighed how he felt about hospitals.

Surely if their suspect was on shift they wouldn't dare try anything, with him liable to pop up in their face at any moment. He noticed the looks on their faces as he appeared from nowhere whilst they were going about their duties. He watched as they went to the drug cupboards and followed when they went into the clinical room to check and draw up their drugs. He didn't take his eyes of them, even though he wasn't quite sure what he was looking for. He was listening to them repeat the name of the drug, check the prescription charts and re-check it. He assumed the re-checking was done for his benefit. Never the less he was reassured to see them doing it.

Cate and her team were feeling the discomfort of Charlie wandering about their ward. He certainly knew what he was doing, his presence unsettling them all perfectly. Did he think they were going to crack and come running to him and confess to being the murderer? Life just wasn't as simple as that surely.

'I hope he gets out of here soon, I can't take much more of his popping up in my face. Surely he can let us get on with our patient care.' Tim was getting really fed up with Charlie that morning. 'It's as if he doesn't trust us with our patients.'

'Of course he doesn't trust us Tim,' Cate was speaking in a hushed tone, unlike Tim; she really didn't want any of their patients overhearing their conversation. 'Four of them are bloody dead. Someone is accountable, and until we find out whom then we have to put up with him here.' From the expression on his face Cate could see that she had shocked him with her reply.

'I know. I just want to be able to do my job properly. How can I when the patients see a detective watching my every move?' She took a deep breath to calm herself. 'Do the best you can and use his presence as a positive. Whilst he is here surely nothing will happen. No one would be that stupid.'

'I'm off. Got to check some observations. Let me know when I have to go for my interrogation won't you. I want to get it over and done with so I can tell that idiot that I am not responsible for any of this.'

'Tim! Don't say it like that. He is just doing his job, and if you think about it, he is protecting ours. You are going to have to change your attitude before you are interviewed, otherwise you are going to land yourself in trouble with the detectives whether you like it or not.'

'I haven't done anything!' *'Change his attitude, who exactly did she think she was all of a sudden? Detective's little pet or what?'* he thought.

'I know that Tim, but Detective Hammond doesn't, does he? You will make yourself sound guilty if you go in with an attitude like that,' she added.

'Point taken.' Tim turned and walked briskly down the ward, away from Cate. She was beginning to have second thoughts about him. She didn't like his attitude and wasn't sure that his reaction was entirely how it should have been.

She was fed up with Charlie popping his head up when

they least expected him to, but somehow she felt safer whilst he was there. If one of her staff was responsible for the deaths then surely his presence was an asset. She would have to keep a close eye on Tim herself, just in case. Something just didn't feel right, she had only known him a few months so really didn't know him at all. He had come with glowing references so she'd had no hesitation in employing him. She just wasn't happy with his attitude at the moment. Maybe she was wrong, but in the present climate she needed to follow her gut instinct with anything and everything she thought was out of the ordinary.

Cate sat at the nurses' station. She could see Tim with the patients towards the bottom end of the ward from there. She could see him checking their observations and charts. He had the blood pressure monitor with him and was filling in a chart at the bottom of Mr Williams' bed. Cate was beginning to wonder if she was becoming totally paranoid.

Was she wrongly jumping to conclusions about her staff? Did she want to find one of them guilty of causing the deaths? It was that detectives fault; he was rapidly instilling his cynicism into her. The whole situation was causing paranoia that was spiralling beyond her control she just wanted things to return to 'normal', whatever that was!

'Sister!' called a voice from the bed opposite the nurses' station. Cate had gone into a world of her own for a moment and hadn't heard the call the first time. She rose from her stool and approached the patient's bedside.

'Yes, Mrs Carr, what can I do for you?' Mrs Carr was a 68 year old woman who had come in to the ward four days ago, following hip replacement surgery. She was progressing well and gradually regaining her mobility with the help of the physiotherapists. A couple more days and she would be discharged home.

'Sister can you tell me what exactly is happening here?' her voice sounded panicky.

'What do you mean, what is happening?' Cate half knelt down beside her bed.

'Come on, you and the other staff are all so jumpy and that man in the dark suit keeps wandering about the ward, he is very nice,' she said, 'but who is he? Is he meant to be here on the ward just wandering about? I am not daft you know.' Mrs Carr was smiling sweetly at Cate, attempting to gain her confidence.

Cate really didn't know how to answer, she thought about her reply carefully, for what she thought was an eternity but was probably only a few seconds. 'Mrs Carr, he is a detective and he has a job to do on the ward. Unfortunately he is able to come on to the ward; I have no jurisdiction over his actions or his wanderings. He is here to make sure that we are doing our job and that our patients are safe.'

'Safe, Sister? Surely it is your job to make sure we are

looked after and safe? Why on earth would we not be safe on the ward?' She was giving Cate the chance to tell her exactly what was going on. To confirm or deny the news reports. Maybe they'd overlooked the fact that she had heard the news on her portable radio.

Cate was beginning to think that she had said too much. She couldn't avoid the issue as soon enough all her patients would be hearing the news bulletins and be aware of what they thought had happened on her ward. 'Something happened on the ward and there has to be an investigation Mrs Carr. It will all be resolved soon. I am sure that the detective won't be here for too much longer.'

'Am I safe on this ward Sister?'

Cate felt like crying. Never before had she been asked by a patient if they were safe on her ward. It had never been an issue before. She wrongly assumed that her patients felt safe in her care.

'Of course you are, now I am sitting opposite you at the nurses' station so if anything bothers you, all you have to do is call out.' Cate put a hand on her shoulder hoping that it would give her some degree of reassurance.

12

Tim was checking some medications in the clinic room with Sally. She had arrived on the late shift and was eager to catch up on all the gossip regarding the interviews.

They had decided to talk in the clinic room as that was the only place where they could close the door and speak in private. The sound of the code being punched in to the door lock would alert them to someone coming in.

'I haven't even been interviewed yet and I have been here all morning. I wish he would get on with it and let me have my say,' Tim said with an air of anxiousness.

'Not like you to be so outspoken Tim, he will get round to all of us soon enough. Can't say that I relish the thought of the interview myself. They can take as long as they like getting round to me.'

'Me neither, but all this is really annoying me now. I feel as though I can't get on with my job. That damned

116

copper has been popping up when you least expect him, all morning. It's just so hard to do the job when you are being watched,' he replied.

'If you have nothing to hide then why let him bother you?' Sally said seriously.

'Tell me that when you have done a shift with him poking around and popping up behind you all the time. He is like an itchy rash that just won't go away. It merely gets more irritating.'

Sally laughed, threw her head back and continued to chuckle. 'Hasn't he been doing the interviews himself?'

'Yes, I think so; he must be popping out in between. I have seen him half a dozen times this morning, here, there and everywhere. Probably meet him in the toilet next.'

'I'm sure he isn't that bad,' she said.

'Believe me, he is, wait and see how he operates, shifty piece of work that guy.'

'He's a detective! What do you expect, coffee with him? Help with the fluid charts and commodes? Wake up Tim!'

'You just don't get it do you.'

'Have you spoken to anyone who has been in to see him yet?'

'Only the domestic staff. Cate hasn't said anything to me, oh well unless you count the time when she practically told me to pull myself together.'

'What?' Sally said surprised.

'Yes, I think it's all getting to her. Told me to change my attitude! The cheek of her!'

'Why would she say that?'

'Don't know really. All I said was that I didn't like that detective in my face all the time when I was trying to look after my patients.'

'Forget it Tim, think of the stress she must be under. Think how you feel, she is accountable for all of us and the ward. If anyone is going to get in trouble she will surely be the first in the firing line. No wonder she is being like that to you. Just ignore her and merely answer what he asks you. You can't do any more than that.'

'I know, but…' Tim said pausing.

'But what? Surely the more they question us the quicker they are going to find out what really happened. We all know that it wasn't one of us, so the sooner we answer their questions the sooner they will realise that too and find out what really happened.'

'Yes, I suppose you are right.'

'Of course I am,' said Sally with a smile on her face. 'Soon all will be over, then we can get back to how things should be around here.' She patted him on the back. Friendly reassurance goes a long way, she thought.

'Soon we won't be able to remember what normal is. I'm not sure I want to stay working here Sally, might have a word and see if I can go back to the medical admissions unit. I don't want to be caught up in this rubbish.'

'What are you on about? If you jump ship now surely they are going to wonder why? That will get them asking you more questions! It will make you look guilty. I'm sure that they wouldn't let you jump ship yet anyway!'

'I am not guilty of anything! For goodness sake Sally. I just don't want to be part of this and I don't want to work for Cate.'

'No Tim, if you start shouting about wanting to move wards then they are going to be asking why.'

'Yes, and I will tell them why.'

'What if they don't see it your way and see you as running away from a problem?'

'Sure, yes I will be running away from a problem, but one that isn't mine. I am only a couple of years in to my career and I need to protect my registration.'

'Don't we all?'

'I know that, but how is it going to look on my CV when I go for another job and the employer sees that I worked on the ward where the cops were in investigating patient deaths? No one is going to forget this in a long time. If I go now then I can leave it off my CV and get rid of any connections to this damned ward.'

'Tim, if you have nothing to do with the deaths then...'
Tim butted into her sentence.

'What do you mean IF?!'

'Let me finish Tim.'

'Fuck off.'

'Tim!'

'You think I want to work with you after you have said that?' Scorn resonated in his voice.

'IF you have nothing to do with the deaths then surely you have nothing to fear from the investigation.'

'Of course I have nothing to fear that way. I just don't want to be associated with all this. It could ruin my career.'

'Oh and the rest of us will be ok, huh?'

'I didn't mean it like that. Maybe you should think about what I am saying and get the hell out of here too.'

'When they have found out what is going on we will be able to make our decisions. What if it is just a dodgy batch of drugs? All this will have been for nothing. Well, not all of it, but the patients will have been worried about our care for no reason. Look how it's got us arguing already. Damned police investigation is out to destroy this team and succeeding on their first day.'

'I still think that I need to get out of this ward before I am tarred with the stigma that is going to be attached to here. Everyone will know 73 as the ward where the patients died. What if they shut the ward down? We will be moved to other wards then anyway won't we?'

'I know what you are saying Tim, but I still think you are overreacting here. I have Lorraine in one ear at home, panicking about being interviewed by the cops in case she says something wrong. You are on about moving wards, and I have Chloe in the other ear wanting to leave nursing all together. This really is turning out just fine.'

With that Sally turned and left the clinic room, slamming the door behind her. She forgot that she had gone there to check some tablets with him.

Sally was concerned about Tim; in fact there wasn't much on the ward today that wasn't concerning her. He was not the level-headed professional nurse that she was used to and seemed different from usual, uptight and outspoken. His attitude wasn't his usual jovial one; she began to wonder if she should speak to Cate about him. She wasn't sure if this was the right thing to do or if it would land him in trouble with the police investigation. She was also wary of approaching Cate in case what Tim said was true and she merely jumped down her throat instead of listening to her.

Sally saw Cate standing by the nurses' station; she didn't appear to have moved since she passed her on the way to the clinic room earlier.

Sally walked up to Cate, still unsure whether to speak to her or not. Something was bothering her though, something just didn't feel right. She was just going to have to take her chance and go for it.

Cate looked up as Sally arrived at her side. She appeared

to be working her way through a mound of papers, Sally couldn't see what the documents were though.

'Can I have a word with you?'

'Of course, what's up Sally?'

'Is there anywhere else we can go for a minute, I don't want any of the others to see that we are discussing anything.'

'That's fine but Detective Hammond is still in my office, the only sanctuary I can offer you is the store room or the canteen. Is there something bothering you?'

'It's everyone really. Tim, Lorraine, Chloe, well it is Tim mostly,' Sally stated quietly, looking around to check that Tim wasn't within earshot.

'Tim?' Cate looked surprised, or at least she tried to, bearing in mind the concerns she had herself regarding him.

'I have just had a conversation with him,' Sally continued, 'he seems to be different from his usual self. He usually gets on with his work and doesn't bother anyone; today he is being stroppy and talking about leaving the ward, saying he doesn't want to be part of a ward under police investigation. I don't know Cate, I really don't, I don't want to sound like I am telling tales on him, but something isn't right.'

'I'll take on board what you are saying to me. Leave it with me. You are right to come to me and tell me what you are thinking. I will deal with this myself. Don't worry nothing will get back to Tim about this. I am just glad that someone at least is coming to me and telling me what is going on around here.'

Cate couldn't afford to comment or judge, especially having concerns of her own on the subject. She just hoped Sally would accept her loose reply.

'I just want the team back how it was Cate. Chloe came out of her interview in pieces and Lorraine is freaking out about being interviewed by the cops.'

'Lorraine? Why?'

'I don't know, she won't say anything except that she hates the cops and doesn't want to speak to them.'

'Well, unfortunately she doesn't have a choice; do you want me to have a word with her about it?'

'No, not really, I don't want her to know that I have said anything to you.'

'I wouldn't say that Sally, I could merely ask how she was feeling about things on the ward, have a general chat with her.'

'Oh, Cate, why can't things just go back to normal around here? The team just aren't gelling like usual, can't we get things back how they were? There is so much tension here at the moment; no one can get on with their work properly. I have only just come on shift and feel the tension gripping me already.'

'I know, and they soon will be Sally. Go back to your shift now and leave things with me. I am sure that once the detectives get things straight we will all be back to how we were.'

Cate really wanted to believe what she was telling Sally but she just wasn't sure if things on ward 73 would ever be the same again.

Cate knew that she had to go and speak to Charlie. She would take him a coffee and see if she could approach the subject of Tim and the other staff with him. Something had to be said, yet she didn't want to land him in trouble that wasn't his. She just hoped he didn't start interrogating her again with her voluntary visit.

With two cups of coffee in her left hand, Cate knocked on her office door. She heard Charlie shout to come in.

'Coffee?' Again she worked hard at faking a smile towards him. She noticed that he looked tired, with a hint of rough stubble, and wondered if he had been up all night pondering this investigation himself.

'Thanks Cate,' Charlie smiled across at her. He realised it was the first time for hours he had smiled, the sight of her had raised his spirits.

'Sit down, join me, I could do with a few minutes time out before the next interview.'

'Well, I am not sure if you will get a break once I tell you why I have come to see you.'

'Have you found something?'

'No. Nothing that is really going to help. Sorry. I just

have some concerns about some of my staff that I need to voice to you.'

'Go on.'

'Well, maybe this is not significant but I have just had another member of staff come to me and voice the same concerns. Tim, one of the staff nurses is acting quite out of character, in fact,' she said with a heavy sigh, 'they all are really.' Her immediate thoughts were not to single him out to start with. I just can't put my finger on it but he isn't his usual self at the moment. You haven't interviewed him yet have you?'

'Tim? No I haven't seen him yet. I called him in earlier but he was caught up with a patient, I am due to see him this afternoon. What's the problem?'

'Well, he is usually so professional, quiet mannered and softly spoken. He hasn't been with us here very long, but so far has fitted in to our team very well. Today he is very loud, outspoken and almost bolshie in his attitude. He has developed an attitude to the investigation, to being interviewed and from what I have been told he wants to leave the ward. His work is faultless I can assure you on that score. It's just his attitude that is unusual and the other staff are concerned too. I thought I should warn you before you have him in for questioning.'

'Was he on duty at the time of any of the deaths?'

'No he wasn't. He was part of the team on shift when two

of the patients were nursed on the ward though, but not on duty when the two deaths occurred on the ward, or when the two happened in theatre. He had worked the night shift when they were in theatre.'

'Ok. You are certainly right to let me know what is going on Cate. Sometimes people react in this manner during an investigation like this. If a person has some involvement in a case like this they often act out of character and therefore draw attention to them. Not always a reaction of a killer, but quite typical in a case like this.'

'Oh.' Cate hesitated and felt herself dip her head downwards, avoiding Charlie's gaze.

'It doesn't mean to say that he has anything to do with the deaths Cate.'

'Ok, I didn't mean to make it sound that strong, what I was saying detective. I just meant to alert you to his change in attitude. It is just so out of character for him, it could be that he is feeling the stress of it all, as we all are.'

'I realise that but everything is relevant Cate. This is why I am here. I find out information then decide what is relevant to the case.' Once again he was pulling rank over her whether it be intentional or not.

Charlie didn't want to tell her too much, maybe he shouldn't have told her about suspects bringing themselves to the forefront of the investigation, after all, Cate herself was a suspect still, until he proved otherwise. He really couldn't decide about her involvement, deep down he hoped she had nothing to do with the events, he wasn't sure he could handle arresting her himself.

'Just out of interest, who came to you to tell you about him?'

'Sally, one of the other staff nurses. She actually raised the same concerns that were mulling around in my head. Once she came to me I couldn't do anything else but come to you really. Just in case it is relevant.'

'No, you couldn't. Everything has its place in this investigation Cate. Anything you feel that is out of character or unusual in the behaviour of the staff needs to be reported. In most instances it will be nothing, but maybe something will lead us to more. I don't think I have met Sally yet.'

'I feel that I am letting him down. He's stressed like the rest of us. I am sorry, I shouldn't have come to you.' Cate got up to leave the office. Charlie walked slowly towards her and caught hold of her forearm. She turned to him, tears welling up in her eyes.

For a moment Charlie again forgot where he was, the only thought in his head was that he wanted to kiss her. She was so close to him, she felt as vulnerable as she looked, so kissable, he wanted her and he hadn't felt this way about a woman for years.

She was lighting up his world, was she aware of the impact she was having on him, he couldn't risk that just yet.

The two of them stood motionless, Cate didn't attempt to move his hand. That was all the reassurance that he needed. She certainly wasn't pushing him away. He just felt so comfortable and alive touching her; he wanted that moment to last forever, he wanted to hold her and take care of her, to give himself up totally, but she was a murder suspect and until he had solved this case there was nothing he could do or say. He desperately told himself this so he could regain his professional composure. His internal argument was in full force.

She surprised herself with the reaction he stirred within her, shocked, more like. She was unable to move for what seemed like an eternity. She felt the sex appeal oozing from him, escaping his every pore, infusing into her, overtaking her senses and upturning logic.

There was a knock at the door, Charlie immediately removed his hand and remembered where he was. Cate was still looking straight at him, transfixed by his eyes, looking into them beyond the surface, seeking his real personality. They were both saying nothing, yet saying everything at once.

Charlie noticed her full, well-defined lips and was immersed in imagining their first tender kiss. He knew it couldn't happen, any other time and this moment would have been perfect. This was however the most imperfect, perfect moment he had ever experienced. Cate Carter was the most exciting secret that he had ever detected, he could not afford to lose her by jumping in too soon and messing things up. He would have to bide his time, however frustrating and confusing this was for him.

A second knock at the door broke their silence.

Charlie cleared his throat and managed a mere, 'Come in.'

'I need Cate to take a call on the ward,' the voice stated.

The unwelcome interruption was Tim. Cate immediately felt guilty. After all it was to speak about him that had brought her to see Charlie in the first place. She felt as though he knew what she was telling him, maybe she was getting totally paranoid now.

With his appearance at the doorway Cate and Charlie immediately broke their lengthy elongated eye contact. Charlie instead looked directly at Tim and awaited his reason for the interruption. It better be damned good, he thought. Cate however avoided Tim's gaze totally. She looked past him and towards the floor as if she was searching for something she had dropped.

Cate wasn't sure if the words would come out if she attempted to speak, never the less she gave it a go. 'Who is it?' She was so thankful that her words came out. She thought for a moment that Charlie had taken her breath away merely by touching her arm, and prayed that the words would come out as coherently as her mind told them to.

'Frances, she says she needs to talk to you specifically.'

'Ok, go back and tell her I will be there in one minute will you.'

'Fine.' With that Tim was gone. Damned detective, he thought, refusing to look anywhere near Charlie's direction. He didn't wish to stay in his company any longer than he really had to.

Charlie returned to his seat behind her desk. Cate looked across at him, almost fearing how she would react. 'I need to go and sort this out.'

'When you are done, come back so we can finish our discussion Cate.' Charlie winked at her as she exited the door, silently wishing his professionalism had held tighter. He didn't seem to be able to help himself where she was concerned. He was as astonished at his reaction as she would surely be. Not once since he lost Valerie had he even looked at another woman, and here he was unable to control himself and flirting with a damned suspect. What on earth did he think he was doing? If he wasn't careful he would be looking at enforced early retirement!

Closing the door behind her, Cate let out a massive sigh, stopping to allow the door to prop her up, whilst she re-entered reality. She hoped that Charlie couldn't hear her through the closed door. She felt as if her sigh would be heard bellowing and echoing miles away. It was a sigh of total contentment and anticipation. The feelings she had now were so different to how he made her feel earlier during the interview. Why on earth was this guy having this effect on her, it was so long since she had felt like this that she didn't remember how good she could feel. Yet she told herself that she had to remain professional. After all he was the detective and she, the ward sister whose team was under criminal investigation. She really had to control her feelings and tell herself he was just doing his job.

She was scared by her own fragility and the feelings that he had stirred up inside her. That long forgotten sensation of butterflies amassing in her stomach.

That certainly wouldn't go away, even if her sense of reality towards him did kick in.

As Charlie had watched the last of Cate leaving he shook his head in disbelief. He was now standing directly behind the office door and had heard her let out an almighty sigh. She sounded content; at least that is what he was telling himself during his own internal argument.

What on earth was this woman doing to him? It was as though she had some sort of hold on him, he struggled to remember what he was going to do next as he forced himself to think about the investigation and not the beautiful woman that was taking over his mind.

Cate took the call from Frances at the main phone at the nurses' station. Fortunately she was merely after an update regarding the status of interviews on the ward. Cate felt that she couldn't cope with any further questions from her at the moment. She felt mentally exhausted and was totally confused by the signals she was getting from Charlie. One minute things were extremely formal and he was interviewing her, the next she really didn't know what was going on! She knew what she felt, and thought maybe she was mistaken about what was happening, he was leading the investigation on her ward for goodness sake! What was she thinking?

She had nothing more to say and ended the call as soon as she could without feeling she was being rude. Frances too had been interviewed by two detectives who merely turned up in her office to speak to her. Frances was the head of the senior nursing team that covered the whole hospital site. She was one of the team of senior nurses who the wards referred to for advice, sorted out where patients were moved to in a bed crisis and monitored staffing levels to ensure adequate cover. Accountable for everything that happened at ward level across the hospital site and now accountable for suspicious deaths.

Cate wondered if she should go back in to see Charlie or not. If she ran back to the office immediately would he see her as desperate? Would he think she just wanted to jump in to bed with him? Maybe he would just be pleased that his tactics were working on her?

What if he thought that she was being immature and attempting to gain favouritism from him to persuade him of her innocence?

No, she couldn't go back to her office; he would get the wrong impression, whatever that was.

She was hardly sure of what the right impression was or what impression she wanted to portray. She was just acutely aware that she was a murder suspect. That, she thought, was the impression he had of her and that was enough to shock her in to momentary sanity, or was she reading the signs the wrong way!

Cate need not have worried; she looked up and could see Charlie approaching. He was carrying the two cups of coffee that she had made them just a few minutes earlier.

'Sister Carter, your coffee,' he said smiling towards her.

'Thank you detective.' She couldn't help but flash a smile at him and hoped none of her staff were watching. She thought it unusual that he called her Sister Carter, then remembered they were out on the ward in full view of the staff, maybe he was maintaining his level of professionalism very well, she thought. She had immediately forgotten all her self-control and had awkward thoughts at the sight of him.

'Sick of my office yet?'

'Actually yes, I think I am, and I am well overdue a lunch

break. Are you going to show me where the canteen is? I have just about got enough time to grab some carbs before the next interview is scheduled.'

Cate looked around her ward, she wondered if she really should be thinking about leaving the ward at all. Yet she was feeling compelled to accept his invitation. She wanted to be in his company and didn't want to miss out on an opportunity to have him all to herself even if it was in a crowded hospital canteen. She might also learn about how his investigations were progressing, whether or not he would take his detective hat off and gossip was another matter!

Anything he uncovered that she wasn't aware of she wanted to know! She hoped that he would tell her if he had come across something, maybe she would ask him later.

She called out to a passing Sally. 'Sally, I am going for a short lunch break, bleep me if you need anything will you.'

'Of course, Sister.' Sally thought she'd better stick to Cate's professional title with the detective in their midst. She just felt uneasy in his presence. She didn't like him creeping about the ward any more than any of the others did. She just chose not to voice how she was feeling about this.

Charlie put a hand in the crook of Cate's back and gently directed her forward. Cate didn't want to move, she was comfortable with his hand there, it felt reassuring and right now that was just what she needed. There was

134

something about his touch that made her feel secure, whole and complete.

How on earth was he making her feeling like that she wondered? She had spent years with Gareth and never felt at all like Charlie was making her feel at this moment.

'Lead on Sister,' he said.

As they walked out of ward 73 Cate noticed how Charlie smiled at Sally and patted her shoulder lightly as he passed her, his hand resting there for longer than it should have. She pondered for a moment before the realisation hit her head on.

Cate immediately became conscious that Charlie was trying to win the trust of her and the staff and she didn't like the way he was going about it. He was charming them all and lulling them all into a false sense of security. One minute he was Mr Nice Guy the next he turned detective and was firing questions at them. She didn't appreciate his methods.

She felt that he had merely gained her trust to extract information from her. He was after all the detective. These thoughts hit her with a tremendous sense of reality. She felt physically sick at the thought that she had fallen for his strategies and schemes. She didn't appreciate his approach even though he was there to gain information from them all. Now she had to spend her lunch time with him. Well she wouldn't be forthcoming and certainly would be keeping a check on herself and her responses towards him.

If he had merely asked her she would have given him any answers she could, without coercion, he didn't have to employ these dirty tactics to gain her support.

Suddenly she felt intimidated and vulnerable. She had to retain her composure through lunch, the way he was scrutinising her he would notice a change in her in an instant if she wasn't careful. She walked alongside him towards the canteen, managing to keep silent. He was probably thinking out his next move of intimidation, she thought. Her mind just wasn't clear, her thoughts and hormones were all over the place. He was already causing her to question herself.

She had felt as though their lunch date was in fact that, a date. Somehow she had allowed her mind to believe this, how she wanted it to be, not how it really was. She had to pull herself together and stop responding to his alluring charisma. Over lunch he began to question her further about her staff and their characters, their moods and clinical practice. It was the reality check that she needed.

He was a detective through and through, she was useful to him and he wanted to keep her sweet so she would give him the information. His mole on ward 73!

Well, she wasn't going to have it, no more, but she knew she couldn't shake off her hidden feeling for him! She was beginning to feel jealous towards his job! She knew she shouldn't panda to him anymore, she had to distance herself from him and concentrate on keeping her team together.

She was cross with herself for exposing herself to his charms, allowing him to reel her in and penetrate her defences. So very rarely did anyone actually manage to do this. She needed to toughen up where Detective Sergeant Charlie Hammond was concerned, and quickly.

She called their lunch date to a halt, making out that her bleeper was vibrating. She briskly informed him that Sally must be in need of her on the ward and she was going to head back there. She left him to finish his chips alone.

13

Back at the station, Vicky sat silently reading and re-reading the police reports about David Waters. Fortunately she had never come across anyone like him when she'd been nursing. *'Why on earth do these people even enter the profession,'* she thought, *'surely this is the last place you would expect someone with such a warped or sick mind to be working, in an environment where they had to care for others.'*

She had just organised teams to interview the porters, the theatre staff and the recovery nurses and needed to read up about Waters before Charlie returned to the station.

Now she was a police officer knee-deep in an investigation that was beginning to look like someone was trying their hand at a repeat of his work.

She was arresting all sorts of undesirables nowadays but it never ceased to amaze her the depths people would sink to in committing their crimes. Whilst many murders were spontaneous and appeared to have no motive at all, it seemed that in other cases crimes were becoming more serious and carefully thought out.

She didn't think anyone would be so stupid to try the same thing again. They would be picked up quickly if the pattern re-emerged. So far, at Westwood General though, they didn't have any pattern, merely a weak link and that wasn't going to solve their investigation.

Maybe there was another evil mind out there with another way of doing this. She just had no idea herself what this could be. There had been no reports of any needle marks on the victims. The only route of administration for intravenous drugs would have been the cannulas. That couldn't be the method, Vicky knew that. There were many staff about in theatre and in the recovery room so no individual could give a patient any form of a drug that was not prescribed without being discovered. They would be checking all the intravenous drugs there with two staff. No margin for error, surely.

'Got another one Vicky.'

'Charlie? I thought you were interviewing on 73?' Vicky turned to see Charlie standing in the office doorway; he was leaning to one side on the door frame. He had a couple of report files in his hand and was waving them at her. He had startled her whilst she was deep in thought.

'Another body at the General, this time in ward 68, nowhere near 73. Other end of the corridor. Had to get extra cover to continue with the interviews whilst I came back here to get a handle on this one and get more teams organised.'

'Shit Charlie, does Chalmers know?'

'Not sure, although if he did I would have expected him down here to see us by now.'

'Point taken. What the hell is happening there? This situation is becoming incomprehensible.'

'Goodness knows. The more people we speak to, the less we seem to know. Now we have another victim.'

'Five damn bodies! Now a young, fit 23 year old. No reason to have complications. Understandably the family are going berserk,' Charlie said and sat down before continuing. 'Apparently her parents were in the senior nurse's office shouting and bawling at her, threatening to sue the hospital. You can hardly blame them really can you? I have only just got myself out of that place and now I am going to have to go back and sort this one out. I am up to my eyes interviewing the staff on ward 73, now we have to set up on 68. We will have to set up another team to go in there. I can't take any more on at the moment; there is enough to keep me going already for months there! If I take that ward on too I am going to end up missing something on 73. I haven't finished with that lot there, not by a long shot.'

'Oh the press are going to love this one! Any of the same staff work on 73 and 68?'

'Nope, already had that one checked out. Usually the bank nurses work on random wards but they are now being monitored and kept on the same wards as far as possible. That way we can track them easier. The ward managers put a stop to any avoidable movement of staff since 73's deaths. Even the doctors are from different teams. Any staff that do have to move to cover the other wards if someone goes off sick etc are now documented in the ward duty rota on a separate sheet. Everyone's movements are accounted for. There are no members of nursing, medical or ancillary staff that have worked on both the wards.'

'There must have been surely? Who was it that checked the staff rota?'

'Sister Cate went through her rotas and got the sister from ward 68 to bring a copy of her rota down to her. I have a copy somewhere amongst all the paperwork here, just had it faxed through to me. I have got Myers checking out the bank staff though, just in case we can get a link there. We could have missed something, a member of staff who worked on the ward who wasn't recorded on the duty rota or who was moved from one area to another to help out perhaps. The bank staff, I understand, are not always marked down on the ward rotas.'

'Something could have been missed there then; we need some form of link soon. Let's face it, it would make our job a hell of a lot easier.'

'We bloody better find the link. This is getting right out of hand. Someone is having a laugh at us and so far I haven't come across anything that is vaguely going to help us uncover the truth. How can patients be dying on another ward when the staff are not moving from one ward to another and neither are the patients? It just doesn't add up. Some son of a bitch is going down for these patients and it's going to be soon. Where the bloody hell are the post mortem reports? How can we be expected to link these people or their reason for death if we don't know why they died?'

'We don't want to drive them underground and find ourselves with a recurring problem in a few months time do we.'

'If we are barking up the wrong tree here and it turns out to be dodgy drugs we are going to make ourselves look like a bunch of incompetents. The patients will lose faith in the staff and won't want to be treated there, the knock-on situation will be unmanageable for the hospital. So far I have merely asked everyone if they nursed the patients and if they thought that anything was out of the ordinary. I haven't gone in full whack with any of them yet. I'm leaving that for the next round of interviews. None of them have experienced the full-on interview yet,' he said coldly.

14

Detective Inspector Chalmers had to release a press statement about the suspicious deaths at Westwood General Hospital. They would merely say that unexpected deaths were being investigated. No indication of any possible foul play by staff members would be mentioned. That would cause public panic and an outcry at the hospital. They were not ready to consider that option at the moment.

They had to acknowledge what had happened as the news would reach the community soon enough anyway. The relatives of the deceased would see to that at the very least.

He was in no way looking forward to releasing this statement. Murder enquiries always left him feeling powerless, until he had the suspects in custody of course. This investigation was like no other he had been involved with before. Murder of patients in an environment where they were admitted for care was a whole new ball game for him. One he really didn't want to be dealing with.

The flashlights were going off one after the other and there were so many microphones in front of him. Charlie could feel his palms sweating, he was thankful it wasn't him that had to deliver the speeches.

* * * * *

'What news today?' the voices began as the ten o'clock news was about to start.

'What praise will the detective broadcast today?' The voices needed praise to know that the job they asked for was being carried out to the letter.

* * * * *

As an exhausted looking Detective Inspector Chalmers sat at the desk flanked by a uniformed officer on his right and Charlie on his left who looked straight into the cameras as the announcement about their recent findings was conducted.

'The recent spate of unexplained deaths at Westwood General Hospital continues to be an agonising source of mystery for our investigation. Today another victim, who cannot yet be named, was confirmed. We are continuing the investigations and have closed some wards in the hospital to routine and emergency

admissions. A full enquiry is underway. Any further news on this will be brought to you as it breaks.'

All the reporters started to ask their questions at once. Chalmers stood up and put his hand up to signify silence from them.

'That is all I have to say at the moment. I will not be answering any questions. Further announcements will be made in due course. Thank you ladies and gentlemen.'

* * * * *

'Well done my little one. You have done us proud,' the Fallen Angel understood. Today was the day for praise. It was the posh lady that was speaking. She was always full of praise. Her voices sounded happy, and bouncy in their tone.

It was the angry man's voice that they feared. That was the voice that was always nasty.

'We commend you on your good work. You are undoubtedly the best and are proving it to all… No you are not, you need to listen… Do what we say…' The angry man was trying to talk at the same time.

Voices, voices, two of them now, oh the headache, the torture, 'Stop it I can't hear the both of you, STOP IT NOW, you are hurting my head.'

Would shouting out to the voices make them go away? It had to be worth a try. The voices had to go; there was no way to get away from them. Their demands had to be shut out. The Fallen Angel tried not to listen but the commotion faded and one became clearer...

'To have killed on your own ward was good; to manage another on a ward you have not worked on is excellent. That will really get them running. They will never be able to work out how you have managed that! We need more like that, see to it that you have as many as you can on as many wards as you can. You know how to do this; you have proved yourself so well. Get them all running, give them the headaches and yours will fade. You know how to do it little one, you have proved that to us perfectly.'

With that there were no more voices, for the time being anyway.

'Sleep, I need sleep, I need to rest from the voices whilst they rest too. Leave me alone whilst I sleep.'

With that a long and peaceful sleep followed whilst the voices temporarily abated.

15

Charlie had returned to ward 73 with some reluctance, he would have much preferred to handle things from the station; he couldn't stop thinking about what Cate had said to him about Tim. He had to conduct his interview as a matter of priority now, just in case he turned out to have something to hide. He had sent Barry Foster, one of his up and coming young detective constables into ward 68.

He knew when to delegate, and this was certainly the time to handover some of the interviews. This was beginning to drive his head to exploding point. He hadn't been without a headache for the last twenty-four hours, he popped a couple of aspirin, swigged down with his ever faithful caffeine fix and settled himself in Cate's office for the foreseeable future.

His next task was to bring Tim in and put some very well chosen questions to him, he was going to go for the third degree tactics. It sounded like this guy had a problem with the investigation and Charlie was going to ensure that he was at least one step ahead of him at all times.

Charlie rang through to the ward; as usual it was Cate who answered the phone.

'Cate, can you send Tim down.'

'Alright, I will go and find him and send him into you as soon as I can.'

'If you would, I'll let you know when I am through with him and need the next one in.'

'Fine.' Cate really wasn't sure how to take him. The more she interacted with him, the further he added to her confusion. He seemed to slip from human being to detective in one smooth move, like a snake shedding its skin. It was almost as if he didn't notice this transformation himself. Or, maybe he did and that was part of who he was, how he worked.

Her head was pounding, was it the day's events, the search for a murderer amongst her staff, or Detective Charlie Hammond. Cate really didn't know. She shook her head, laughed at herself.

Enough of this she thought. She went looking for Tim, she better get him to Detective Hammond soon or he would be after her wondering what the delay was. She really didn't want to chance a further encounter with him if he was in detective mode, not just yet anyway.

Cate walked down the ward, Tim was allocated to the patients in the beds in the side rooms and she couldn't see him evident in the ward. She stopped at the closed door of the first side room, the curtain was closed in the little window and she decided not to disturb its occupant.

'Seen Tim?' she posed to Sally.

'I think he is in room seven, with Mr Stanley. At least that was where he was going a minute ago, to do his dressing I think. Why? Is something up?'

'No, I just need to find him, thanks.'

Sally pulled a face behind Cate. What was happening to her these days? She really wasn't her usual self; this dammed investigation was definitely getting to her and indeed the whole of the ward staff.

'Sally, I just need to find Tim so that the detective can do his interview.'

'Right. But you are ok aren't you? It's just that you don't seem to be yourself.'

'Are any of us?' she said to her.

'Not really, it feels like this ward team is cracking up, falling apart in a heartbeat. They don't even know for sure if it is a member of staff who has done anything to those patients. They just don't seem to have any respect for us as individuals; they march in here, interrogate us all to see if we think any of our friends killed our patients, but have no proof to show us that the deaths were suspicious. When is this all going to end? I see Tim's point now. Maybe I was too hasty coming to you about him, he was bolshie, but maybe he is right. The cops are tearing us apart and maybe for no reason, we now have no trust in each other.'

'I wasn't sure you were going to draw breath there Sally.'

'Sorry to rant on, but this is really annoying me now.'

Just as Cate was about to respond to that last comment, Tim exited from the door of Mr Stanley's room. She called out to him; he was only a few yards in front of her.

'Tim, one moment please.'

'I just need to get some gauze, be back in a minute.'

He was heading to the clinical room to collect his dressings, Cate called him back.

'Tim, I mean now,' she ordered, raising her voice uncharacteristically.

He almost recoiled back with shock, wondering who had rattled her cage to get her so het up.

She was usually so calm.

He approached her with some caution, thinking it was better to find out what she wanted rather than cause any more bad feeling on the ward.

'Detective Hammond is ready to interview you now, can you go along to my office.' MY office, what a joke she thought, she said it out of habit, but wasn't really sure if she would ever be able to return to it and call it her office again.

'I am in the middle of Mr Stanley's dressing Sister, can I just finish this first?'

'Tim, I think you are missing the point here, go now

please. He is the detective investigating patient deaths on our ward, I don't think it was a social invitation he was extending to you. You don't get a choice in your time of appearance.' He was really trying her patience now and the frustration of it all showed through in her voice. 'I will finish it for you,' she said kindly.

'Mr Stanley is expecting me, whatever happened to the priority of patient care? Doesn't that exist in the detective's book?' His voice was getting louder and he realised that some of the patients in the beds opposite the side rooms could hear him.

'I said I will finish off the dressing for you. Off you go. He is waiting!' she said. 'No further discussion Tim, go now,' she sounded pitiful in her plea.

Tim merely turned and walked towards the top of the ward to face the budding Sherlock Holmes and his crackpot theories about ward 73. He had all the intention of winding him up in his interview; because this damned detective was annoying him by his mere existence in their professional space, but carrying it out was another point entirely...

16

Tim was unsure whether to merely enter the office or knock on the door. Logic told him to knock, his new-found emancipation and resentment towards Detective Sergeant Charlie Hammond's presence on the ward told him to barge in and sit down. Too late, decision taken out of his hands, the door was opening and there he stood, the detective from his worst nightmare.

Tim didn't even bother to feign a smile.

'Ah, I was just coming to look for you, come in.'

Charlie was looking forward to this interview. If this guy was coming to him with a pre-formed bolshie attitude then let him bring it on. He could eat Tim for breakfast, tie him up in knots and have him begging to get out of his presence. It was times like these he really enjoyed his job!

'Sit down Tim.' Charlie put his arm forward to direct him to his chosen seating position. He began by introducing Harry Webster, his only response involved a momentary nodding of his head followed by an immediate return to his scribing. Tim was wondering why he had two dectectives present at his interview when the others said they only had DS Hammond.

'I will tell you the same as I have told the others that I have interviewed. I am conducting these initial enquiries on the ward, you are not under arrest and our conversation is not being recorded. If further questioning is required this will be undertaken down at the station.'

'Right, what do you want to know then?' Tim snapped.

Whoa thought Charlie, this little upstart needs sorting out and quickly.

First get him talking, anything to get him to interact and answer his simple questions, then out with the relevant ones. Take him by surprise.

'Tim, how long have you been in nursing?'

'Four years.'

'And on ward 73?'

'Two months.'

'Why did you move from your previous ward?'

'I wanted surgical experience,' he replied curtly, not seeing the relevance of the question.

'Did you encounter any problems whist working there?'

'What sort of problems?

'How were your working relationships with the staff there?'

'You know your presence is unsettling everyone! Don't

153

you just want to know if any of us killed the patients on this ward?' Tim said ignoring DS Hammond's question.

'Well if that is what you want to talk about Tim, go ahead. Did you kill any of the patients on ward 73? Do you prefer me to go down that line of enquiry?'

Silence.

'You didn't answer my question, Tim.'

'You really want me to dignify that with a reply?'

Charlie got up from his seat, walked towards Tim and stood alongside him, level with his shoulders.

Leaning down to whispering distance, he uttered a few choice words directly into Tim's ear.

'I beg your pardon detective?' Tim stuttered.

'You heard me Tim, did you do it?'

'Oh come on here, you didn't ask the others this so why me?'

'The others do not come in to the equation of this interview. All the discussions are confidential; if those are the rumours of the content of these interviews, we will be re-questioning each and every one of them, explaining that you are the reason for this.'

'Oh come on.'

'I suggest you decide on another tone for you discussion with me Mr Simpson. Otherwise you will find that life gets worse than you could ever imagine.' Charlie turned to face Harry, hoping that he wasn't recording his dialogue word for word.

'Are you threatening me detective?'

Charlie positioned himself so that he was perched on the edge of the desk, almost in Tim's face, but far enough away to allow him only minimal personal space. Tim could feel his breath on his neck, heavy and smelling of fresh coffee.

'I don't make threats Mr Simpson. I can assure you that I follow through with all my promises.' A smirk broke through involuntarily.

Tim, nearly fell off his chair. He hadn't expected it to be like this at all. He wondered if he should ask if Cate could come in with him, so that he had a witness, but logic told him he would only make things worse for himself by asking this now.

'I thought that you were going to ask me about clinical practice on the ward, that's all, not ask me questions about being a killer!' he stuttered.

'Well then, how about we start again. Start with clinical issues, and then we can talk about what else you want to tell me about.'

'Round one to me,' thought Charlie, *'that will teach this little upstart to mess with me.'* If he tried anything else he would find himself being interviewed down at the station, just because Charlie felt like doing so. Just to annoy Tim. He hadn't been a good detective all these years to be messed about by someone as insignificant as him.

17

'What on earth are you doing Loz?' Sally said, looking at the sprawl of papers on the floor of their lounge all neatly positioned in the middle of their deep brown faux fur rug.

'Cutting out some of the articles about the ward. Look, they are all about the murders on the ward!' she said with a coy grin.

'What on earth are you doing this for?' Sally questioned Loz's motives for this, it just didn't feel right, her sitting there with a pile of cuttings about the deaths on their ward.

'I want to try and follow what is going on here.'

'Err, Loz, that's what the detective is for.'

'No one is really telling us anything at work are they? I just wanted to keep a record of what the press has to say about it all.'

'Oh come on Loz, what part of those reports are true? The newspapers write what they think will sell the papers.

Not what is actually happening?'

'Seems to be accurate so far with what I have read Sal.'

'Oh come on, it's a waste of time. Do you really want to have those clippings to remind you of deaths?'

'Yes actually I do. Because when all this is over it will be part of history in our profession. One day lessons will be learnt as a result of all this. If it is something to do with dodgy drugs there will be a massive lawsuit against the pharmaceutical company won't there?' She took a deep breath, 'maybe I'll change my career and be a forensic detective!'

'What? Anyway, of course I get that bit but what if one of the staff is a murderer Lorraine? What then? Will you want to save the reports of that? Of one of our colleagues who turns out to be a psycho?'

'I just want to follow what the press are saying that's all. I think it is fascinating. Could be a good basis for further research for a masters, that is if I go on that far with my studies. I could do a thesis on nurses that have murdered their patients.'

'They are few and far between Lorraine. This doesn't seem very healthy to me. Can't you get rid of them, what if someone finds out we have them, it might look suspicious.'

'Oh come on Sal, there is nothing suspicious about having a few newspaper cuttings.'

'Well if you are sure but don't leave them laying about

MAGGIE WILSON

will you. If anyone comes round I don't want them visible, ok?'

'This has happened before hasn't it?'

'What?'

'What about that guy the detective was on about. Nurses have been jailed for acts like this. It's real Sally. Nurses who intentionally kill their patients.'

'Seems as though you have developed some morbid fascination here Loz.'

'Not really.'

'Hospitals are full of people who are ill, and some of those people will die, whatever we try and do for them. Sometimes several patients die within a short space of time. Occasionally one or two of the staff are particularly unlucky in being on duty when too many deaths occur. It doesn't mean that they are directly responsible for their deaths. Or, as you are suggesting, they killed them on purpose,' Sally questioned.

'It's real Sal, you know that and let's face it there are days that I'd like to shut them up myself!'

'I know, I'm sure we all often joke about it, but truth is none of us want to be on duty when a cardiac arrest ends in death. None of us also ever think that it is one of our colleagues that have caused the death intentionally. We need to stop this conversation Lorraine. You are doing my head in with all this.'

'How would you know Sal? What does a killer nurse look like? Any ideas on that one?'

'Same as you and me I expect, they are not going to walk around with a name badge outing themselves are they?'

'Sal, murder of patients on the wards by anyone employed to provide their care is going to be so rare that we won't ever come across it.'

'Can't you see that we have come across it? We are living the nightmare, right here, right now. You need to wake up to reality Lorraine and quickly.'

'But I thought they had no evidence of the deaths being intentional? They are just being cautious surely, just in case something is going on.'

'Can we agree to drop the subject for the time being? Fancy putting all that away and coming out for a few drinks with me? I need some time out; the atmosphere on the ward certainly wasn't very pleasant today. It's as if we are all looking at each other accusing each other of being 'the one'. Come on; say you will come out with me, just for a couple.'

'What now? You have changed your tune. It feels a little inappropriate to be going out drinking with all this going on around us.'

'Yes, now. I really have had enough of all this today and need to let off some steam. Everyone is telling me their side of things, dumping their views on me and I just need a break from it. So, let's go out for a few drinks before I end up sulking on my own with a headache. I haven't been able to shift this headache these last few hours, so a couple of pints and an early night will do the trick for me. That detective is still hanging about on the ward, seems to be working his way through all of us with his questioning.'

'I didn't mean to upset you, don't let us fall out over this, and I am sorry if I have been moaning at you too much about it all. I just can't bear the thought of the cops interviewing me. It's all getting on top of me and I just thought by following what the papers say I can be one step ahead.'

'Ahead of who?' she paused and took a long hard look at her friend. 'Look let's forget this for now huh? The pub awaits.' Sally didn't wait to hear what Lorraine was going to tell her about her paranoia regarding her forthcoming police interview and her reasoning for her trepidation. 'Anyone would think with your sudden enthusiasm you had something to do with the deaths!'

'What?' Lorraine questioned, and then laughed, 'I've seen that type of suspect on CSI.'

* * * * *

Charlie was beginning to enjoy his day on the ward. The interview with Tim had cheered him up no end, he loved a challenge and this guy was giving it to him on a plate. He would break him in half and have him talking in no time. Having decided to recommence their discussion about the clinical issues, Tim seemed to be answering each given question without so much attitude. Charlie was almost disappointed with Tim's new-found compliance. He continued his questioning this time trying to provoke him. He could at least amuse himself whilst trudging through the investigation.

'Tim, do you have any ideas to explain how these patients died?' Charlie enquired.

'I have no idea; shouldn't you be talking to pathology or something?'

'But I am here talking to you, so I am asking you.'

'Obviously I have no idea.'

'Are you sure about that?'

'Of course. What makes you think I would know anything?'

'I am seeking answers and asking you questions, that is my job. It is your job to answer questions about your patients, so I will ask you again. What do you know about the deaths of these patients?'

'Nothing, just that they died, they were all fit for their surgery and they died after failed resuscitation attempts.'

'And?' Charlie waited for his reply, watching his face as Tim pondered an answer.

'And what?'

'Nothing else you want to tell me?'

'Nothing.'

'Alright Tim. That is enough for now. Go back to the ward; I will let you know when we need to speak to you again.'

'When you need to speak to me again? I thought you said you were seeing us here. Now you say that you are interviewing us all again?'

'I said I will let you know when I need to talk to you again. Goodbye Mr Simpson.'

Oh he can go to hell, Tim thought. He really has no idea about patient care or the wards. All he was doing was messing their whole team up and putting suspicion on them when there was no evidence against any one of them.

Tim, against his better judgement left in silence. He wanted to leave with a great parting shot but decided against it. This detective obviously didn't like him and he got the feeling that if he said anything else he would be taken in without hesitation and have something pinned on him.

He wasn't going to risk that. He seemed to be in enough trouble with him already.

Tim was in no mood for the disarray of toys he found greeting him when he opened the door to the flat he shared with his wife Caroline and their 18 month old daughter, Bethany. Usually this would not bother him, he would smile at the thought of her playing as he saw her toys strewn across the floor. Today was the exception. Tripping over her favourite teddy was the final straw. Teddy had ambushed him as soon as he entered. The one place he thought he could finally find some sanctuary at the end of his tortuous day was maybe not going to give him the escape that he so desperately needed.

Caroline could hear him cuss as soon as the front door banged. Two very obvious signs to her that he had experienced a bad day. She was unaccustomed to seeing him in this frame of mind. For a moment she thought it best to leave him until he came through to her. She could hear him banging the cupboard door as he hung his coat, continuing to cuss and mutter as he did so.

'Tim?' she called out softly, peering round the corner at him, she could only imagine what stress he must be going through right now! 'Are you ok love?'

'No, not really!'

Caroline thought it better to keep out of his way until he was ready to talk, but asked anyway, 'Wanna talk about it?'

Tim arrived alongside her in the kitchen moments later. 'Bloody ward. You are not going to believe what is happening there now.'

'That bad? Fancy a cup of tea?'

'I'll put it on,' he said picking up the kettle. 'It really couldn't be any worse.'

'Come on, do you want to talk about it?'

'I am not sure that I do. But...' he hesitated, 'it's necessary so that you know what shits I work with.'

'Oh Tim. Haven't you learnt to back off from the gossips? Just get on with your work and ignore them.'

'You better sit down. There's a lot more to it than that.'

'Sounds ominous.'

'It sure is. I am going to resign, get myself out of there before I get caught up in the shit that they are causing themselves.'

'Oh come on, slow down Tim, you are not making any sense. What exactly has happened?' She looked at her husband, studied the lines of worry appearing across his face. She hadn't ever noticed him showing them before, he looked tired, then when didn't they both? Since Bethany's arrival they hardly had any time together and were always tired, perhaps she more than he realised.

'What's happened?' Caroline repeated.

'Where do I start?' He put his head in his hands and sank down into the armchair, as if retreating into himself.

'You haven't done something that has caused you to be reprimanded have you?' she enquired cautiously.

'Caroline, please don't speculate. I need a minute. This is all getting confusing in my head. The fucking bastards have got me all confused. My head is banging, I have a hell of a headache coming, I can just feel it.'

She sat on the edge of the armchair and put her arm

around him, offering him what little comfort she could. Something was obviously bothering him, maybe he just wasn't ready to tell her.

'I am getting out of ward 73. That I am sure about,' he stated emphatically.

'Why?' she enquired.

'Fucking detectives that's why.'

'Tim, you are making no sense here, what have detectives got to do with anything?'

'Bloody detective on the ward. Been saying that our patients have been killed by one of us! That's what.'

'What the…?' she stopped herself in time, not wishing Bethany, who was now playing at her feet, to hear what she was about to say.

'There were a couple of patients that died last week, but one died in the theatre, so it wasn't anything to do with us on the ward. Bloody detective comes in and takes over our ward, telling us he wants to speak to us all and ask what we know about these deaths.'

'Do you know anything?'

'Oh come on, not you as well. Of all people I wouldn't have expected that from you.'

'I was only asking Tim. You really aren't telling me much here.'

'Can't can I? I s'pose I shouldn't have even told you what I have. Patient confidentiality and all that shit.'

'So are they going to speak to you more about all this?'

'Seems like it.'

'So what's your problem?'

'Are you for real? My problem is that the damned detectives think that one of us is responsible for the deaths of our patients that's what. Why do they think we spend so much time caring for them and putting up with the obnoxious ones? Just so we can find the right moment to bump them off?'

'You are probably getting the wrong end of the stick here. Surely if they thought that they would have the suspects down the cop shop.'

'Maybe there are just too many staff to suspect? Can't get all of us in the cells there can they? Could be a nurse, doctor, porter, anyone really. Could even be a patient. The plods just don't know what they are on about. That is why I have decided to get out of ward 73. Find a new job as soon as I can. It won't take long before anyone who has worked there will be associated with whatever it is that is really going on and none of us will get a job anywhere else again. Best to get the hell out of there whilst I can,' Tim stated without pause for breath.

'Don't you think you are being a bit hasty? If there are detectives on the ward then it's not surprising that you are a bit nervous about being there. You haven't done anything wrong but if you start drawing attention to yourself by jumping ship you might just have something to regret. Don't you think? Especially as you have only just started working there.'

'Oh I don't know. That detective really is some bastard you know. Pissed me right off today.'

'Surely if you quit the ward that is going to encourage more suspicion towards you. If it is as bad as you are saying, drawing attention to yourself is the last thing you should be doing.'

'I have to get out of there. Whoever is responsible could try and pin it on someone else, I am sure as hell not going to wait around and let it be me.'

'Come on. Just ride this out. See what happens. It could all turn out to be nothing, couldn't it?'

'It could, but I don't think that is going to happen.'

18

The post mortem results were in and Chalmers couldn't get his head around them. He just kept staring at the reports, reading and re-reading their contents. Reaching for his phone, he dialled Charlie's desk and summoned both him and Vicky to his office. Much to Charlie's relief further teams of detectives had arrived at Westwood giving him an excuse to leave and return to the sanctuary of the station. However temporary, he was just relieved to get out of there and be able to breathe non-antiseptic air for a while.

The two of them sat across from Chalmers at his desk. The only item resting on its surface was a report in a dark grey A4 sized folder. Chalmers was looking at it pensively, like it was going to burst into flames at any moment.

He broke the stony silence. 'The post mortem reports are in and we now need to get results with this investigation. The public are not going to remain oblivious to the escalating number of deaths for much longer. We need to make sense of these post mortem results. As far as I can see there is just no link. Forces are to be drafted in from neighbouring areas to provide extra bodies in uniform to man the hospital. That place is going to be crawling with uniform soon; no one will be able to move unless we know about it. Right now we need to go through the victims' details and organise the board for further investigations.'

Chalmers had his Detective Inspector head on and was avoiding all eye contact whilst speaking to them. He had hardly taken his eyes off the typed words on the pages of the report all the time he spoke. He was overseeing this investigation and it was becoming increasingly apparent to him that he had to be more involved in order to get the result they needed.

'Each victim has a varying cause of death, a different drug found in their bloodstream on post mortem. Listen up guys, this is going to take some time and concentration to get through…'

He paused to ensure they were ready, knowing full well that there was no way they could be prepared for what they were about to hear.

'Victim one, had lethal levels of insulin, as did victim two. Victim three had lethal levels of digoxin, victim four, potassium. I have had the pharmacy go through this with me. Insulin as we know is a drug for diabetes, digoxin is a cardiac medicine, to slow and regulate the heart rate. Potassium is given as a supplement when the body is depleted in it. When given in excess this drug can cause heart problems, at least this is how it has been explained to me by the pathologist.' Chalmers read from the medical report, briefly looking up at Vicky and Charlie as he wanted to see if their expressions confirmed they were following him with this, knowing full well there was not much chance that they were. They were both staring right at him, their gazes fixed. He continued reading the report out to them. 'And secondly to increase the systemic vascular resistance and restore through this way, a better tissue perfusion. That's not my version of that, I might add. I seem to have swallowed the pharmacist's words there sorry. What I understand is that if this drug is given to a patient who does not require it, it will induce the tachycardia, the fast pulse, and, or a heart rhythm that could cause death.'

'David Waters!' Charlie flippantly added.

'By the sound of it yes. Same conclusion.' He wasn't quite following all the medical jargon he was reading himself, how was a hospital phobic like Hammond going to cope he wondered?

'All these drugs are available on most wards in the hospital. Insulin is kept in a drug fridge; some of the wards keep their drug fridges locked, whilst others are not so meticulous about this,' Charlie said and drew another breath before reeling out his notes on the other drugs, 'Digoxin is kept in a locked cupboard along with potassium and Adrenaline. The Adrenaline is also kept on the ward resuscitation trolleys but is kept in a sealed drug box. If this had been tampered with it would be noticeable, and of course the drug would be accounted for. If taken from this trolley the daily check on the trolley and drug box would show this up. No wards have reported the Adrenaline from the arrest trolleys missing and the pharmacy department keeps a regular check on these boxes, mainly to ensure the drugs are in date.' He finished with a deep sigh. 'The rest of the drugs that are kept in the medicine cupboard, they are kept locked at all times, or should be. The keys to these are held by, as I understand it, any qualified member of staff who is on shift. That gives several people access to the drugs that are not accounted for in any way. Medicines that are controlled drugs, morphine, diamorphine etc are counted and signed for each time they are administered. Other medications are not. There is a potential minefield here as we cannot track the movement of these drugs. Whoever they are, they are not touching drugs that can be accounted for and would be noticed to be missing.'

'But not one of these patients had the drug that was found to be in their body prescribed to them. So what the hell is going on? How could this be happening? I can just about run with someone injecting the drugs directly to the patient but the PM's are clear for any additional needle marks on these victims. The only marks they have are where the cannulas were,' Vicky added.

'Is this idiot totally trying to take the piss? Playing with drugs, changing their mind about what they are using? Or is it just what they can get their hands on?' Charlie posed.

'Are we assuming that they administered the drugs via the cannulas then?' questioned Vicky quickly adding her thoughts.

Chalmers responded after a short pause for some well needed thought. 'Not at all. I understand that this is a risky method for anyone to be using. There would be far too great a risk of someone witnessing it being done. But not to be totally ruled out though at this stage.'

'Have any of the wards reported missing stock drugs?' added Vicky.

'None. It's difficult to assess apparently, as there are no specified stock levels and no records kept of how many of a certain drug are in the cupboard. Only the controlled drugs are counted and documented, I have checked that one with Cate on the ward already.'

'How the hell have they got victims on two different wards? That doesn't sound possible. If someone is giving the patients random drugs then they have to have access to those patients.'

'Have we got more than one sick mind here? Surely the

thought of that is beyond comprehension! One would be one too many.'

'One competing with the other for the acclaim and attention maybe?'

'For that to be the case then they would have to be in collusion. In my opinion that would be far too great a risk to take, having another know what you are doing.'

'Well, so far not one of the staff that I have interviewed has had anything to say that helps us in any way. Maybe a second round of questioning will unearth something.'

Walking over towards the investigation board Chalmers began to put up pictures of the victims, one by one. As he did so he stated each and every person's details.

'Victim one, Betty Adams, aged 71, was admitted to ward 73 on 2nd April for routine surgery. She had a total hip replacement on the 3rd. She died on the table in the orthopaedic theatre, before surgery was completed. There was a resuscitation attempt. She had an intravenous infusion commenced on the ward and the bag that was put up was still the bag that was attached to her drip when she died. The post mortem showed that she had abnormally high levels of the drug insulin in her blood. Betty wasn't a diabetic and at no stage in her treatment had she been prescribed insulin.

'Victim two, Hannah Brown, female, aged 64 was admitted to ward 73 on 3rd April for surgery on the 4th. She died in the recovery room adjacent to the general theatre. She was admitted for a cholysystectomy.'

'What?' muttered Charlie.

'To have her gall bladder removed, apparently. She had an intravenous infusion running when she arrived in theatre and had a new bag of fluid put up when she was in recovery. She had been in the recovery unit for an hour and a half before the staff had to undertake the resuscitation process. Again unsuccessful. Again her toxicology showed abnormally high levels of insulin. She too was never prescribed insulin and was not a diabetic.

'Victim three, female, Martha Jones, aged 78, admitted to ward 73 on 3rd April. She was transferred from the accident and emergency department where she had come in as an emergency admission to the orthopaedic theatre. She had an intravenous infusion started in the A & E department and further bags of fluid given both on ward 73, and in the recovery unit. There was a resuscitation attempt but again it failed. Martha's toxicology report showed abnormally high levels of digoxin, a drug used to slow and steady the heart rate. Martha had no history of heart problems and had never been prescribed this drug.

'Victim four, Harriet Skillen, 67 year old female, she was a routine admission to ward 73 for a hip replacement, came in 6th April, had surgery on 7th and died in the early hours of 8th after being back on the ward only a few hours. The post mortem showed that she had lethal levels of the drug potassium in her body.

'Victim five, female, 23, that's all we know at the moment. We should have the post mortem in over the next day or so. We also cannot assume that this is linked!'

'The only links between these victims is that they all had intravenous infusions, and they all had surgery. There are no other common links with consultants, nursing or ancillary staff, surgery or allergies. They were operated on in a variety of theatres; the only bloody link is the drips; even then that gives us nothing. All the batch numbers of the bags used are different. They were signed for by different members of staff who checked and set the drips up. So no bloody link really at all.'

'What if the batches are faulty or expired fluids were put into the wrong bags, or even worse that someone at the manufacturing end had wrongly labelled the bags?' Vicky said.

'So don't just sit there Vicky, get uniform to pay them a visit and report back to me as soon as you can. If there are dodgy bags of fluid we need to get all the fluids withdrawn from the hospital as soon as possible. Get someone on to the drug manufacturers too, check out batches of drugs delivered to Westwood General recently and double-check from pharmacy's end,' Charlie ordered.

'Ok, right on it,' Vicky stated as she got up to leave.

'Get extra uniform to man the wards too, I want two officers at the entrances to all the wards. Anyone and I mean absolutely anyone who wants access to the wards will be logged, who they are, who they are visiting, and how long they are there. Record down to what they had for lunch if it helps us find this son of a bitch. If they are staff, I want it logged how long they are on the ward and why they are going on to the ward if they are not on a shift there and what ward they have come from. If they are there to borrow something full details must be logged. Within the hour I want Westwood General crawling with uniform,' Chalmers ordered. 'Where the hell are we going wrong here? Where is the little bastard hiding? And how the hell are they doing this?' Chalmers slammed his fist down hard on the desk, instantly regretting his decision to do so.

Alone in his office Chalmers reflected the gravity of the situation. Whilst awaiting other forces to draft in additional detectives it was looking likely that he would have to head a team at Westwood general himself.

There were so many interviews to get through they already had six detectives interviewing there. So far not one of the staff interviewed had noticed anything that was of any help to them in their investigation. He wondered at what point would they get their well-deserved breakthrough and be able to stop these unnecessary deaths.

He would have to send someone to take charge of the interviews on ward 68, if no one suitable was available then he knew he would have to attend there himself.

Re-interviewing random members of staff on ward 73 would be his first priority and of course the pharmaceutical staff. He was unsure if Charlie had actually interviewed the whole team there or not. He would chase this issue up with him once he had allocated the additional teams to the other wards. Organising the presence of uniform at the doors of all the wards was more pressing in his mind.

He wondered at what point he would have to consider closing the ward down to protect the patients' interests. He really wasn't sure if the hospital should be running at all, but he had no proof of any foul play right now. What if it was one of the patients? He couldn't afford to think about that, a patient with little medical knowledge seeing the opportunity to steal drugs from an open cupboard and inserting them in to the cannula of another patient? Possible though maybe not so probable.

That was unheard of and almost unthinkable. Stranger things happened though. He deliberated for a moment. No, he was definitely thinking off track here or at least he hoped he was. Surely the ward staff would have noticed something before a patient reached the drug cupboards. He shuddered at the thought and pushed it to the back of his mind.

Chalmers was heading for despair. Could he bring forensics in? He wondered where they would start? The victims all died in different places, the wards and theatres. The domestic services would have been in to clean those areas countless times since the deaths.

He would have to contact DS Harvey and see if he could bring in a criminal profiler, maybe then they would have some more ideas as to what type of person they were looking for. See if there was any help that he could give them.

He was in total panic; the death count was rising and he just had no control, no leads and none of the staff had admitted to having ever seen anything suspicious. Had they already spoken to the Fallen Angel during the preliminary interviews on the wards? Usually Chalmers could smell guilt from fifty paces but today he had absolutely no clue. Was he losing it? He hated himself when he couldn't solve a crime, especially when murder was involved and some smartarse was on the loose. He would not stand for it. No stone could be left unturned. He was adamant about that.

Chalmers was beginning to dream of his golf clubs. He was approaching retirement and this morning began wishing that he could end all of this right now. He should be out in the brilliant sunshine swinging his clubs. Instead he was heading a team who had absolutely no leads in what was turning out to be the nightmare crime of his career. Give him a body and a murder weapon and he would get his perpetrator. But with no motive and no murder weapon he was stumped. Totally lost and knee-deep in bodies at Westwood General and he didn't want to be there. He promised himself when this was all over he was resigning, he would take his pension and run. He really couldn't do this anymore; if he took three months sick leave it would lead him up to his retirement date perfectly. He would be out of this as soon as he could, or as soon as this was over. If indeed it would ever be over. If he didn't solve this soon he knew that he would be pushed out without the element of choice.

19

Her feet were sluggish, Cate did not relish the thought of reaching the ward. For one moment she thought she could see two uniformed officers standing like century guards either side of the ward door, she rubbed her eyes, thinking she was still half asleep. Nearing them the reality of the situation hit her, she really did have two uniformed police officers at the entrance to her ward.

WPC Lorna Wilkes and PC John Henderson introduced themselves to her when she revealed that she was the ward sister. She was requested to produce her ID to them to confirm this. Shocked at this turn of events, the seriousness of the situation again slapped her in the face.

They informed her that they were to be taking notes of who entered and left her ward, how long they were on the ward and what business they had there.

Lorna wasn't looking forward to the day ahead of her, standing at the entrance to the ward wasn't exactly the idealistic image of police work that she'd had in her mind when she joined the force. As an officer with less than a year's experience she was one of the first in line for Westwood's duties. It was the not knowing if she would be here today or tomorrow as well, or the next day, she saw no end to it. Fortunately John, her colleague, was amiable and spending the day logging activities of the ward visitors perhaps wouldn't be so bad after all with his company to divert her.

Cate, however, wasn't so impressed.

Weren't they taking this just a little too far? Why wasn't she told this was going to happen? Did no one bother to keep her in the loop, after all it was still her ward? Just about. She was struggling to hold on to her team, had restrictions on her admissions and cops based at the entrance. Nope. Cate certainly wasn't in charge of ward 73 anymore and she was desperate to find out who was responsible for upsetting her life like this.

She thought she may as well offer hospitality, she didn't want to upset them so early in their shift.

'Can I get either of you some coffee?' she smiled as she spoke, thinking it best to be agreeable with them if they were going to be there for a while.

'That would be great, in fact, I will come with you and you can show me where we can make it if that is ok?' replied Lorna.

'No problem, come with me,' added Cate as she reached

for the door.

She led Lorna a few paces on to the ward, entering the main ward kitchen.

'So whose idea is this then?' Cate posed.

'Probably come from the top.'

'The detectives who are here on the ward? Would they have requested you?'

'No, when I say top I mean the guys who rarely come out of their offices. Believe me they are all out of their little comfort zones now, trying to sort Westwood out. They are dusting off their desk shoes, putting down their pipes and out with the best of us now.'

'Oh.'

'It's murder isn't it, it always gets them running and this is a hospital where the public come to be cared for. When there is risk to the public they are not going to take any chances, they are all going mad trying to get this one sorted.'

'Oh shit.'

'Sorry I didn't mean to imply it was something to do with you or your ward Cate.'

'Don't worry about it. Let's face it, it is something to do with me and my ward isn't it. They were all our patients.'

She could hear her phone ringing in her office as she approached it. She flung open the door and reached for the receiver, her heart leapt as she realised it was her favourite detective. Almost as quickly she remembered she was mad at him for attempting to manipulate her.

'How are you today Cate? Bearing up?' She almost identified a sparkle in his voice.

'Just about. Are you coming to the ward today?'

Why on earth did she have to say that? She could have kicked herself! Why did she lie about how she was feeling? Surely he would understand, given the circumstances. She didn't want to appear out of control though, didn't want him to think she couldn't handle her job. She had to raise her defences where he was concerned until she was sure that she could trust him.

'Just to let you know that there will be a team of forensics down at some stage today, I will be down in a couple of hours. A few things I have to check out first then I will be resuming interviews on the ward. I will try and be there for coffee!'

Bastard, he was still trying to be jovial with her, she wasn't falling for it but would let him think she was, to some degree at least. She had to play him at his own game. She just wasn't sure that she could balance the love-hate feelings that she had for him.

Cate could almost see him smile as he made the comment about the coffee. She really would have to get some proper coffee for him if he was going to take root on her ward for much longer. Just to placate him, that was.

At last, someone was finally bringing her up to date with

what was happening around her. Usually she was the one calling the shots and informing everyone what was taking place. How the tables had turned on her in a matter of days and she wasn't at all comfortable with it.

'Oh, I already have your colleagues here.'

'Uniform?'

'Yes, two officers standing either side of the ward entrance as we speak. Right pair of bookends,' she struggled not to laugh at her own comment.

'That's good, we need to have everyone logged as they enter and leave the ward.'

'Surely that won't help us now, the patients died last week?'

'It could prevent further deaths Cate.'

By the time Charlie returned, the forensic team, consisting of three officers, were making their presence felt on ward 73.

They were white-clad from head to toe, in what looked like cheap paper boiler suits. How they held together to resemble an item of clothing was a mystery.

They were crawling on their hands and knees taking swabs for DNA. There was no lead to give them, no clue where to start so random samples were being taken. Maybe a pattern would emerge. If nothing else it would shake the staff up, he thought. At best, they may discover something that would help uncover their Fallen Angel.

There was already a growing pile of plastic bags, all tagged, with what appeared to be completed swabs in them.

The curtains around the other patients' beds had been drawn in such a way that the staff could see their patients but the patients couldn't quite see what was going on out on the ward. They had been told by the staff that a deep clean was being performed and that their beds were being moved temporarily to allow the procedure. This bluff would only work for them if the patients stayed within the confines of their beds and didn't attempt to wander along the ward. Cate was being vigilant in case this happened.

The forensic team were taking swabs from the drug trolley, Cate watching, walked up to them, 'You know you are going to find fingerprints and DNA from each and every one of us on there.'

The lab guy barely looked up, 'Just doing my job, you'd be surprised what turns up that isn't expected,' the white-clad vision in front of her was heard to say.

'So what next? Are we all going to be swabbed? What use is DNA to you if you have nothing to compare it with?'

He had no intention of further interaction with Cate and continued with his face firmly fixed on the surface of the trolley and the swab he was taking.

'How am I meant to run a surgical ward with you lot crawling around? Answer me that would you?' Cate saw she was going to get nowhere with him, receiving no response from him.

She was also scanning round to see if any of the patients had realised what was happening. How could she expect them to miss something like this?! They usually knew when the staff went for a sneaky coffee, they may be ill, but their senses were as sharp as. Who was she kidding? Should she admit defeat now? Go and see Frances and bail out? Give up ward 73, back out of nursing altogether perhaps. She was seeing logic according to Chloe now. Before Chloe had left for her days off Cate had thought she was overreacting saying that she didn't want to be part of the profession if it was going to be like this. Cate thought it was just Chloe's inexperience talking, but now she was beginning to think she had the right idea. Throwing in the towel and quitting wasn't usually Cate's style, she had put far too much work into her career and into ward 73 to walk away from it now.

Cate was scanning the room, at any given moment waiting for Charlie to arrive, then she heard from one of the domestic team that he was already sitting rather too comfortably in her office. Surveillance obviously wasn't her strong point.

He needed to advise her of the post mortem results. He knew he shouldn't but he wanted to see the reaction on her face himself, one to one when he told her. He would know then if he could eliminate her from his list of suspects in his mind and allow himself further illicit thoughts about her.

He had to know for his own peace of mind. Even if she wasn't officially eliminated from their enquiries. No one could be at this stage but he would go by his gut instinct and her reactions for the time being. His gut instinct very rarely failed him.

'Cate, here,' Charlie was calling out towards her down the ward. He was beckoning to her, signalling for her to come to the office.

She just couldn't get used to being asked to come to her office. Surely this nightmare had to end soon.

'Detective?' she questioned.

'Come in and sit down. We have the results from the first four of the post mortems.'

'You do?' her tone suddenly softened.

'All of the first four patients were found to have evidence of drugs in their system. Not one of them had these particular drugs prescribed to them.'

'Shit... Was it the same drug?'

'No, a variety.'

'Bloody hell. What now?'

'It's definitely murder. Someone had to have given those patients the drugs. The question is who and how,' he paused before adding, 'and indeed why.' He sank back into the comfort of her black leather desk chair, he looked far too comfortable for her liking. She felt like shouting at him to get out of her chair, her office and her ward. She thought better of it, just for now.

'But the patients weren't looked after by the same staff, you know that, so it can't be one person.'

'So either we are looking for more than one, or someone extremely devious in their crime.'

'So you think it is one of my staff then?' Cate hardly dare await his answer. Her heart pounding at the directness of her question to him.

'Not necessarily. The first four deaths were arguably your patients but they didn't all actually die on the ward. That puts a slightly different light on it.'

'So where does that leave us?' she said.

'Although we know that it is highly likely that an individual is responsible for giving the patients unprescribed drugs we don't know when, where or who. It's back to square one, unless he or she slips up and shows their face, we have an almost impossible task on our hands,' Charlie simply added.

20

The discussion with the fluid manufacturer had drawn nothing. Vicky, fed up stuck at the station, and longing to be part of the investigation at the hospital, had been handed the report from Matt in uniform. It turned out that the factory always tested random bags prior to the dispatch of their products. Each stage of the manufacture and bagging of the fluids had stringent double checking and testing in process so there was no element for error. They informed her that due to the nature of the investigation they would be running tests on all the current batches of fluids as a safeguard. They had requested samples of the bags of fluid from Westwood General to be returned to their labs, if the hospital had any of the same batches left in stock.

That meant that Vicky needed to check the prescription charts of all the victims and find out the batch numbers of the bags of fluid and get those numbers back to the factory as soon as possible. She rang through to Matt and requested that he come back up to her office and collect the copies of the charts. She could pass the buck on this one at least. She would then ask him to attend the General and go through the fluids on wards 73, 68, theatres and recovery. They would need to locate bags with the same batch number on them for further investigations and testing of the fluid.

She requested additional random checks to be done. She couldn't afford to miss anything out at this stage of their enquiries.

She also asked him to bring some other bags of fluid chosen at random with different batch numbers from a selection of the wards. This just had to be their link and she was out to prove it. Although it would still be headline news, it would be far better than finding out that a member of staff was premeditating the murder of their patients.

Chalmers would ask her to do this when he was informed so she thought it better to get them started on it.

By the time he asked her to sort it, she hoped that they would be coming back to her with some results.

Having found no common link other than the fact that all the victims had drips up at the time they died, or just before, Vicky had come up with another idea. She just had to get Detective Inspector Chalmers to run with it. That, she thought, was the hard bit. She had to do something whilst Matt was investigating the fluids. Just in case they did have a murderer on their hands. She thought it unlikely but had an idea how she could eliminate this possibility.

She went straight up to Chalmers' office. Charlie, she presumed, would be at Westwood, she'd deal with him later.

'Sir, can I have a minute please?' she enquired.

'Come in Vicky. What have you got for me?'

'Not exactly, well not directly got anything. The fluid manufacturers are coming up clear so far, but I do have an idea how we can get inside this case.'

'Go on.' He was staring intently at her, awaiting her thoughts.

'Well, obviously you know that I was once a trained nurse, I know it was a long time ago now, but I could go undercover as an auxiliary nurse to see if I can come up with anything? I would be able to observe much easier if I was part of the team and maybe hear some of the gossip from ground level? See what the staff are talking about? If they have any suspicions they will certainly all be talking about them despite being told by you and Charlie not to! The ward gossip can be second to none sometimes! The only person who would recognise me would be Cate Carter, the ward sister. So we would have to bring her in on this, though if she is part of this in any way I am sure she will trip herself up sometime.'

Not once had she paused to draw breath during her well-rehearsed speech.

'Not bad thinking, I'll see what I can do, are you sure

you can remember enough to keep your cover?... and forget enough to keep your cover,' he added.

'I'm sure I will remember as I go along and it's not as though I would be working as a qualified anyway, my registration expired years ago. But at least I can be in on the ground and be there to observe. Might just come up against the Fallen Angel?' she said, almost believing what she was saying to him.

'Leave it with me and I'll get back to you later this morning. Somehow we would have to explain your appearance on the wards when we have been so stringent in telling them not to move staff. I'm sure we could come up with something though. In the meantime see what Charlie has come up with when he gets back would you and I'll see who I can get to work with Charlie if you go in.'

Vicky hoped that Chalmers would take her request seriously. This was her chance to prove herself and maybe take her one step nearer to the promotion she so craved.

In the meantime Charlie had finished conducting the interviews with the ward staff for that morning and once again caught up with Cate. There was much more he needed to know. It was the technicalities that he just didn't understand and that he needed explaining to him.

He called out to her as she was just leaving a patient's bedside.

'Charlie!' He had startled her. What was it with this

guy always appearing out of nowhere? She certainly wasn't complaining about it though, she just preferred warning!

'Cate, would you share a coffee with me? I need you to go through a few more things,' said Charlie.

'I have got to go through this paperwork first then I am free, is that alright?' For once, Cate was going to make him wait for her until she was ready. No more jumping to his tune, even if he was a Detective Sergeant. He had to remember that this was still her ward, she didn't know for how much longer but today she was still in charge of her patients and she was going to remind them all of that.

Charlie turned and made his way to her office, he contemplated making himself a coffee but thought he would see if Cate volunteered that service herself. If not he would surely have to ask. He was desperately in need of his caffeine fix. A sandwich would have gone down well too but he knew it would be many hours before he got time to get himself some lunch, in fact, he was pretty sure it would be supper time before he even got around to lunch.

Cate actually hurried up the paperwork as she couldn't resist the thought of being with him alone, even if it was just to go through procedure.

'I need you to take me through the process of what happens with patients that are coming in for surgery as routine admissions. I need to know the exact process from admission to the hospital to post surgery. Everything. What checks do you do? Whose decision is it that someone is fit for surgery? Explain to me exactly. Criminal I can deal with but this medical stuff you are going to have to explain to me step by step,' Charlie said as she sat in the chair opposite him.

Cate felt as though this was no meeting but an interrogation that would never end. She took a deep breath and began to explain the process.

'Ok, let's start with Betty then, Betty Adams. She came as a booked admission. That means not as an emergency, she knew that she was coming in for planned surgery. Before Betty even got here to us on 73, she would have been seen by the nurse practitioner at the pre-operative assessment clinic. She would have gone through the full screening procedure of bloods (full blood count, haemoglobin, crp, u+e), a full medical history, a check to see if she had any known allergies, vital observations would have been taken (temperature, pulse, respirations, blood pressure, oxygen saturation levels) and she would have been asked if she'd had any previous surgery and if so any adverse reaction to an anaesthetic. She would also have had a routine ECG, a tracing of the heart, to check for any abnormalities that would preclude her from surgery. Any previous hospital notes would also have been sent to the clinic to check any information she gave and to document this current information in. The full procedure for surgery would have been explained to Betty at the clinic too, she would have been given the opportunity to ask any questions she may have had about the surgery or recovery time. She would have been told what to expect when she woke from the anaesthetic, like a drip or a catheter for instance.' She paused for a momentary breath before continuing.

'It would be at this point that she would sign the consent form for surgery. Some admissions come directly to the ward where the junior doctors would take all the patient's history on the ward and the same checks would be made, only whilst the patient was on the ward. If this happens they are usually admitted the day before surgery so that there is time to complete all these tests. When she was admitted as a patient to our ward, her admission procedure would involve all these details being re-checked. All the results of her blood tests and observations would be checked and the results available in her notes. She would also have been seen by the anaesthetist on the ward so that they could go through everything with her prior to her being in theatre. They would have the final say as to whether she was fit for anaesthetic. All this information would have been sent down to theatre with her so the surgeons had access to all the relevant information. On the day of her surgery one of the staff would have gone through a check list with her, which is sent to theatre on the front of her medical notes. She would also have had an identification bracelet put on when she was admitted to the ward. This would have her name, hospital number, date of birth and address on it. One of the patient's printed labels is used and stuck onto an ID bracelet. You see Detective, every possible attempt is made to ensure nothing is missed or overlooked to ensure the safe transfer of our patients from the ward to the theatre and back to us on the ward.'

'What about this check list then, remind me exactly what checks are made on that? I only really checked the signatures on those forms before. I didn't exactly digest the information it provided.'

Again Cate took a deep breath, gathered her thoughts, and began.

'Her vital signs, temperature, blood pressure, pulse, respirations, weight and height would all be checked and recorded again the day of surgery. The following would also be checked: name band, any allergies, medical history and blood sugar. If she used glasses or a hearing aid and needed to wear these to go to theatre it would be documented that these were going with her. If there were any prostheses that needed to be removed before she went and that the site of the proposed surgery had been marked. For example, having surgery on her left hip would mean there would be a mark made by a permanent marker so that there were no questions once she was anaesthetised as to which limb it was she was having surgery on,' she paused and sighed, 'Yet you have all this information.'

'I know, I just cannot get my head around it and there doesn't seem to be any pattern at all!' He paused, 'there is always a pattern!'

'There is?' Cate questioned.

He simply nodded, 'What about the procedure for checking the drips?'

'The fluids we put up you mean or checking the lines?'

'The fluids,' he said.

'The fluid is prescribed on a separate intravenous fluid chart, one separate from the main drug chart. Each bag is clearly labelled with the name of the fluid, the volume in the bag, bar code, batch number and expiry date. The formula for the fluid is also listed printed on the bag. That is what the fluid comprises of. The bag is also marked with lines and numbers showing how much fluid is in the bag. These markers are somewhat inaccurate so if we are using fluid containing potassium the drip set, or line as you would call it, is put in a pump to regulate the speed at which the patient gets the fluid. Also on the bag by the bar code is the manufacturer's name and address.'

'Yes, Vicky has had all that checked already.'

'Oh, she has, that's good,' Cate said with a heavy heart before carrying on with her breakdown of events. 'Before putting up a bag of fluid the prescription is checked to ensure the doctor has prescribed it correctly and has signed the prescription. If the fluid is NaCl (Sodium Chloride), 5% Glucose or Hartmann's Solution (Compound Sodium Lactate) then one trained nurse can read the prescription, check the bag of fluid themselves and administer it to the patient. Only when the bag of fluid is prescribed to contain potassium does it require two trained nurses to check the bag and to sign the prescription chart. One of the nurses then administers the bag of fluid by attaching it to the patient's drip line. The signatures and batch number of the bag, expiry date and the date and time of administration are all recorded on the prescription chart. When the two nurses check this bag we do not require that the two nurses both go to the patient. It is more of a safeguard that the bags are checked as they contain potassium - K. This is because the bags come with either K 20 mmol/l or 40 mmol/l. You see detective...'

'Call me Charlie, please.'

'Charlie,' she said with a smile, 'we do check these things with precision because as you will realise if these drugs are given to patients who are not prescribed them then adverse effects are involved and the results can be devastating.'

'Five counts of devastation in this case!' he flippantly added.

'Sadly, yes!' she said, again being thrown from her train of thought, it was hard enough for her to be in the same room as him without clamming up she didn't need him to keep butting in with snarky comments too. 'Sometimes these bags of fluid have drugs added to them for administration. Let me take an example; when we give a drug such as digoxin, we do not put the few mls that the drug consists of in its neat form into the cannula. The drug is added to a small bag of fluid (NaCl) and then given as a drip over the prescribed timescale. As I have told you there is a port on the fluid bag where drugs can be added. One thing I might add at this point is that most of the drugs that we add to these bags of fluid are clear and colourless fluids, so when the drug is added to the clear fluid the bag appears as it would before the drug was added. To avoid any confusion or drug error a bright yellow sticky label is completed and stuck on the back of the bag of fluid. The label states the patient's name, hospital number, what the drug is that has been added, its dose, when it was prepared and when it expires. The whole process is checked by two trained nurses and they both have to sign the label to say they have checked it. There is no margin for error here. The bag of fluid then is administered to the patient by one trained nurse. Two nurses are not required to check the patient.' She knew she was repeating herself now, there was so much she wanted to get through but she suddenly felt overemotional.

'We can stop if you'd prefer?' he asked placing his hand

on hers.

'No, I will be fine, but thank you,' she said embracing his touch before carrying on. 'The only exception to this rule is when drugs like morphine are being used. These drugs are kept in a double locked cupboard and the drugs are counted and checked by two trained nurses. There is a separate register to record how many of the drugs remain in the stock. In this instance the two nurses are required to go to the patient and check the prescription against the patient details and their ID bracelet.'

'Coffee?' he said hoping that she too was ready to take a short break.

'Coffee?' she questioned.

'I am sure that you could do with a cup, I know I could.' He smiled down at her as he stood and reached for the phone. 'Tell me, could someone get around the system?'

Before she could answer he was picking up her phone and ordering coffee for two to be brought in. At this stage Charlie felt like his body had given up caffeine as it had been so long!

Cate was also feeling the lack of caffeine, she really did have one humdinger of a headache on its way; she could just feel it brewing. She would have to treat herself to two paracetamol with her caffeine hit, in a vague attempt to rid herself of it.

Charlie and Cate continued their conversation with coffee in hand. Cate remained the one who was doing all the talking. The caffeine aided Charlie's concentration levels, which were rapidly wearing thin. He hoped that she didn't realise how out of his depth he was with the information that she was giving him.

'With regard to the administration of intravenous drugs, this procedure requires two nurses to check the drugs but only one to go to the patient with the drugs to give them. The two both check the drug prescription chart to check the drug name, dose, and the due time for administration. The signature of a doctor also has to be on the prescription. For example benzylpenicillin is a commonly used antibiotic that is administered intravenously. It is not available in tablet or any other form than for intravenous use. This particular drug comes in a small glass vial less than an inch tall. It is required to be dissolved in NaCl. To do this the saline used is in sterile plastic vials. Again the vial is checked for its contents and expiry date. The same is done for the antibiotic that is being used. The saline is drawn up into a syringe and then added to the vial of the benzylpenicillin. The vial is secured by a small colour-coded cap that is snapped off to reveal a plastic bung that is used to insert the needle through to add the saline. The contents are mixed by shaking the vial and the needle re-inserted in to the vial to withdraw the drug that is now a clear dissolved liquid. This liquid is then added to a bag of 100 mls of NaCl so that it can be given to the patient via a drip. As recent as the past few years this particular drug used to be given without adding it to the bag of fluid. Changes for the administration of drugs were made though and we changed our practice to give many drugs added to bags of saline. This reduces the risk of the drug being given too quickly and also dilutes it so there is reduced risk of burning the vein with a concentrated drug. Some drugs and antibiotics are given into the cannula when dissolved in fifteen to twenty mls of saline or water, depending on which drug is used, bolus administration, as we call it.'

'Any of our *vics* need this?'

He had just done it again she thought, losing her trail of thought she simply added, 'Er, no, I don't think so!' She continued, 'Other intravenous antibiotics and drugs that we give directly into the cannula are checked by two trained nurses. Again though, it is not required that the two nurses go to the patient when the drug is given. Just that the drug is checked.'

'So they could be changed before they got to the patient?'

'Well seeing you put it like that, then yes. What you are saying is right, it would also be possible for the nurse to take the drug and give it to another patient.'

'One that it wasn't prescribed to?'

'Technically yes, but it wouldn't happen. That would

constitute a drug error.'

'That's exactly what it could be, it could all just be possible.'

'Possible yes, in practice no. A nurse who has trained for three years has their registration to uphold. No one in their right mind would risk their registration or do something so stupid,' she ranted. 'We are here to care for our patients, they are vulnerable and often frightened when in hospital and we have a duty of care to provide to them. That's what we do here detective. Care for our patients. If the patient was allergic to that particular drug, which often happens with antibiotics, then it could cause such a severe reaction that death could ensue.'

'Just remember you said that Cate. Not me.'

'I am stating facts here Detective and answering your questions. It would indeed be possible. It's just quite impossible someone would even think of doing it, let alone actually carry it out.'

'But is it?' he added.

For a second they both stayed silent.

'Cate, you have to remember we are looking for a really sick individual here. Someone is actually doing this intentionally.'

As far as Cate was concerned their conversation was over. She felt like she was the one under interrogation, she was beginning to take this personally and she just wanted him to go, to get out of her life and get off her ward. She just wanted to get on with her job and get her ward running normally as it usually did. She had a long uphill struggle ahead of her trying to support her staff. Who was going to support her through this?

They both sat in silence, each trawling through a variety of confused thoughts in their mind. He enjoyed being with her, for him it was as simple as that!

Charlie's head really was aching with all this technical information, maybe he should have sent Vicky along to speak to Cate. Why hadn't he thought of that earlier and saved himself this entire information overload? He was enjoying listening to Cate and watching how she showed such enthusiasm about her profession, and he thought, such a wealth of knowledge. He wasn't sure about having Vicky there anyway, he wanted Cate to himself at the moment and Vicky clucking about acting like his mother was something that he really didn't need right now.

Charlie had noticed some time ago that Vicky mothered him far too much. He often wondered if she carried a torch for him, but dismissed that one out of turn. She knew him better than that surely.

Charlie had been frantically trying to note down what Cate had been telling him. He'd got the salient points he needed and he could always request her to come to the station to go through it again, couldn't he. Some parts of this investigation he was actually enjoying, for once. It made a change to have someone as vibrant as Cate to talk with.

He was beginning to wonder what was happening to him. He was becoming preoccupied with thoughts of Cate; it certainly wasn't just her professionalism and enthusiasm that was holding his attention.

He wasn't used to his mind having thoughts of a woman, none other than Valerie anyway. He wasn't sure how to handle what he was beginning to feel. He dealt with it the only way he knew how and that was to bury his head in his work. He wouldn't allow himself those thoughts of luxury because there was no room in his life for getting hurt. No room at all for that. He snapped himself back to reality. Stood up from his chair and looked directly at Cate. He tried to perfect his serious face but felt himself fail slightly. She was certainly having some form of effect on him, although he wasn't quite sure what it was just yet. He had to remember that she was part of his investigation on ward 73. Until the deaths were explained or a murderer caught, then Cate too was under suspicion. That thought alone snapped Charlie back to the reality of his investigation.

'Cate, before I go, I need you to make sure that the procedures for the drug administration are secure. Any drugs that are prescribed for intravenous use, I need you to ensure that two trained nurses do the checking from start to finish. By that I mean that they both go to the patient and that they are both present whilst the drug is given. Every part of the procedure is to be witnessed by the second nurse. Both need to sign the drug chart, not just the normal procedure of the nurse that has given the drug signing the prescription chart. There should be no way that drugs can be given to the wrong patient or indeed not given.'

'Ok, that's fine, something we should be thinking about implementing anyway,' Cate said.

'Your staff will feel happier if there are two of them anyway. Working under these circumstances I am sure nobody is going to complain about that procedure,' he said. 'Just try not to arouse suspicion in the patients, especially in their family or friends. A public outcry and mass panic about the state of our healthcare is all we need at the moment, I'm not sure if the Detective Inspector will be too happy about that!'

Cate managed a smile.

'If the public get a hold of our suspicions then the world will be upside down before the bulletin is over,' he added.

He was desperate to leave the hospital, nothing he wanted more than a long drawn in breath of fresh spring air to rid him of the ever lingering hospital smell that seemed to cling to his insides as well as his clothes. It was the first time he had noticed the newsagent's shop, the coffee bar and the florist all in a row adjacent to the main entrance. He found himself lingering by the flowers, a striking array of many different coloured roses in a green plastic bucket had caught his attention. He selected the colour that he knew she would like, a delicate yet vibrant shade of pink.

As he approached to pay for his choice he noticed the assistant was older than on first glance, chubby and fairly innocuous, not a face that would stand out in a crowd.

'You realise they are two for one, we always sell them off cheaper at the end of the day son.'

It was years since anyone had called him that, he allowed a smile to escape gradually. 'She'd appreciate that,' he said with a smile.

'I am sure the young lady will love you all the more when you give her two!'

Charlie simply smiled.

From her position at the front of the queue at the coffee shop, Cate witnessed the whole episode intently, unsure if she felt anger or hatred towards him or just the woman he was buying the roses for. She paid for her sandwich and made a hasty retreat back to ward 73.

Charlie was now in possession of twice the roses he wanted, and an idea struck him. One was sufficient for where he intended them to go.

'Here, lad,' he called out.

'Me?' enquired the lanky porter that was passing him by.

'Yes, lad. Do me a favour and take these up to ward 73. Make sure that they are put in the sisters office would you.'

'73 is only along the corridor, can't you take them yourself mate?' he replied.

Charlie wasn't in the mood for a smartarse, he opened his suit jacket, reached into his inner pocket and produced what looked like a rather thin battered black wallet and proceeded to flip it open.

'DS Hammond, CID,' he voiced authoritatively.

His ID badge reinforced this information rather rapidly and the young porter took a step back and put out his hand towards Charlie to take the flowers without speaking another word.

Returning to the police station Charlie was in need of some further serious caffeine and some effective headache pills. He stopped at the vending machine on the way up to see Vicky, choosing a cappuccino with extra sugar.

He sipped from the lid of his coffee cup. He savoured the tang, as he knocked back a swig. It felt like hours since he had had a fix of his desired beverage even though it wasn't really that long. He desperately needed to rid himself of the bitter taste at the back of his throat and the lingering smell of antiseptic.

Charlie had taken half an hour out on his way back to

the station to stop at the cemetery and put flowers on his wife's grave. Westwood and the investigation would have to wait. It was the anniversary of Valerie's death, three years now.

As he stood at the graveside he held back his tears, intense emotion always hit him when he visited her but today he would have to keep a check of himself. Time to reflect extensively was a luxury that he just couldn't afford. He would save that for the sanctuary of home when his meetings were all done.

Sometimes it felt like it was yesterday, others it felt like an eternity since she had been there with him. Valerie had died after suffering with cancer. Neither she, nor Charlie, had much warning that they were to be parted. He knew he had left ward 73 abruptly but he had to visit Valerie and keep his regular appointment with her.

That was what got to Charlie most, not having had enough time with her before he lost her. He would often wonder what would have been enough time. Eternity wouldn't have been long enough to come to terms with the prospect of losing her. Charlie had shut himself away following his loss not knowing how to deal with it. The only way he could cope was to throw himself totally into his work. He did this rather well, too well in fact. He socialised as little as he could get away with. It wasn't as though he was antisocial; he just didn't want to go to parties and dinners or any other social gathering without her. It just didn't feel right. After a while his friends stopped nagging him to socialise. He appeared to be happy as he was. It appeared to be his way of coping.

Charlie didn't spend enough time on himself or his flat. He did what was necessary, the bare minimum, at home. He cleaned up when he needed to, usually when he had no clean cups. He wasn't dirty or lazy he had merely lost interest in almost anything other than his work.

His music was important to him, he would immerse himself in his music and escape, forgetting about things for a while. Charlie hadn't known how to handle things when Valerie was ill, the only way of dealing with it had been to bury his head in his work.

The guilt he carried with him came directly from the fact that he wasn't actually with her when she fell into a coma; he was told over the phone while he was sat at his desk in work. Her condition had deteriorated rapidly following her diagnosis, the disease being advanced by this stage. The shock of losing her so swiftly and almost without warning had shattered him beyond his comprehension.

The Westwood investigation was just a reminder of the guilt he held, he would always have that sick feeling inside, even when thinking about the place, let alone having to walk on to the wards and appear the professional that he was.

He now realised that he should have taken some time

off work to be with her. He just didn't realise how little time they would have together.

He felt that he would always carry the guilt with him. He knew he should have been dropping his caseload when she received her diagnosis but that was just the way he coped with it, since her death he hadn't crawled out of that hole.

He certainly had not looked at another woman since; he saw that as a betrayal of his love for Valerie. Now for some weird reason he really couldn't stop thinking about Cate. Thoughts of her kept popping in to his mind. He knew he shouldn't allow himself these feelings, but seemed unable to control them.

He knew that he shouldn't and in fact couldn't ask her out. She was a suspect like all the staff, until they had the investigation concluded. But somehow Cate made him feel alive again and he was enjoying that feeling.

A feeling he never envisaged himself experiencing again.

21

In the early hours Charlie was woken by a phone call, as he peered through his sleepy eyes he could just make out the time on the clock that sat next to him on the cabinet, 2.34.

'Hello?' his voice muffled.

Within seconds he had flung his duvet off and was pulling on his trousers, while dialling Harry's number.

'Sir?' he simply said as he answered the phone.

'I want you on the ward, and round up all the staff, do not let any of them go!' Charlie said.

'Now?'

'There has been another death,' he said calmly. 'I'm not sure how we are going to catch this one Harry, they seem to be too cute,' he continued reluctantly, with the thought of the murderer prominent in his thoughts.

'I'm on it sir!'

They had been striving to ensure the deaths reached no

more than five, although they were still not sure if the death of the fifth victim, the 23 year old female was at all linked at this stage, but now here they were with a sixth death and things were just not getting easier.

Ward 23 had cause to report an unsuspected female death, age 42, failed resuscitation attempt - post appendicectomy, initial uneventful post operative recovery for the first twelve hours. She had an intravenous infusion running at the time of her death. She had been taking oral fluids, eaten and tolerated breakfast and was recovering as expected.

She was due to have the intravenous fluids discontinued that morning if her breakfast was tolerated and hopefully to be discharged home the following day.

Charlie knew that there was something glaringly obvious that he just wasn't seeing. How could the drips be the only link when all the fluids came from different batches? And put up by different members of staff. Yet was there a link, so obvious he couldn't see it, a doctor, nurse, porter? He thought he had this hospital on lockdown, but it seemed not!

Interviewing the ward sister proved inconclusive. Charlie and Harry had spoken to Helen Franks, a ward sister with almost twenty years experience in the profession. All their clinical notes were complete and their fluid charts filled in, listing the IV fluids she received. Her drug chart proved unhelpful, showing minimal intake of analgesia only. Nothing to link this victim to any of the other deaths. None of their victims appeared to have anything in common.

Charlie had asked Helen for a printed list of staff on duty when the patient died and for the night shift prior to that. She duly provided him with of a photocopy of their ward duty rota. There was nothing that stood out to alert them; it merely confirmed that their own staff had nursed their patients on the ward.

Their patient had been found in an unrousable state in the bathroom. Previous to that she had shown a positive post operative recovery and was progressing well. The staff had documented her planned discharge as aimed at being within the next day or two.

Harry interviewed two other staff nurses that were on duty during the shift when their patient died. His efforts so far had proved inconclusive. Harry was aided by PC Jackson, who was furiously taking notes of the initial interviews in his notebook.

Charlie spoke to the two health care assistants and the domestic assistant who was also on duty, assisted by one of the uniformed officers he pulled from the ward entrance. Again, nothing of note was discovered in their questioning. Charlie felt as though he was chasing the invisible criminal.

'Check the staff list for 68, and I want to know when the

staff on 73 have been contacted!'

Tina was filling in extra hours cleaning whilst studying at college. She'd worked on ward 23 for eight months. She was shaking and hardly able to get her words out all through Charlie's interview. Charlie actually felt quite sorry for her, caught in the middle of their murder enquiries. He knew she had nothing to tell him about the patient, she had been in the top three bays for most of her shift. She was part of the investigation and however she was reacting Charlie still had to ask her what she was doing and what she saw during her shift.

Charlie advised them all that they may be required for further questioning down at the police station. He would be in contact with them if the need arose, which he was almost positive it would. Chalmers was definitely right drafting other forces in. There was no way Charlie and his station team of five detectives could cover the volume of interviews alone. He had no choice at that time but to call detectives off the other wards.

'None of the staff had time to leave the ward during their shift sir.'

'None?' Charlie was clutching at straws and he knew

questioning the intelligence of his uniformed was wrong, but he didn't seem to have anything left at this stage.

'Their records showed no incidents of any of the six members of staff on shift having left the ward at any time during their shift sir. The staff members who had been noted to enter ward 23 had duly been recorded. Their reasons for attending the ward varied. Doctors calling in to see patients and for the daily doctors' rounds, a physiotherapist visiting four patients, a pharmacist doing the daily stock level check for the ward drug ordering and several porters. The list of visitors numbered twenty-nine. Two had visited their victim, three hours before she had died.'

The records showed these two visitors returning to the ward later that evening. The officer really hadn't known how to react to the questioning.

Charlie slumped into the chair at the desk where the log-in book sat, 'How?' he whispered to himself.

'Sir?' the young officer questioned.

'How could the IV fluids be involved?' Charlie just couldn't get his head around all this. He just couldn't see how they could be the link to these deaths, however much he scratched his head in search of the answer.

Charlie went through in his mind what Cate had told him. He could see the vision of her in his mind's eye, relating the information to him. It was almost as if he had a photographic impression of her within his grey matter. The bags came in different sizes, 100 mls, 250 mls, 500 mls and 1 litre. They were all clearly marked by the manufacturer with the name of the fluid the bags contained. No margin for error he deduced.

'I want forensics all over these wards, I want every inch scanned!' he said.

The young officer looked on at him, he knew he wasn't authorised to make these actions.

'Sir?' he simply said again.

Charlie sighed, 'Tell them I authorised it!'

'Yes sir!' he said, 'Thank you sir.'

Charlie wandered down to the store room; he just couldn't shift the fact that the fluid bags had something to do with it. He needed some time to examine these fluid bags for himself.

Following this theory he picked up a random bag of fluid, this time one that had not been opened. Each clear bag of IV fluid was sealed in another thicker plastic bag that was vacuum sealed. There were tear points along the top edge so that the bag could be opened and the fluid bag revealed.

They were tamper proof; whichever way Charlie looked at them he could see no way that anyone could put something in a bag that was contained within another sealed bag.

Vicky had been in contact with the fluid manufacturer and they had tested random fluids and found nothing untoward. All the bags were as stated and the process of sealing them scrutinised to exhaustion and found to be secure.

Another brilliant theory out the proverbial window. He had to be missing something here; he just had no idea what it was.

There were hundreds of nursing staff at the General… all able to have access to drugs legitimately and without question.

So what the hell was going on here?

He had already ordered a post mortem to be carried out on the new victim so for now it was a waiting game. He knew he had no option but to agree with the DI that someone had to go in undercover.

Back at the station, Vicky had been called in by Detective Inspector Chalmers. She sat directly opposite him in his ever neat and organised office.

'I have got authorisation to put you in undercover on ward 73; I've cleared it with the hospital. The ward sister Cate Carter will be the only one who is in the loop. You start tomorrow. I want a detailed report after each shift. Report directly to Charlie who will keep me informed. We are running with the suspicion that it is one of the staff, you need to gain their trust. I can hear you thinking that it's going to be impossible but even if you keep up with the gossip, find out what's the word on the ground we might gain something from that to take a lead from.'

'It's not going to be easy sir, they will have closed ranks now.'

'Yes but we have a lot of temps going in to help secure the place and double up on nurses so there shouldn't be too much suspicion.'

'Thank you.' Part of her was relieved that he was sending her in, part of her was terrified she wouldn't come up with anything to help them, without exposing herself by asking too many questions. 'Of course I will keep close contact with Charlie. He is aware of this I take it?'

'I have spoken to him yes, he isn't happy, but none of us are!' Chalmers replied. 'Let me worry about that one, ok,' he added.

Vicky was excited yet filled with fear that she was actually going to be working alongside someone who could be the Fallen Angel. It was her first experience undercover and she was determined to prove her worth. She was under no illusion that going undercover on ward 73 would either make or break her career in the force. She intended to make sure it was the making of her.

Charlie was given the job of informing Cate that Vicky was to go undercover on her ward. Her initial reaction was as he expected. She was protesting that it would too suspicious having a new member of staff that wasn't recognised on the ward when they were trying to keep to their own staff and not have any movement of staff.

Charlie was dubious about Vicky's forthcoming presence on the ward. Would she be able to make out that she didn't know him? Could she resist mothering him? She would have to draw upon every ounce of her professionalism for this one, especially as it was to be her first experience of undercover work. It would be challenging for her to do this right under his nose.

Charlie had expressed concerns to Chalmers about sending Vicky in, but he knew she, if anyone, was the one person stubborn enough to do it, cope with it and thrive on it.

There was an uncanny hush on ward 73. Surgery was continuing as normal but the staff were checking and re-checking everything they did. They were also checking and re-checking everything their colleagues were doing. They were looking over their shoulders at each other in case 'it was them'. The atmosphere was almost unbearable. No one was beyond suspicion. The ever present uniformed officers at the door of their ward were a constant reminder of that.

They had all been told by Cate about the double checking and in fact were relieved in a way. They were all to give drugs in pairs so that they would have the signature of another trained professional to confirm what they had done was right – a time wasting exercise she thought.

Sally and Lorraine were both on the late shift. In the clinical room they were checking some morphine for a post operative patient who needed some pain relief. They as usual checked it in the controlled drug register, counted the remaining morphine vials and both signed the register.

Lorraine was pensive. 'You know Sal, just looking at what drugs we have in the cupboard makes you realise how easy it would be to get hold of them.'

'What?'

'Well, take a look, there's the digoxin, lignocaine, midaxolam, potassium, diazepam, atropine, heparin, lanoxin, everything! In theory anyone who has hold of the keys could just take those vials out of the cupboard and put them in their pocket. I've never really thought about that before.'

In their clinical room, there were two floor to ceiling cupboards that were locked. Any of the qualified members of staff had access to these cupboards if they had the ward bunch of keys. No member of qualified staff would be queried if they wanted the keys and certainly wouldn't be questioned if they went to the cupboards in the clinical room for medications. Except now maybe. With the police presence on their ward and the constant reminder to check all drugs administered, each and every one of them expected to be challenged at any moment, whether it be by each other, Sister Carter, or indeed the police.

The door of their clinical room had a key pad lock on it, so again they needed the code, but all the staff on the ward knew it. It was more to keep the patients out of there as some may enter by accident or indeed some on purpose. The locks had been introduced when the medical unit experienced a patient who had been found in a clinical room rooting through a drug cupboard. The staff on that ward had shut the clinical room door but hadn't locked their drug cupboard. The result was the patient, a known drug addict, was helping himself to vials of drugs. He had tried to take vials of diazepam but been found in time to apprehend by the hospital security staff. From then on the doors of all their clinical rooms had key pad locks installed on them.

'Where I last worked it didn't work like that,' Sally said.

'What do you mean?' Lorraine added.

'The drug cupboards were in clinical rooms but they were small areas like bays on the ward and didn't have doors, and some of our wards had the drug cupboards behind the nurse's station, it depended which ward you were on. The older wards didn't have separate clinical rooms, just cupboards on ward.'

'Makes you think though doesn't it, how easy it would be if you were so inclined,' Lorraine agreed.

'Bit worrying really. Especially when you think someone has already thought of this and done it by the sounds of things.'

'Yes Sal, but if the drugs were given to the patient then whoever was doing it would surely be seen by someone. What if the patient wasn't prescribed the drugs, which is what that detective guy was saying? Surely if I was giving IV drugs to someone that didn't have them prescribed to them then you or whoever I was working with would see what I was doing. There's no way someone would take a risk like that. They would be found out in an instant.'

'I hadn't really thought about it. You are right though. We really need to make sure that our practice of drug administration is by the book all the time. I'm damned if that detective is going to start pinning things on me or any of us for that matter. It would be unbearable if they started accusing one of the staff we work with wouldn't it. I just wouldn't be able to believe it.'

'It's not going to happen Sal, no way are any of our lot involved.'

22

That night Sally and Lorraine decided on takeaway pizza. Neither was in the mood for going out and somehow they had recently slipped in to a lazy routine of takeaways and microwave meals. There was a pizza restaurant alongside the General and they stopped to pick it up on their walk home. Lorraine picked up her ritual couple of newspapers in order to keep the scrap book up to date, which had become a habit of late for both of them.

'Bloody hell,' screeched Lorraine, 'they are only going and broadcasting it!' she exclaimed as she plonked herself on the sofa and flicked on the television.

They both managed a stunned silence whilst the newsreader recounted events.

'The patients aren't going to trust us at all now, are they? Shit they are going to have a bad shift tonight if the patients start getting twitchy,' Lorraine said.

'Do you really think they will let this be on in the ward?'

Sally questioned sarcastically.

'S'pose not! But what about their relatives watching it? Nothing we can do about that!'

'I know that but how are we going to face the patients? What if they think it's us? Not exactly going to be easy to work is it,' Sally said.

'Umm, I hadn't thought of it that way,' Lorraine answered with a horrified look.

'Well, you better, tomorrow's shift isn't that far away, and the way I see it, it is going to be unbearable, for us and for them. What did the reporter say about surgery? I didn't quite catch it!'

'All surgery is cancelled; routine and emergency, yet Cate said they were continuing surgery as normal. Something doesn't fit there does it?' Sally said shifting uncomfortably.

'I wonder if we will be moved to other wards to work then. They won't keep us there if there aren't many patients, will they?'

'Loz, wake up. If they think one of us is slipping them something then there is no way they are going to let any of us go and work anywhere else is there? Anyway I told you before, the reports and the papers don't always give the right story.'

'Oh.'

'Yes, oh. You heard what that detective said to us. The deaths are being treated as suspicious, that makes all of us murder suspects.'

'Oh come on, I'm no murderer Sal!' Lorraine grinned nervously, 'Would they… Could they really think that?'

'It's not me saying it is it? Face it, until they find out what's going on then we have to keep our heads down. You have got to get real with this Loz and soon.'

'Surely if someone is doing this on purpose then they would have it all planned out. None of the guys on 73 would do that; you and I both know that,' Lorraine said.

'Loz, we just have to be extra careful, watch out that no one tries to frame us either. That could be on the cards with this too.'

'Shit, yes, can we just stop the conversation about this now? We are going to have to go through it all again when we get to work tomorrow anyway.'

'We have the interviews with the cops to look forward to as well,' Sally grumbled back.

'Don't remind me, maybe I just won't go in!'

'What are you on about? Loz you don't get a choice when it comes to the cops requesting to see you! They may see us more than once too, I've heard of that happening.'

'I hate the cops Sal; I don't think I can cope with it. I get too stressed out and start talking crap.' She curled herself up into a ball on the sofa, hugging her knees to her body.

'Just say what you know!'

'I haven't done anything, I don't know anything!'

'Then there's nothing to worry about, is there?' Sally questioned. Turning to face Lorraine she noticed tears falling down the side of her face.

She drew herself closer on the sofa and gave her a big hug.

'Come on, pull yourself together.'

'SSSal,' sobbed Lorraine, 'I can't deal with the cops, I really can't.' Her eyes were beginning to puff up and redden with her tears. 'What if they try to blame me?'

'Why would they? Silly girl!' Sally said, holding her tightly. She realised nothing that she said was going to help at that moment and so just cuddled into her.

The next morning Sally and Lorraine walked into work to be greeted by a staff meeting.

'I take it you will have all seen the news last night?' Cate said to a very silent audience. She then proceeded to fill them in on the new staff situation and the fact that they would be joined by an extra team of care assistants on each and every shift - Vicky being one of them.

She was to work a morning shift on ward 73, followed the next day by a night shift. Chalmers was initially giving her two shifts to see what she could come up with. As far as the other staff knew she was just another burden to their jobs!

She hadn't been told how long exactly her undercover work was going to last so she had to make use of every minute that she was there. She just had to come up with something. She would feel such a failure at the station if she couldn't come up with even the smallest snippet that would help them gain their conviction.

She would have to be careful about asking questions though, she didn't want to arouse their suspicion. The idea was to remain behind the scenes, not draw attention to herself but try to examine practice of the staff. They had been asked to tighten up their drug administration procedures and she would be able to take note of that during the course of the shift.

She'd asked Cate if she could do a night shift as she thought things would be quieter and give her more observing and thinking time.

Vicky found the first shift quite trying, she had forgotten how demanding the job actually was and realised just how frustrating it could be too. She watched the best she could when staff went to give the medications and the intravenous drugs; at least she saw that they were indeed going in pairs to the patients. She couldn't extend her view to the actual checking of the drugs because she wasn't really able to hang about in the clinical room. She did once go in to get some dressings when Sally and Cate were checking something but that was the nearest she could get.

The general feeling of the investigation was that their suspect was a qualified member of staff yet so far she wasn't finding it easy to get near the drugs as a health care assistant. She knew that was the way it should be; and at least some protocols were being followed, but that wasn't helping her get close to the staff that had the authority.

Vicky wanted to really test her theory, but she had to find a reason to go off the ward. Maybe she would have to leave it until she had her tea break as she wouldn't get away with leaving the ward without a valid reason and she couldn't just disappear, they would notice her absence. She was beginning to find it difficult being accountable to Cate when she was really accountable to Charlie. Trying to fit both roles yet being seen to work as a health care assistant wasn't the easiest task she had set herself.

If she was going to get close to anyone on the ward Vicky knew that she was going to have to have some inside help, she was going to have to rethink her feelings towards Cate and ask her for help. So she went to see if Cate was in her office, as she entered she instantly noticed the most gorgeous bunch of velvet pink roses delicately arranged in a vase on the window sill.

Cate instantly felt out of control by Vicky's manoeuvre. When would these damned detectives learn that sometimes, just sometimes, Cate was in 'her' office and not theirs?

'Cate, I have just had an idea and I need your help with this one.'

Well, Cate thought, that is certainly a first, she looked directly at Vicky in surprise at this announcement.

'Right... What is it you need me to do?'

'I need to go and see if I can 'borrow' some drugs from another ward. I want to see if as a health care assistant I can get access to drugs without arousing suspicion. I need to go off the ward for a few minutes or so, but I also need you to know what I am doing in case any of the wards ring to see if I have been sent to borrow anything.'

Cate pulled a face, 'If you are sure.'

'I am, this needs to be done,' she added decisively. 'Roses are nice by the way, anyone special?'

'Maybe,' Cate added hesitantly not wishing to enlighten her any further. There was enough tension between them without adding to it by mentioning DS Hammond. 'I see what you are thinking about here, we often send our auxiliary staff to wards to borrow things or collect drugs that we need, and I don't have a problem with you going to do that.'

'Ok, but will the staff on the ward question me when I ask for something, that's what I want to test out, ok. So if they are on to me, as I hope they would be, seeing that the use and movement of all drugs is being scrutinised at the moment, I'll tell them Sister Carter sent me, ok?'

'Ok.'

'Oh, give me the names of a couple of drugs that I can ask for, I'm a bit out of date on things like that now. Something that could cause problems if it was given to the wrong patient for example.'

'Well, any drug given to the wrong person could cause them problems. Any medication given that wasn't specifically prescribed for the individual could cause adverse effects, drug interactions or allergy. I suggest you ask for diazepam, which is Valium, ask for it for IV use, five milligrams/one ml and also ask for atropine sulphate six hundred mcg/one ml, hang on I'll write that down for you. Don't ask for both on the same ward will you. They will wonder why you are asking for that combination of drugs.'

'Ok, thanks.'

Cate handed Vicky the scrap of paper with the drug names and doses on.

'Won't be long,' said Vicky. As she neared the door she turned and delivered a comment that cut straight into Cate's heart. 'Pink roses are DS Hammond's wife's favourite.' She shut the door behind her adding to the impact of her parting shot.

She left Cate to ponder the consequences of the newly acquired information.

Vicky decided to pick wards at random to test her theory, as she walked along the corridor passing visitors and hospital staff alike, she quickly reached ward 72. First ward she got to would do for the first attempt at access to drugs.

She duly gave her name and showed her ID badge to the uniformed officers at the ward entrance, shooting them a scowl incase either verbalised their recognition of her.

As Vicky entered the ward she checked the piece of paper Cate had given her and memorised the first drug. She walked past a couple of patients in bed and stopped at the nurse's station. Two qualified nurses were sitting writing their patients' notes.

'Hi, I'm on the scrounge, have you got any Diazepam, five milligram's for IV use?'

Vicky purposefully didn't say her name or which ward she was from, she wanted to see what questions the staff would ask of her if she gave them no information, merely turned up in her uniform. She was wearing a hospital ID badge but she wore it inside her pocket instead of outside on display like the staff were meant to.

'Hang on, I think so,' one of them said, then proceeded to get up and go towards the drug cupboard. She had the keys in her pocket and opened the door.

'Yes, we have, how many do you want?'

'Two please.'

Vicky was then handed two very small five ml glass vials,

she read the writing on the side of them; they were indeed the diazepam she had asked for.

'Thanks,' said Vicky and turned and left the ward.

Vicky couldn't believe how easy that was. The qualified nurse not only hadn't seen whether she had an ID badge, but hadn't even queried Vicky as a health care assistant asking for drugs that only the qualified staff had access to with the keys. Here she was now about to walk through the hospital with two vials of what was a strong sedative in her pocket. She hadn't even been asked what ward it was that needed the drugs so no check could be made as to where the drugs were going.

With the recent spate of unexplained deaths how on earth could this still be happening? Ok so they had asked the staff to implement stricter procedures for checking and giving these intravenous drugs but she thought it would have gone without saying that the drugs themselves should be monitored too!

Maybe that was a one off. She would try several wards.

Vicky repeated the process on a further four wards that she chose at random on her walk along the hospital corridor. The same happened on each ward, not once was she asked what ward she was from or if she had hospital ID. Vicky was largely unimpressed; she wanted to test her theory but didn't expect the collection of drugs within the hospital to have been so easy. She wasn't sure if she was helping or hindering their investigation, now their enquiries had to extend as far as the auxiliary staff as she had exposed the ease of access to the drugs by any level of nurse.

Didn't these girls realise the street value of this stuff? She was now in possession of seven vials of diazepam, commonly known as valium. On the street to the drug user these vials would be great, they would know that it was good stuff as it was in a hospital vial and couldn't have been tampered with... good job she was planning to give them to Cate when she got back to 73.

Vicky also managed to get three vials of atropine on her travels. Vicky knew that atropine was used in emergency situations and cardiac arrests, any more than that, she had no idea.

She was decidedly unimpressed with the hospitals blasé procedure on borrowing drugs from other wards like this. When she got back to Cate she would have to get her to do something about this. Bloody quickly. This was with the uniformed police presence in the hospital; still no one was questioning her about borrowing drugs. 'If their suspect was going around borrowing drugs this easily then heaven help them all,' she thought.

Stopping off at one of the public toilets in the corridor Vicky sent a text to Charlie. She hadn't been in touch with him for a few hours, now she felt she had something constructive to say. Maybe the ease with which she had managed to obtain these medications would have some bearing on the investigation.

> *'EASY TO GET ACCESS TO DRUGS.*
> *COULD BE UN-QUAL STAFF TOO.*
> *WILL REPORT BACK IN AN HOUR.'*

Leaving without waiting for him to reply, Vicky went straight back to see Cate.

'Cate this really is beyond a joke you know.'

'What are you on about?' Cate forgot she was talking to a detective.

Vicky emptied out the contents of her uniform pocket for Cate to see - seven vials of diazepam for IV use and three vials of atropine, along with two syringes and three needles, these now lay on Cate's desk.

'Do you know what? No one questioned me at all, didn't even ask what ward I was from.' Vicky sported a disapproving look on her face.

'What wards did you say you went to?'

'72, 34 and 38 too I think? Yes, as well as 62!'

'Wow!' Cate simply said in shock, 'I get your point, but what does that have to do with me or my ward?' said Cate. She really wasn't sure how much of this she was able to take. This wasn't her fault she couldn't be held accountable for this.

'I am merely illustrating how easy it is for even an unqualified member of staff to get hold of drugs within this hospital, without resorting to crime to get hold of them.'

'Where did you get the needles and syringes?' Cate asked.

'Stock cupboard on here, no one noticed, I shut the door and bingo took what I wanted. All this uniformed police presence and I can still pocket things without being seen. Shows just how easy it is to obtain these items doesn't it. I could have taken the valium and sold it for a good few quid if I was that way inclined or indeed gone to the toilet and injected the whole lot in to myself,' she stated purposefully.

'If you injected that lot into yourself you'd be dead, not sitting there talking to me now,' Cate snapped.

'Exactly,' said Vicky and gave Cate a long hard *I'm a copper and not a nurse* look. One strike to me Vicky thought.

'You see why I am stressing the seriousness of this?'

'That's a bit far-fetched don't you think? Can you be that sure?' Cate said.

'Sister!' She paused for a moment, looking down at Cate in a patronising manner, which made Cate feel slightly uncomfortable.

'I am going off now,' stated Vicky, 'back for the night shift tomorrow; make sure the other ward sister's get the message about not lending drugs from their ward to another won't you? We'll speak to pharmacy too about this. In the meantime make sure you get your drug policy tightened up.'

With that Vicky was gone, not even giving Cate the chance to vocalise her reply.

'*Nice tactics,*' thought Cate. '*You sure are going to make friends in life with that attitude. How on earth Charlie could work with her day in day out, she had no clue.*' Certainly not a woman she would choose to be friends with, she concluded.

Cate had to sort this drug borrowing issue out but she knew it would be a time-consuming task.

So she decided to start with a simple poster on all drug store doors:

NO DRUGS TO BE LENT TO OTHER WARDS
NO DRUGS TO BE BORROWED FROM OTHER WARDS
STOCK FROM PHARMACY ONLY
NO EXCEPTIONS
SR CARTER

That covered what she wanted to say, at least her staff wouldn't be implicated in giving drugs out to all and sundry. Covering her backside and those of her staff was getting to be more than she could cope with. She was running round in circles trying to comply and she now had to do what Vicky had asked and sort the other wards borrowing policies out. She decided that if she rang the hospital co-ordinator, who was in charge of the whole of the hospital for that shift, she could pass the buck somewhat and then leave her shift for home.

23

Cate's life the past few days had been one long headache. She just hoped that she would be able to get some sleep tonight. Another shift like this tomorrow and she would just about be finished off. She couldn't take time out, not during times like this, and as it stood, it was looking like she would be coming in on her days off for the foreseeable future too. She longed for some solitary time out, right now she couldn't even remember what her interests outside work were, let alone plan a day out to do whatever they were.

As she sat motionless waiting for the traffic lights to change to green, Cate noticed a familiar figure walking alone on the pavement in front of her. Her spirits raised, she felt butterflies in her stomach and intrigued by these unconscious feelings and the captivating effect he was having on her she decided to park up and follow him to see where he was going. *'Was he meeting with his wife as DC*

Trent had so readily informed her?' she flippantly thought.

He looked different without his suit, casually dressed in dark chinos and a light shirt. He definitely looked like someone she would like to get to know further, or at least find out more about his habits and indeed his wife. If indeed he really did have one. She noticed that he didn't wear a wedding ring, knowing perfectly well that this wasn't a sure-fire answer to her query. She had to know before she built up the feelings she had into something that she wasn't able to control.

She found him sat alone in a wine bar and built up the courage to join him, 'I never said thank you,' she whispered as she stood nervously behind him.

'What?' Charlie looked up and saw an almost perfect vision before him. He could not have dared hope for such a beautiful companion. He wondered how she could look so fresh in her stonewashed jeans and crisp white shirt at the end of such a harrowing day. He knew how stressful work was for her at the moment, he was suffering the same fate.

'You heard me. Less of the questions from you now.' A smile appeared, gradually lighting up first one corner of her mouth then the other, highlighting her rosy pink glossed lips. He was taking in every available detail about her as he watched the sun shining down on the gold strands of her bountiful curls.

He smiled, he really admired her style. She just wasn't

afraid to say what was on her mind.

'Are you waiting for someone or can I sit down?' she continued.

'No, I am not waiting for anyone.' He pulled a chair forward for her. 'Just needed a pint, no way to clear my head at the moment, so I thought I would take temporary leave of my senses to see if that worked!'

'Well I can certainly empathise with that, is it working?'

'Oh sorry, I haven't even offered you a drink, what would you like?' he got up to go to the bar for her.

'I'll join you with a beer. This headache is bad enough today, I can't see a few drinks making it any worse.'

'Don't think I go getting drunk all the time,' he said in all seriousness. 'Oh and it's too early to tell if it's working by the way!' Charlie added, picking up on her earlier enquiry.

So she intended staying a while, his heart skipped a beat, in anticipation. Maybe he could remember how to get it right, chatting with a woman outside of work wasn't his specialist subject, it hadn't been for many years. He hadn't allowed himself this luxury. He approached the bar with a novel spring in his step, enjoying every pace and sporting the brightest grin.

'Won't your wife be expecting you home?' Cate questioned. She just had to know the answer, realising the only way she was going to know was actually to ask him outright.

'No,' he paused. Should he tell her more?

'Oh, right. It's just that DC Trent mentioned her today…'

'She did what?' he asked surprised at this revelation.

'Said that the pink roses were her favourite, that you get her them all the time.' Ok, so she knew she was adding her own point to the information she had been given, but she needed to hear the truth from him. If only to snap her back to reality and stop herself wasting so much time thinking about him.

'She is right there,' he hesitated before adding, 'but not on all counts.'

'Sorry, it's none of my business. Maybe I better go…' she felt his hand on her arm as she attempted to rise to leave.

'Please stay Cate. It isn't as straight forward as Vicky said.'

'It never is Detective. It never is,' she added in a rather cynical tone.

'No, Cate. Please, just sit down and listen for a minute.'

He looked at her with sadness in his eyes. She got the feeling that he wanted to tell her something, and she sat back down to hear all about his widowed life.

24

Over the last few days Lorraine had grown increasingly intrigued by the story Cate had told them about David Waters. At home that night she started to do some research about him and what exactly he had done. Sitting at the table in the corner of their living room she settled herself in for what she thought could be a long night of research. She searched the internet and found more references to him and his handy work than she had expected there to be. She was fascinated by what he had done, she really couldn't believe that a nurse could do that to his patients. How could he have got away with it for so long she wondered? It sounded so simple too, swapping the syringe of saline for an identical syringe of insulin. The amount of insulin he had given was way over the lethal dose and she began to research the effects of insulin in the body and the effects of such an overdose.

How long would it take before the patient became ill

or showed side effects? She knew that depended on what drug they were given, even with insulin there were different types. Lorraine began reading the articles about the two types of insulin, quick acting and a long acting. With the quick acting insulin the onset of the action of the insulin was anything from ten minutes to two hours for the commonly used doses. The peak absorption varied from one to eight hours with the duration of action lasting for up to twenty-four hours. She wondered if a huge overdose would cause immediate death. It sounded like it to her.

For the long acting insulins, the onset of action was anything from four hours up to twenty-four hours.

On that score then if anyone was using insulin then they would have used a quick acting insulin in excessive dose to cause an almost immediate effect, or so she had concluded from her evening's reading.

She was getting herself all confused. She knew that if she gave a patient their normal dose of quick acting insulin then their blood sugar reduced quickly. The diabetics that used the longer acting drug often just used that twice daily to keep their blood sugars stable due to its longer action.

Could it really be done? No she shouldn't be thinking like this, but found that the curiosity of possibility was compelling.

Her mind was spinning in a million directions, the insulin on ward 73 was kept in the drug fridge in their clinical room. Although it was hidden from the patients' view if any member of staff went to get something from the fridge they would be seen entering the room, using the key pad lock to get in. She knew that nobody would question a qualified member of staff doing this.

It did have a lock on it and the key was kept on the general ward bunch of keys that all the qualified staff had access to. Admittedly it was easy to get access to and the stock levels were never checked or recorded. They just re-ordered when they needed more and pharmacy brought more vials up to the ward. How often had she gone to get something from the drug fridge and found it open? Countless times throughout her career, this too added to her concerns and intrigue. Maybe someone without access to the drug keys could get hold of insulin.

She pondered further on this. If the staff were busy around the ward it would be so easy for a vial or two of insulin to go missing and remain undetected.

She couldn't get it out of her head though. Was it really a staff member who had caused these deaths on their ward?

She just didn't understand how it was being done on several different wards?

Who was this person? The obvious observation was that it was someone she knew. Had she worked with them?

What would a sick bastard like that look like? Would she know it was them if she worked with them?

Too many questions and she was starting to feel dizzy with it all, Sally wouldn't be home for a couple of hours, having stayed on to do a double shift.

She flicked through some of the articles she had printed off from the internet. It really did make for fascinating reading. Putting them aside she picked up a small shoe box that Sally had put on the coffee table earlier. Inside it she had several newspaper cuttings containing reports of the deaths at Westwood General and the events of ward 73. Carefully lifting them out, Lorraine read them all again and placed them back safely in to Sally's cutting box. After all Sally had said to her about not keeping the cuttings Sally herself was the one who had kept them.

If she was lucky she could get a couple of hours kip to rid herself of this awful headache she was struggling with and be up in time to have supper with Sally when she got in.

She got herself a glass of water from the kitchen, two paracetamol from the bathroom cabinet and settled down on the sofa for a nap.

*****

Vicky had been on the ward for a few days now, but it seemed like months as she sat preparing her report for

Charlie and Chalmers about her investigations.

'We know that the intravenous fluids are the only link. I have shown that it is not difficult for any member of staff to go to a ward and "borrow" almost any drug they ask for. What I just can't work out is how the drugs are linked to the intravenous fluids and how these deaths are happening on several wards? The only way for this to happen is if someone is adding the drugs to the bags of fluid, but the staff have already said that these bags are checked before they are used and come in sealed packages. We have to rule out the fluid bags containing the drugs. That only leaves the person giving the patient the drugs directly. No nurse has looked after all these patients though.'

'What the bloody hell is going on then? And who are they?' Chalmers said as she began briefing him.

'I don't know sir… any news from the fluid manufacturer?'

'No, all their tests were clear and nothing further has come from them.'

Vicky was going to be reporting about the mental state of the staff to Charlie. It was interacting with the staff on the ward that was the most challenging part of her role. They were happy to moan to each other, Vicky could pick that up, but they were not so forthcoming towards her. She could understand this, after all she was a stranger in their midst at a time they were all under surveillance for murder!

She was decidedly unimpressed with Cate. For one, she was always following Charlie with her eyes and Vicky didn't want her getting close to him at all. He didn't date, she knew that, maybe she should inform Cate of that little gem... maybe when the opportunity arose she would throw that one at her, just for good measure and get her off his back. Stop her making puppy dog eyes at him.

Maybe the staff were being so professional and vigilant because of the investigation? Vicky could identify no glaring gaps in their clinical practice. She had witnessed two members of staff checking and double-checking when they administered drugs, and indeed when they attended their patients. It was as if they were trying to safeguard themselves by not dealing with their patients alone. Great practice under the circumstances, but this afforded her no avenue to pick them up on their skills.

Vicky was dismayed that none of the staff were forthcoming about the deaths to her. She couldn't exactly start asking questions either. As an unknown quantity on the ward, she was just about getting away with being there, if she started quizzing them she would merely draw suspicion towards herself and blow the operation apart. She felt that she was achieving very little so far with her time on the ward. She had to come up with something constructive to justify her presence there to Chalmers. She wanted to prove herself to him, and Charlie. Show herself worthy of her place on their team. But right now, she couldn't even justify this to herself.

If the staff were gossiping about the investigation, they were certainly not doing it within her earshot. She hadn't even seen evidence of them talking to each other about it. Maybe Charlie had done his part too well, telling them not to discuss the events.

* * * * *

After a sleepless night and an equally restless day Lorraine was working with Tim, she'd not worked with him before and wasn't too sure of him. Unbeknown to her Tim was feeling exactly the same about working with her.

Tim had worked on 73 for only a few months, having transferred from the medical admissions unit. Although he was known in the hospital he was feeling uncomfortable on the ward knowing there were some members of staff he had yet to work with and whose trust he had to gain.

Lorraine wondered if she could test out her theory about giving one of the patients something that they shouldn't have. She wouldn't actually do it; she just wanted to see how it could have been done.

The drug fridge was in the clinical room, she knew she could get insulin from there. Tim had begun to go around his patients doing their obs, as they called it. He was checking the blood pressures etc and would be at it for a while she thought.

Lorraine walked down to the clinical room and went in as though everything was normal. The drug fridge wasn't locked, it had a lock on it but true to typical bad practice it was unlocked. The staff had always been a little blasé about this, thinking it was safe as the main door was locked. She did indeed find six different vials of insulin in the fridge. Taking one out she quickly put it in her pocket. The syringes they used to draw up insulin were tiny. She knew that insulin was measured in international units and even a large prescribed dose wouldn't equate to half a ml of fluid if put in an ordinary syringe. Knowing this Lorraine picked up a five ml syringe and a green needle. She put all three items in her uniform pocket and left the clinical room, ensuring the door was locked behind her.

Lorraine then followed Tim's lead and did her patients' observations. That took her just over half an hour, she only had eight patients to look after so hopefully was looking at a quiet shift. Tim had ten but they had two health care assistants, Rachel and Joe, to help them so were well staffed.

Lorraine told Tim she was popping off to the toilet… the bits and pieces she had in her pocket were intriguing her and she had to try it, she really had to see if it could be done. In theory. She didn't stop to think about what she was getting involved with.

Once safely in the female staff toilet, she took out the contents of her uniform pocket. She opened the packets containing the needle and syringe and connected the two together. She then inserted the needle into the top of the insulin vial.

She withdrew almost the full contents of the vial, which amounted to almost five mls. Just enough to fill her syringe. She put the drawn up syringe into her left hand uniform pocket and the empty vial and rubbish into her right hand pocket. She wasn't sure if she felt excitement or horror at what she was doing. She just had to see if she could do this. In theory that was.

To make matters worse there were two coppers within feet from where she was, keeping their guard on the ward. What if they came in and checked her pockets? This was no time to allow paranoia to take hold. It wasn't as though she was going to harm a patient.

Exiting the staff toilet Lorraine walked straight to the clinical room, keyed in the code for the door lock, entered and made sure the door had shut firmly behind her.

Taking the rubbish out of her right pocket she put it straight into the bin. She took out the empty insulin vial and put it in the 'sharps bin'. This was a yellow plastic bin that was specifically for the disposal of needles, syringes and glass, anything that could cause injury if disposed of in a normal dustbin. Nothing to arouse suspicion so far, she thought.

The first part of her theory had been proved to herself. She had managed to dispose of the evidence. The yellow bin was opaque. There was no way to tell that there was an empty vial in there and the chute to insert the rubbish didn't allow for the retrieval of anything from the bin. At least there was a safety system in place somewhere.

Lorraine then began to get things set out for her antibiotics. These were to be given intravenously. She would have to go and get Tim to come and check them with her.

She started by drawing up the five mls of saline she needed to flush the cannula before she gave the antibiotics. A five ml syringe now contained a clear fluid, saline. She left the plastic saline container for Tim so he could check it later. She was sure he wouldn't question her about drawing up something as innocent as saline without being present when she did it.

She took out the syringe from her pocket and held the two up to the light. The insulin she had drawn up was also clear. She had chosen correctly. As she went to put the syringes back down she heard someone tapping in the security code in the door lock. Tim then entered the clinical room.

Lorraine had no choice but to put both the syringes down on the worktop next to the antibiotics.

'Want those checking?' Tim asked.

'Yes, when you have time, it's not urgent.'

'I'll do it now, save me coming back later.' Tim proceeded to check the vials of antibiotic, and the prescription charts.

'Fine, is that the saline?'

Tim had picked up the syringe of insulin; the second syringe was now lying underneath the drug chart. It was obscured from his view.

'Yes,' she stammered.

'Yep, fine,' he said as he checked the empty saline vial. The only thing was he had just checked the empty saline vial and not actually seen her draw it up.

He placed the five ml syringe on the foil tray.

Lorraine had almost finished drawing the antibiotic up into a twenty ml syringe.

'I will come with you now so you can give it; we are best taking no chances with all these accusations we are all facing at the moment. Safer that way, we don't want to be caught leaving drugs drawn up in syringes do we?'

Lorraine tried not to look as horrified as she felt. She almost dropped the syringe, her palms were so sweaty.

Tim picked up the tray and walked towards the door.

Now or never thought Lorraine as she picked up the drug chart. She couldn't even reach back to get the syringe of saline. She knew she should say something to him, but the words just weren't coming out.

Shit, this is really going to happen, if I give that insulin to flush the cannula I am going to cause a death. ME?

Shit, what to do, Lorraine began to panic, her heart was racing.

Someone is going to get a bloody fatal dose of insulin and there is nothing that I can do about it, unless I tell him what I have done. Her mind too was leaping about all over the place. Panic. Total panic. What to do?

She told herself to stay calm, any sign of panic and the cops would be all over her jumping to the wrong conclusions.

The only thing she could do was get that tray from Tim, knock it on the floor perhaps? That's what she would do, when she got to the patient.

As she followed Tim down the ward to where her patient, Graham Stewart, was she suddenly felt a huge rush of adrenaline. She had the overwhelming urge to actually allow this to happen. She was going to be in control of the situation, she could make out she just noticed he was ill when 'it' happened couldn't she. At least she would know that he needed glucose, she'd know what they would have to do.

One of her other patients stopped her as she walked by asking her for a commode. 'I won't be a minute.'

'No dear, I need it now, I'm bursting to go, please dear get me the commode.'

'Go and get it for her and I will give this for you, you can watch me go to Graham when you get back with the commode,' Tim announced.

Lorraine's blood almost ran cold, shit, Tim was going to give the fatal dose. She was so pumped up with adrenaline; her heart was nearly beating outside of her chest. She had a real feeling of excitement, combined with total nausea. Suddenly she wanted this to happen.

'Ok,' was all she managed as she hurried to get a commode. She had to be quick; she had to see what he was doing. She had to know he had done it. She really was feeling powerful now, she would know what was wrong with her patient and sort it out. No problem. She might even be praised for her quick actions.

But what would happen if they had another death on the ward, if she got it wrong? If Tim thought it was something else wrong with Graham?

The fucking cops were crawling all over the place, yards from where they were now. They just would not get away with it.

They? Tim, she thought. Nothing to do with her. That's what she would tell the cops. She was thinking in a blind panic now.

She wasn't giving the patient any drugs was she? Tim was giving them, if they started asking her questions about the patient becoming ill she would be able to say Tim gave him the antibiotics, but they had both checked the drug prior to it being given. Anyway the patient wouldn't die because she knew what was wrong didn't she. She could sort this out and Graham would be fine.

Hell this was exciting in a weird sort of way. Lorraine hadn't known a feeling like this before. She felt like she had all the power, for once in her life Lorraine had the power and she liked it.

Lorraine came back with the commode and glanced over to where Tim was standing at the side of Graham's bed, chatting with him. Graham was 32 years old and a customer services manager for a telecommunications company in the city. Lorraine began to feel guilty about what she was allowing to happen and how ill this guy was about to become. She stood in silence, perfectly still watching them chatting.

Transfixed.

She knew though that he would be ok, she would see to that.

Tim raised his hand to Lorraine indicating to her that he knew she'd seen him at the bedside of the right patient for the antibiotics.

Lorraine could hardly raise her eyes to make eye contact with him but knew she had to, to allow Tim to continue without arousing suspicion.

Either that or shout out to him and tell him to stop. What reason could she give? How long would it take the cops to run from the door of the ward to her wrists and cuff her if she did that she wondered.

Returning to Mrs Gray behind the curtain, Lorraine was frantic inside, she positioned the commode by the bed, bashing it into the bed end in the process.

'Mind my legs dear,' said Mrs Gray.

'S... Sorry, I didn't mean to,' stuttered Lorraine.

Lorraine knew she had to pull herself together. She also knew that in only a few moments Tim would be shouting out to her to come and help him.

Lorraine left Mrs Gray on the commode and gave her the call bell to ring when she was finished. She couldn't just stay there with her knowing, yet not knowing what was happening to Graham.

Calling out to a passing Rachel, the health care assistant Lorraine asked her to listen out for Mrs Gray ringing to help her back into bed.

Lorraine, after ensuring her patient was safe, slowly walked up to where Tim was with Graham, she had to do something.

'I'm just going to ward 72 to see if I can borrow some

fluid charts, none in the cabinet, won't be a minute.'

'Alright.' Her announcement didn't worry him in the slightest.

She really had to have five minutes to herself. How was she allowing this to happen? She knew that a patient was being given a fatal dose of insulin, and what was she doing? She was walking away from it.

If she left the ward and was legitimately doing something else then it wouldn't be her fault. If she told herself that, maybe she would begin to believe it.

To get to 72 she had to exit 73. First problem. Telling herself to get a grip she attempted a smile at the two male uniformed officers who were outside the door of the ward.

'Excuse me; we need to record who you are and where you are going.'

'Of course, Lorraine Harris, staff nurse, I am going to ward 72 to get some fluid charts.'

'Ok Lorraine, how long will you be?' He was noting everything down as she spoke.

'Oh only a few minutes,' she stated.

'See you soon then.'

Lorraine took a slow walk to ward 72, even though it was only twenty or thirty yards along the corridor. There were two more uniformed police, this time both female officers, walking towards her on their patrol around the hospital.

She was using all her self-control to hold on to her

composure attempting to cover up her terror at the situation she had engineered.

Was that meant to make them feel safer she wondered? Was that meant to stop any more unexpected deaths on their wards? How could it, she had just drawn up legal drugs and a patient was being given them now, so that theory was out the window wasn't it.

Lorraine felt the uncontrolled urge to run. She was off the ward, didn't have to go back. She could run. Where to? No idea. Nowhere to go. What reason would she give when they caught up with her for leaving the ward?

No, running wouldn't do. She would have run away from a death. Put her right in the frame for the other deaths. She had to keep calm, walk slowly and deliberately past them.

25

The taller of the two duty police officers acknowledged Lorraine and said hello as she made sure that her reply was coherent and clear, and she composed herself enough to flash them a smile. It took a lot to raise a natural smile but she had to ensure that they remembered passing her in the corridor that night. Wasn't that convenient, she thought, not only did Tim give the drugs, the time of administration would be documented and she wouldn't be on the ward when the patient became ill. The cops would be recording having seen her along the corridor. She would have two sets of the recording of her leaving ward 73 and entering ward 72, which would seem nothing out of the ordinary, just a nurse going to collect some charts.

As she approached the ward door she saw two uniformed officers flanking it, male officers, both appearing underage for the job, but none the less forbidding in their presence.

'Excuse me, I need to take your details,' the young blonde

officer stated.

'Lorraine, staff nurse from ward 73. I am here to collect some fluid charts. The other officer has just logged me coming from 73.'

'Ok Miss, will you be long?'

'No, a few minutes tops.'

'See you when you come back then.'

The officer smiled at her. Lorraine thought that they must be so bored just standing there. There wouldn't be many staff walking the corridors overnight.

'Long night for you two huh?' she managed.

'Beats walking the streets or spending the night bringing in the drunks.'

'Well you won't be too far from them in here either!' she said putting her hand out to the door of the ward, pushing it and entering.

Walking onto ward 72, Lorraine approached the desk; she had to remind herself what it was she had gone there for. Dora was at the desk, Lorraine had met her in passing once or twice but the two didn't really know each other more than that. Lorraine duly asked for the fluid charts, which Dora pulled out from a drawer in the cupboard at the side of the desk.

'How things here Dora?' Lorraine asked.

'Not bad, should be a good shift with a bit of luck, although I'm not sure I like the police popping their heads in so often, it's unnerving the patients. It's reassuring for us maybe, but some of the patients are definitely being affected and I feel as though I am in the wrong every time I give one of them any drugs.'

'I know, it is unnerving isn't it. At least if it is a member of staff then they are at hand aren't they,' added Lorraine.

'I suppose so, I just wish it was all over and they find it was a dodgy batch of drugs or fluids or something. Can't imagine it being a member of the nursing staff. What about the medical staff, no one checks what they are giving the patients? We may check the drugs but how many of us actually go with them to the patient? We don't do we, we trust them. *Trust me I am a doctor,* well, what happened to *trust me I'm a nurse?*' Dora was off on her little rant.

'Mmm, must be dodgy drugs, so who are you on with Dora?'

'Oh, Sarah is on and we have Annie and Marc as the health care. Fortunately we have a good team this shift.'

'That's nice, I'm on with Tim. I haven't worked with him before. He seems ok.'

'He always seems nice; he always speaks to me when I go over to 73. I've met him two or three times now,' Dora replied.

'Anyway, I better get back he will be wondering where I have got to.' Lorraine cut their conversation short. She felt the sudden urge to go back to the ward and make sure that Graham Stewart was alright. Maybe if she got back quickly she would be able to do something to help him. She thought she should at least give it a try.

'Have a good shift.'

'Bye,' muttered Lorraine.

Lorraine turned to walk out of the ward, was it safe to go back to 73? How was Graham? What if he had a cardiac arrest? Or worse what if he was ok and became poorly later when she was there. Shit, she would have to deal with him.

The enormity of what she had just done had just hit her. Oh shit, Graham could be dead and it's all my fault. Tim and I would instantly be the two suspects and Tim would be saying it was me. After all he was innocent wasn't he, poor bastard, he hadn't a clue what he had just done.

Lorraine was too scared to open the ward door when she got to it, yet she couldn't afford to hesitate; she had two uniformed police officers right beside her watching her every move, or lack of.

Lorraine didn't have to worry about opening the door to ward 73, just as she was contemplating the impossibility of doing so several doctors and Frances, head of the senior nursing team, ran past her pushing open the door.

'Come on Lorraine,' shouted Frances, 'cardiac arrest, quick!'

Lorraine went into autopilot and ran in behind them, she had to remain cool and calm and do as she would normally do in a situation like this.

'*What the hell have I done?*' she thought. She just hoped she hadn't said it out loud.

Lorraine hastily followed them, running down the ward.

She found herself passing Graham's bed and down to Mrs Gray's. What on earth was happening?

Behind the curtains, Tim and another junior doctor who Lorraine didn't know were in full cardiac arrest mode, trying to resuscitate Mrs Gray.

Frances, Tim and a team of what was now three doctors were more than enough bodies around the bed. Lorraine backed off and looked around the ward. She would be needed to run for anything they wanted if they shouted for her. She had to stay close by.

She had to be on the ward to reassure the other patients. Had they seen what had happened?

If they had seen her arrest then they would be upset. If they knew she died then they would have no trust in Tim or Lorraine at all. They would be seen as being the nurses who killed all the patients, whether they had done or not. She had to remain in professional mode.

Lorraine walked along the ward in the direction of Graham's bed. Curiosity about hat she had done took the better of her. She had to take a look at him and see how he was.

He looked as though he was sleeping. Relief for Lorraine was temporary.

Going up to him Lorraine called out his name softly.

'Graham, Graham,' she called.

No answer.

Did she really expect him to answer?

Hell, she wanted him to.

'GRAHAM!' she raised her voice this time and put a hand to his forehead. She tried to rouse him by placing a hand on his sternum and rubbing hard. No response. The internal panic she felt was rising by the second.

He was cold and clammy, sweat dripping from his brow.

Oh! Hypoglycaemia. Obviously, she thought.

He'd had fast acting insulin of abnormal quantity of course he would be hypoglycaemic, comatose in fact. Who was she kidding?

'I need some help here!' she shouted. 'NOW!' raising her voice to ensure that everyone heard her cries.

Lorraine pulled out the bed from the wall to allow access to the head of the bed and started to pull one of the curtains around the bed.

Frances appeared at her side and drew the other curtains, she shouted to another nurse to run to the next ward and get their arrest trolley, 'NOW!'

It wasn't common place to be shouting at all and sundry

on the ward in the middle of a cardiac arrest. Usually they tried to remain calm so not to alert the other patients. Frances had left Tim with Mrs Gray and was keeping an ear out for him in case he needed her help too.

Frances passed Lorraine the cuff for the blood pressure machine and Lorraine duly wrapped it around Graham's upper arm. She was trying to attach him to the cardiac monitor that was at the head of his bed but the sticky pads wouldn't stick to his chest as he was so clammy and sweaty.

'Must be a low blood sugar, look at him he is sweating, pass me a blood sugar monitor someone!' she shouted with an air of urgency.

The least she could do was to alert them to what the problem was, seeing that she was the only one who knew what had happened to him.

Lorraine had gone into professional mode and forgotten all about the nervousness of her feelings about what she had done. She was pumped full of adrenaline in the excitement of the emergency.

Rachel handed her the blood sugar monitor, a lancet and the test strip. Lorraine pricked Graham's finger and quickly obtained a small blob of blood from its tip.

It seemed like an eternity for the blood sugar result to appear on the monitor.

'Good thinking Lorraine,' said Frances, momentarily wondering how Lorraine thought of a low blood sugar before any other options.

A nurse arrived hastily with the resus trolley; he threw the bag, valve and mask (bvm) across to Lorraine, from his position at the foot of the bed. Frances took hold of it as Lorraine began the cardiac compressions. He had no cardiac output on the monitor, no heartbeat.

Frances was trying to ventilate Graham using the bvm; a mask was now over his nose and mouth, a bag attached. She was squeezing the bag to try to inflate his lungs.

One of the doctors had joined them from Mrs Gray's bedside and was now trying to get the defibrillator pads to stay on his chest but they were sliding about. He took over cardiac massage from Lorraine.

'Blood sugar registering LO,' reported Lorraine. It won't read any more accurately, sugar must be really low.'

A second doctor seemed to appear from nowhere and was applying a tourniquet to Graham's arm. Without hesitation he inserted the needle into the vein and took a sample of blood.

He appeared to be in his early twenties, a clean-shaven, fresh-faced young chap, eager not to be responsible for another patient death on 73. His badge informed Lorraine that he was Dr Gordon. No further information was available to her, she was just glad of his presence, maybe now something would be done for Graham and save her having to explain what really had happened.

He shouted towards the two health care assistants, 'Get these to the lab ASAP, ring the lab first and let them know that we are sending urgent bloods down to them.'

The defibrillator pads were in position. No heart rhythm was showing on the monitor. Dr Gordon charged the defibrillator machine. The machine would automatically detect a shockable heart rhythm to indicate when and if they could use it.

Dr Gordon shouted for some Adrenaline. Frances silently handed the pre-loaded syringe to him. He immediately inserted this intravenously.

He turned the dial to set the charging rate. The machine kicked in and lit up indicating the charge was complete and ready for use. A small orange light came on indicating the shockable rhythm they needed. He had some form of cardiac output they could work with.

'Clear.'

Frances and Lorraine quickly stood back.

'Shocking.'

No change in his heart rhythm.

'Clear.'

'Shocking.'

Nothing

The sequence continued. Frances repeated the squeeze of the bag to inflate his lungs each time. Dr Gordon indicated her to do so.

Still no cardiac output appeared on the monitor. No sign of life.

'Does everyone agree we stop?' Dr Gordon questioned, looking around at Frances and Lorraine.

They both nodded. Lorraine appeared to nod in her subconscious. She was in total shock at what had just happened. She stood motionless at the bedside. She was a killer; Lorraine Harris, Registered Nurse was now responsible for the death of her patient. She had done this to him. She alone was responsible for taking another life.

'Pronounced dead at 20:12. Thank you all,' muttered Dr Gordon.

How on earth could he be thanking me for my help,' she thought. If he knew what I had done he would be informing the cops and she would never see the light of day again.

Lorraine remained routed to the spot. She was transfixed by the situation. A situation that she had engineered herself, that had resulted in the death of a patient she was employed to care for. A huge wave of guilt hit her head on. There was no running away to ward 72 now.

Young Dr Gordon turned and left Graham's bedside heading for Cate's office. He would complete his paperwork there.

No one had noticed the two coppers standing at the end of the bed opposite Graham's, watching everything. Dr

Gordon, four months out of university, now found himself part of the murder investigations at Westwood General.

Lorraine and Frances were blissfully unaware that the team leading the cardiac arrest on Mrs Gray had also been unable to save their patient.

* * * * *

The two patients in the beds opposite Graham had been chatting whilst the ward staff had been busy with the two emergencies. They were horrified at what they were seeing. All four patients had been chatting not more than an hour earlier. Laughing and joking to pass the time. Now two out of the four of them were dead, right in front of their eyes, had they witnessed the hand of the Fallen Angel?

Did the staff think they were stupid or something, no way was either of them staying to end up like Graham or the lovely Mrs Gray.

Neither Peter Tyler nor Karl Williams were going to stay about to take any chances. Both men had been admitted that afternoon for surgery in the morning. They were to be fasted from midnight and have their blood tests that night. Not any more they weren't.

Both men had got themselves dressed and were walking up the ward toward the door in tandem, with their bags in their hands, when Frances spotted them.

'Peter, Karl, where are you going?' she called out to them.

'Home. No amount of persuasion will make us stay. So no point trying,' Peter stated.

'Gentlemen, you can't just walk off the ward.'

'With respect Sister, we have just watched two people die. As far as we can see, for absolutely no reason. We were all chatting happily less than an hour ago, now they are dead. Explain that one would you?'

Frances remained silent for want of something to say. She knew whatever she said would be wrong under the circumstances, there really were no words that she could use to explain what had happened, especially as she couldn't even give herself an explanation.

Interrupting her silence Peter spoke again. 'I didn't think you would be able to. We were both unsure about coming in here in the first place.' Peter seemed to have nominated himself as spokesperson for both himself and Karl.

Frances looked surprised at this sudden revolt by patients but deep down she knew that they were right. *'Safer at home until someone uncovered what exactly was going on at Westwood,'* she thought.

'Surely you realise that the story is leaking Sister? We just didn't want to believe it. After this little display there is no way either of us is going to take that chance. I'm sure that a few more in here are getting ready to go home too. This hospital is a disgrace and the bloody papers are going to hear it from us first thing in the morning.'

'Gentlemen, please come back into the ward so we can discuss this.' She racked her brains for something coherent to say, knowing she had failed miserably in her search.

'No thank you. We are going home and going to the press about this shambles you call a ward.'

'In that case please just come and sign a self discharge form. Then you are welcome to go. I am sorry that you find yourselves in this situation. I cannot apologise enough.' Frances was attempting to hold on to every ounce of her professionalism, desperate to scream, cry, shout, anything in fact, to express her frustration at the situation she was swallowed up in.

'Get the forms if you must but we are not staying under any circumstances. Personally I am happy to keep my gall bladder until I can get it out somewhere that I feel I will be in safe hands. Not at the hands of staff who want me dead,' he added abruptly.

She new she could do nothing but get two self discharge forms and hand them to Peter and Karl. She chose not to reply to Peter's last comment, she really couldn't think of anything vaguely appropriate. They both signed their self discharge forms in silence and neither of them said another word as they turned and exited ward 73.

Frances had brought in two other nurses. A quick call to Kiera, the on call hospital co-ordinator for the night had brought Frances two more staff nurses, one from medical admissions and one from orthopaedics to man the ward whilst she dealt with Tim and Lorraine. She hadn't even dared allow herself to think what response they were getting from the ward's remaining patients.

The medical admissions unit would not be able to spare their nurse for long, but she knew that the night staff would be in soon and be able to take charge of the shift.

Frances would decide what was going to happen with the remaining patients after she had dealt with more pressing issues.

She herself would handle the phone calls to Mrs Gray's elderly husband and Graham Stewart's wife. Something of an arduous task but one she had to get on with. Round two of nuclear fallout she thought as she settled into Cate's comfy leather chair and reached for the phone. She couldn't even begin to anticipate what their reactions would be, and certainly didn't have any answers to questions she knew they would ask of her, but knew the calls had to be made without further hesitation.

For Frances her shift was just getting better and better. She had experienced some nightmares in her thirty years of nursing but this was currently making it to number one on her list. Now she had to inform the on call consultant that she had two more suspicious deaths on ward 73. She knew that it wouldn't be too long before the detectives were back there either. Once they heard about this everything would be taken out of her hands. She was trying to stop the vision her mind had created of uniformed officers coming on to the ward to arrest her staff, the image wouldn't shift, her consciousness reinforcing the reality of this, reminding her that she too may be taken off the ward for formal interviewing. All of a sudden she felt a tremendous wave of fear run through her, she could feel her heart pounding, her chest hurt, it was becoming harder for her to breath. Frances tried to calm herself, grabbing on to the side of the desk to steady her quivering legs. She was telling herself to take slow, deep breaths, her physical body following other commands. Fear of losing control of herself as well as the ward was overcoming her. Concentrating on her breathing she slowly began to calm herself, frightened that she was going to become the night's next casualty.

Some days she really hated her job. Today was the best of those bad days.

26

Lorraine and Tim were about as exhausted as they could be. The toll of the shift had mainly been mental. They would be late off shift now; Lorraine wouldn't see Sally before she started her night shift if Frances was going to want them to go through the events. She needed to do some quick thinking to get her story right, adrenaline still pumped around her body from the experience of the cardiac arrests earlier.

They knew that having had two deaths on the ward on their shift would make them public enemy number one and two not only around the hospital but with their patients and their colleagues.

Lorraine wondered if she was just imagining the whispers coming from the other patients.

What the hell had she done? Now she was a murderer. Or was she? She had to pull herself together before she started acting guilty and the others picked up on this. She had to somehow cover her tracks and get herself out of this mess. She desperately needed to talk to Sally, she would have to trust her and tell her what had happened. She would tell her what to do about it.

Who would now trust them as their nurses? Peter and Karl had already left the ward, what about the others? Tim and Lorraine sat in silence in the staff tea room having been sent there for time out by Frances.

Taking a deep breath, she managed to execute her words with enough precision to be understood.

'I have to tell you both that although we do not know the situation fully about Mrs Gray's and Graham's deaths, you both are now suspended from duty pending investigations. There will be no chances taken with either of you continuing to practise.'

Two shocked faces stared back silently at her. She glared them both out before continuing.

'You will each be required to make a statement about the events of tonight. Separate incident report forms also need to be completed before you leave the ward.'

The two of them looked at each other in disbelief. Tim was the first to break eye contact with Lorraine. He hung his head to the floor and remained silent, the shock he felt was overwhelming, his head felt light, spinning in more directions than he realised possible. He was relieved he was sitting down, fearing landing on the floor if he tried to get up.

Tim and Lorraine looked at each other horrified. Lorraine had an immediate elongated pang of guilt but knew she had to keep calm about any questioning that may lie ahead.

She couldn't come clean now and tell Frances what had happened. She had actually made a drug error on purpose. What she didn't understand was Mrs Gray, Tim hadn't gone near her with the syringe. Unless, she thought, if he had given it to her when she had gone to 72?

That was always a possibility, yet if she told the police this, she would show knowledge of the syringe of insulin. She knew she couldn't go down that route.

She certainly hadn't given her any drugs. What was happening? Lorraine knew she was totally out of her depth and decided to say nothing.

Her thoughts were confused and irrational, like the last hour or two of her shift.

Lorraine knew that when they found out what was in Graham's bloodstream they would know he had been given the insulin intravenously. They would look straight to the two of them. Well, Tim would be to blame. Tim had signed the chart for the antibiotics and he had given the insulin. She would deny giving any drugs, after all that bit was actually true. She wasn't anywhere near him, was she, even

Tim would have to agree with that.

She would stick to that story and make out he was lying, it was her only reasonable option. Stitching him up was the only way to preserve her integrity and her nursing registration. It wasn't as if she was a bad nurse, she enjoyed her job and was getting on well here, until today that is. Yes, blame Tim and keep quiet. It was her only chance.

Lorraine knew he didn't know what he had done, but if they found out what she had done she would have to say that he didn't check the saline vial before she drew it up. He merely checked the empty vial and assumed that she had drawn it up in to the syringe. Lorraine wondered what Tim would tell them about that. If she was going down for this, then certainly he would be too, she would make sure of that.

Further investigations and the results of the two post mortems would show the patients' causes of death, she knew that the cops wouldn't have those details for days though. They would not be able to evade questions then. She would have to play daft, answer their questions the best she could but admit to nothing. After all, they had no evidence to prove she had actually done anything, that was one thing she was sure of.

Well, Lorraine could account for the cause of death of Graham couldn't she. As for Mrs Gray she didn't have a clue. She began to wonder if Tim had caused her death.

She was innocent here, regarding Mrs Gray, but could

she pass Graham off as the work of the 'Fallen Angel', surely she would just need to keep her mouth shut.

Was Tim really a killer? Shit! She had been trusting his judgement, clinical skills and patient care. Was this why he had been getting so shirty with the detective on the ward? She didn't know what to think and saw the situation as clearly as her head would allow her to.

Just as Frances had announced their suspension Charlie Hammond appeared, followed by several uniformed officers. His face displaying total danger to anyone who got in his way, causing Frances to take a step back, out of his direct line of fire.

The two resident uniformed officers at the doors of ward 73, had rung Charlie and alerted him as soon as the first cardiac arrest had occurred. Then stood and watched every moment of two cardiac arrests. None of the staff had even noticed their presence, far too busy with the procedure to worry about anything going on around them.

Cate had arrived after she'd had a frantic Frances on the phone to her, she approached Tim and Lorraine, her face displaying anger beyond their comprehension, and she looked as if she was going to burst.

Tim wanted to take a step back but found his limbs unco-operative to his command. He just could not look at her, how he had got into this situation he didn't know but the look she was giving him had him banged to rights already, labelled guilty.

Her normally calm and pleasant demeanour had changed and her face contorted in an all consuming rage, her nostrils flaring, her mouth quivering.

Charlie hadn't noticed quite how feminine Cate looked before. He was taken aback by how beautiful she looked tonight. Wearing a pair of dark blue jeans and a white T shirt Cate looked innocent and just stunning, even in the face of adversity. But it was the sparkle in her eyes that was missing.

Charlie found himself thinking how he would like to see the smile return to her face, to make her happy again and take away her stress, he had to get a grip on his thoughts, right now he was about to take two members of her staff into custody. He knew which he would rather be doing.

He was shocked at himself; again he was taking notice of a woman. Not just any woman, this was Cate.

She kept crossing his path and stirring his dormant emotions. He knew he would have to act on his emotions soon; she was far too precious to lose.

'Excuse me,' she said, directing her words at Charlie. He knew she was about to burst a gasket but was going to allow her to have her moment with them. His moment would keep a little longer.

Cate took a deep breath and edged forward so she was

standing just in front of the two of them, poised to let rip at any second. Two intensely scared faces looked back at her, awaiting the explosion of words they knew was about to dawn on them.

'What the hell is going on you two? I leave you in charge of my ward and what the hell happens? I have more deaths, more bloody deaths! Are you both totally incompetent or just plain sick?' she screamed. Her face flushed scarlet, anger oozing out of her pores. Neither could have imagined the anger that she was now exploding towards them. 'How many more are you two responsible for? Plain sick, the both of you. What is this?' she screeched, waving her arms about her as she vented her rage. 'A bloody double act you sick bastards?' She had hardly drawn breath in her rant at them, she was visibly fuming.

Lorraine couldn't look at Cate. Fear striking her rigid; Tim was almost reduced to tears. Her words had come spewing out filling the room like a volcano releasing its pent up emotions into the daylight, its devastation visible to all.

Charlie turned to Cate, put his hand upon her arm, 'Ok?'

'I'll be fine thanks,' she muttered almost relieved.

'I'll take it from here,' he extended a hand out to her, attempting to lead her to one side. She remained rooted to the spot strangely silent. One of the uniformed officers stepped forward alongside her.

DS Charlie Hammond turned first towards Lorraine.

His moment.

'Lorraine Harris, I am arresting you on suspicion of your involvement in the deaths of Graham Stewart and Alice Mary Gray, and, possibly, several other deaths within this hospital. You do not have to say anything, but it may harm your defence if you do not mention when questioned something, which you later rely on in court. Anything you do say may be given in evidence.'

Lorraine burst into tears and buried her head in her chest as one of the uniformed officers brought the handcuffs towards her. She was physically shaking from the shock of the cold metal clamping around her wrists.

'No, no it's not me you want, I didn't kill them. Don't take me away!' she shouted, aghast at the actual allegations he had presented to her. 'You need to take him, he did it!'

'It bloody well wasn't me!' Tim stated. 'You bitch. You set me up. You fucking psycho bitch!' Suddenly he had found his voice, and pointed his finger adamantly at her.

'Tim...' DS Hammond didn't give him the luxury of continuing to speak, interrupting him almost immediately. 'Shut it, you will have plenty of time to talk down at the station,' interrupted Charlie as Lorraine was ushered away, flanked by two male uniformed officers.

The uniformed officer turned to secure the cuffs as Charlie began to repeat his words to an extremely nervous Staff Nurse Simpson.

Charlie put cuffs on Tim himself, knowing this would add to the satisfaction of his arrest for him.

He accepted them in silence, not knowing how else to cope with the situation he currently found himself in. Internally he was so mad he thought he would have the strength to break out of the cuffs, no trouble. In his mind he wanted to punch Lorraine, in reality his hands were tied. Literally, he thought.

Charlie had had his doubts in the beginning, but over and above Tim's anger he knew he was actually a decent person and a good nurse. However, he couldn't get his thoughts around Lorraine, she just wasn't strong enough to be a killer. *'What part did she have to play in all this?'* he thought, he would never have guessed she was involved.

Cate had encountered the surreal experience of the arrest of two members of her ward team. She was angry to a point she had never felt before. She felt nausea rising and thought she was going to be sick at any moment, she had to concentrate not to vomit there and then.

She could do nothing but watch two of her staff nurses being led out of the staff room in handcuffs. She couldn't have dreamt of seeing anything so horrendous. She hated the sight of both of them.

Charlie saw the look on her face, she looked alone and vulnerable, exhausted and in need of a hug. Now just wasn't the time, yet at that moment she was now no longer his suspect, she was just Cate. Had he pushed it too far with her, he wondered, maybe if he gave her time she would warm to him and see why he behaved as he did. Police procedure after all, he couldn't help that, could he.

Just now, he'd keep those thoughts to himself and for a time more suitable, he hoped it would be soon, right now he had some interrogating to plan.

Cate left the staff room after they had taken Tim and Lorraine out, proceeded directly to the staff toilet and vomited uncontrollably for longer than she could have believed possible.

Cate knew that she would have to stay on the ward and ensure that the paperwork was all correctly completed for the two deaths. She couldn't leave all that to Frances, however much she just wanted to run out of there and not return.

The hospital managers had to be contacted, that she would leave to Frances, after all the hospital was technically her responsibility for the night. That alone was an unenviable task, Cate thought. One she would rather pass over.

She needed to pull herself together sharpish and be of help. She didn't want to be seen in this state of disarray. She washed her face in some cold water at the sink and prepared to show her face out on the ward. She had no idea how she was going to be able to face the rest of the patients. What if they asked her what was going on? She had no idea at all what she would say to them or how much they already knew. She had to summon up every part of courage within her to step back out on to the ward and acknowledge herself as its leader.

Frances found herself in the unenviable position of having to contact the two families and come up with an adequate explanation for their relative's demise. She knew she wouldn't manage the latter.

Her world had crumbled; somehow she was now in the middle of the traumas on ward 73. Would it never end, or maybe it had? She suddenly realised what Cate must have been going through, this last few days, she felt a pang of guilt regarding the lack of support she had been giving her over the investigation.

Lorraine and Tim had been unceremoniously taken off the ward by uniformed officers. She had no idea how many of the remaining twelve patients saw them being taken from the ward, she assumed all of them. Not an everyday sight that could be missed, two members of staff leaving a ward, handcuffed and flanked by detectives and uniformed officers.

She had no idea where Cate had gone, she was secretly hoping that she would come back sometime soon. Since she rushed off she hadn't seen her, at least Cate would be someone she could talk to about all this, no one else would even begin to understand where she was coming from with this one. Then to her dismay the ward suddenly filled with forensic officers and the patients were being moved, all of a sudden she had no control of what was happening.

'Sister?' a police officer said.

'Yes?' she answered emotionless.

'You need to come with me, we have to begin questioning straight away.'

'Yes!'

'You ok Sister?' the woman constable said to her.

She hoped Cate would be back to support her with this. The night staff would be busy enough with their shift responsibilities. They had to continue as normal until she knew for sure when she could find beds for them on other wards. She felt like running far from her present circumstances but there was plenty of unfinished business for her to deal with. She would not be going anywhere for a while yet.

'I'm fine!' she added as she followed her off of the ward.

Frances braved it and walked down the ward, she was only too aware that she was failing to achieve an air of professionalism in her stride.

'Sally, can you gather the others together so I can speak

to you all for a moment?' Cate announced as she arrived back on the ward, relieved that at least the night staff were there. The suits would be along soon, taking control, maybe even closing the ward, but until such time this happened things had to get back to some form of routine.

'No problem, give me a minute.' Sally knew that Mary, who they had sent from the medical admissions unit, was still on the ward, along with Mark and Vicky.

'Hey guys, Cate wants to speak to us all, she's at the nurses station.'

Like animals to the ark they followed her up the ward, the only difference being they filed silently one by one.

'Behind here if you don't mind, the less our patients get to hear about all this the better, for the time being,' stated Cate.

'As you know, Mrs Alice Gray and Mr Graham Stewart died earlier on the late shift; there is cause for suspicion surrounding their deaths. I am advised that in the light of recent events, not only on this ward but within the hospital, Staff Nurse Harris and Staff Nurse Simpson have been taken to the police station for further questioning.'

'Shit,' Sally gasped, she had no idea that this was the reality of the situation. The team were obviously aware of the deaths; they had been left to clear up the mess of the cardiac arrest trolleys and given the task of replenishing them. She had no idea of the fact that the cops had Lorraine.

Without thinking Sally interrupted Cate's address to the staff, 'Can I go down there?'

'What Sally?' Cate paused, 'Down where?'

'To the cop shop of course.'

'In case I have missed something here Sally, you are on shift for the night. I can't afford to lose sight of another member of trained staff.'

'But Lorraine will need me!' exasperation and panic now clear in her voice.

'The only thing she needs right now Sally is a good lawyer,' Cate snapped.

'What do you mean?' Sally was physically shaking now, scared at the prospect of the answer she would receive to her question.

'Look, this is not the conversation I asked you here for. I am informing you all of the situation we find ourselves in. We now have to deal with the aftermath. The main priority has to be our patients. I am keeping you all on here tonight. We need to reassure them that they are all safe and if they ask anything about staff being taken away by the police, not one of you comments. Do you all understand?'

A chorus was heard to mutter 'yes', as if saying amen together in compliance.

'None of us can comment about staff being in custody, we do not know the full story.'

'You said Lorraine had been taken for questioning?'

'I did.'

'So why now say she is in custody that sounds like she is banged up in a cell?'

'Sally, she was arrested and taken to the police station that is all I know.'

'I really need to see her, she will freak out if she is in a cell.'

'As I said, there is no way you are leaving the ward, and you certainly cannot go to the police station, I doubt they would allow you to see her anyway.'

Vicky was attentively watching Sally and her reaction to Lorraine's arrest. Her concern seemed interesting. Why would she need her? She thought that comment a little odd, the urgency in her voice causing her concern.

She couldn't leave the ward to join them at the station; she wanted to continue until the end of her shift. The team had suffered enough shocks tonight without her announcing that she was undercover, in effect spying on them.

She thought perhaps she could find out a little more about how the crime was committed, a long shot but one worth continuing with.

'We have to regain some order here, what is there still to be done? Have the medications been given out yet?' Cate continued.

'All done,' Mark chipped in before Sally could open her mouth and ask to leave the ward again.

'Ok, so what needs doing?'

'Just to settle the patients down, give out a cup of tea perhaps, I don't think that was done earlier. When we came on we were dealing with Mrs Gray and Graham, and sorting out the trolleys.'

'Vicky, you go and get the teas sorted out, the least we can do is give them a cup of tea before settling them down for the night. Sally and Mark, go and check if any further observations need doing. Check your fluid charts and make a list of anything we need to get the junior doctor to do before it gets too late. This ward needs some semblance of order back, so get back out there and sort it out. Oh, and refer any questions from the patients directly to me please.'

* * * * *

Tim and Lorraine had been taken rather hastily to the police station in two separate unmarked police cars. Charlie didn't want the two of them having any chance to converse before he was able to interview them. He requested that Harry Webster remain in the car with Tim and a uniformed officer until they had completed Lorraine's booking in process. He had to ensure that they had no chance to set eyes on each other, let alone collaborate on their story.

He presented Lorraine Harris to the duty custody sergeant. Tonight it was Sergeant Andy Cameron in charge of custody and processing. That pleased him immensely, at least things would get done quickly, the sooner he had the two of them stewing in solitary in the cells the better. A couple of hours thinking time should have both of them ready to squeal he thought. Smiling to himself at the prospect of two convictions.

'What you got boss?' Andy enquired.

'Lorraine Harris. Brought in from ward 73, Westwood General. Cautioned on arrest. Suspected drug error, malpractice and possible murder.'

The horror on Lorraine's face was unmistakable. Every muscle in her face tightened, her eyes appeared huge and surprised, making Charlie wonder if she had any real comprehension of the situation she was in.

'Murder. You said murder…' she stammered as she scanned round her bleak surroundings.

'May I remind you Ms Harris that you are under caution,' said Andy.

'Murder?' she muttered again.

'Ms Harris. You are under caution. Do you understand the meaning of a caution Ms Harris?'

Silence.

'Ms Harris?'

'Yes,' she muttered, 'I think so,' she paused but decided not to speak further, heeding the caution.

'Ms Harris, firstly custody forms need to be completed.

I need you to confirm your name, address and date of birth, for the records.'

Slowly, conscious of forming her words carefully through her stammering, Lorraine complied with his request. She was visibly shaking, shocked and terrified, the reality of the situation kicking in abruptly. The air around her seemed stagnant, stale and cold. A windowless hell closing in on her.

'Ms Harris, you have been arrested in connection with a possible drug error, malpractice and on suspicion of murder,' he paused trying to see if she was actually taking in any of what he was saying. 'I am now informing you of your rights. You have the right to speak with an independent solicitor free of charge, to have someone informed that you have been arrested and you are able to consult the codes of practice covering police procedures and practice… Ms Harris?' She was staring intently at the floor, appearing there in body but certainly not in mind.

'Ms Harris?' he repeated.

'SSSorry, what?' Lorraine stumbled on her words unable to focus on the reality of her situation.

'Do you understand your rights?'

'I'm cold.'

'Do you wish to consult with a solicitor?'

'I don't know. Please just let me out of here.'

'Ms Harris that is your decision. I need to inform you that the service is available to you. You can change your mind at any time and request legal representation at any stage whilst you are detained.'

'Ok.' She noticed a female office appear at her side and took a subconscious step backwards. 'What's she want? Get her away from me!'

'My colleague is now going to search you, Ms Harris.' Lorraine didn't wait for him to continue, interrupting him almost immediately. 'She bloody isn't!' she screeched.

'Ms Harris, my colleague will conduct a pat down search, to check for any concealed weapons or drugs.'

'I don't do drugs.'

Andy signalled to his colleague to commence her search. A non-invasive search was necessary to ensure she was not concealing anything that she could use as a weapon to harm herself or others.

The officer began to pat either side of her arms, over her navy cardigan, working down to her trunk and abdominal area. 'Empty the contents of your pockets on to the counter please,' the female officer requested.

Flanked by DS Hammond and his uniformed colleague Lorraine began to empty the pockets of her uniform tunic. First her breast pocket, from which she withdrew two biros, one red, one black and placed them on the counter in front of Andy. Next she moved on to the lower pockets of her uniform, scissors, a tissue, lip balm, several medi-swabs, a five ml syringe in its plastic covering and a plastic vial of saline.

'Don't look at me like that,' she paused as she stared at Sergeant Andy Cameron, 'nothing there that shouldn't be. Officer,' she added in a perfected sarcastic tone.

Andy was busily listing the produced items on his property sheet, carefully documenting each and every item.

'Your watch too.'

Lorraine carefully unpinned the silver fob watch she had displayed adjacent to her breast pocket.

'Badges too Miss.'

Lorraine looked at him with a sense of emptiness.

'Remove all items from your pockets and uniform Ms Harris,' he said again.

The pat down search nearing completion, Lorraine found hands running through her hair. 'Remove your hair tie please, and your shoes too.' Her limbs were trembling, her lips quivering, scared far beyond her worst nightmares.

Opening her mouth to argue, Lorraine stopped herself before any sound emerged. Visions of previously being searched and interviewed by detectives flashed through her mind. 'Don't, just don't!' she shouted. 'Don't touch me!' she screamed.

'Ms Harris, please calm yourself. The officer is merely doing her job,' came a voice from alongside her.

Lorraine couldn't reply, old images flashed before her, she had been here before, only things had got a whole lot worse for her then, she couldn't let that happen again. Why weren't they listening to her, she really didn't want to be here? They were not taking any notice of what she wanted.

'This is a comprehensive list of your property. You are required to read through this and sign here.' Andy was pointing to the bottom of the form where she needed to sign.

Hesitating, in an attempt to calm her increasing nerves and steady her trembling fingers, Lorraine took a deep breath but felt instant regret at inhaling the stale air of the custody area as it hit her hard and quick with a rancid lingering at the back of her throat.

'These items will be kept in this plastic bag and returned to you when you are able to leave.'

Lorraine started to get sweaty palms as she noticed the fingerprinting procedure being set out in front of her. All she could think about was the past record they already had on file for her!

'Place your hand on here please,' Andy indicated to her.

'Why?'

Frustration was mounting rapidly for Charlie. What a palaver he was witnessing, and he had another one waiting that he had to put through the same process. With no sign of the end of his day he hankered after a satisfying caffeine fix. He would have to quench his desire as soon as this booking process was complete. Maybe he would assign

Harry to bring Tim in he really had had enough of today and he still had two detainees to interview. The mere sight of Lorraine in her uniform was pissing him off right now.

Enough is enough he thought. 'You two sort her out, get her in a cell and I'll be back later to interview her. Get Harry to sort the other one out would you?' Before his colleagues could respond he had left the custody desk.

'We also need to get her risk assessed for interview, see if she is fit for questioning!' he shouted back.

Tim was beginning to feel as though he was a criminal. An hour ago he was on shift on ward 73. Now he found himself under arrest. He just couldn't understand what had happened and how he had ended up under arrest.

'Can I ring my wife? I know she's not expecting me home just yet but I would at least like to get her down here.'

'Calls soon enough lad.'

'Can't I ring her now?'

'Take him to the cells,' was the only reply he received to his request.

He found himself in a small, unwelcoming space, affording him no comfort whatsoever. There was a seat, built into the cell, covered by what appeared to be a thin blue mattress. They were both left in their respective cells for several hours before their interviews commenced.

Charlie and Harry had to gather all the information

from the ward and Frances about the events surrounding Graham and Mrs Gray's death before they could even begin to get their version of events.

Charlie had already decided to interview Tim first. One of the custody team took Tim from the cell that had been his home for the last few hours, to an interview room located in a corridor that he thought was parallel to the cells.

He was surprised by the sparseness of the room as he entered. It was dimly lit, making it appear unfriendly and unwelcoming. He remembered where he was, why would they make it welcoming, after all these were the rooms that they interviewed their criminals in.

He wasn't a criminal. *'What he was doing being taken here?'* he thought. Although the time he spent alone in the cell had given him time to think, the atmosphere had been anything but conducive to his thought process. His mind had been spinning, trying to make sense of the evening's events. He had been more concerned with getting out of there than coming up with an adequate explanation for proceedings on the ward tonight.

There were four chairs, a desk and glaringly bare whitewashed walls. Tim had felt uneasy as he had crossed the threshold into this wasteland. He felt a sense of exposure, unfamiliarity and isolation, he didn't want to sit down as he was told to do, and he desperately wanted to get out of there. It was as though a sense of panic surrounded him as he realised he was trapped there with no escape route.

Tim watched as Harry unwrapped two tapes in front of him, inserting then into a recorder.

For the benefit of the tape Charlie introduced himself and Harry Webster, a detective constable. There was a third person present, Mr Shah. He was formally introduced as the duty solicitor. Tim, made no comment to the introductions.

Tim was asked if he wished to speak with the solicitor alone, prior to the interview commencing, he chose not to. Again the caution was repeated to him. He was asked to confirm that he understood it. One word affirmative was all Tim could manage at this time. He was in total shock at his surroundings and situation and further vocal responses were not forthcoming for him.

'I need to call my wife!'

Charlie looked directly at him, appearing to observe his every move. Tim felt as though he could see right through him and pick up his accelerated heart rate and rising panic. He tried desperately to appear calm and composed but knew that he was failing in this brilliantly.

'You can wait a while Tim,' Charlie said matter of factly, he actually knew this was going to be a quick interview, he now knew Tim wasn't his guy.

Charlie had what appeared to be an inbuilt ability to listen, examine his suspect's non verbal communication and question them all at the same time. He revelled in gaining the confidence of his detainee yet making them feel nervous and uncomfortable.

Charlie didn't sit down, he paced about the room and then settled alongside Tim, he lent down toward him and spoke in a soft voice. He needed to get Tim talking, to start the flow of conversation and being interacting with him before getting on to the nitty-gritty of his questioning. If he could get him to reply to basic, non threatening questions he knew he could lead him on to the essentials with ease.

'Can you please confirm your full name for the tape?'

'Tim Simpson.'

'Your date of birth and home address.'

Tim tried to reduce the tremor in his voice to reply and furnish him with the information requested.

'Who do you live with?'

'My wife and daughter.' He responded to the questioning but just wasn't following why he was being asked these seemingly irrelevant questions.

Charlie saw the look of fright on Tim's face; he knew all of this was getting to the lad. He hated it when he was trying to interview and the suspect remained silent, he had managed to get him talking even though it wasn't about the incident and that pleased him immensely.

'Tim, I would like to start by getting you to recall to me the events of tonight, firstly with what happened to Graham

Stewart and what intravenous drugs he was given.'

Tim took a deep breath and opened his mouth to speak. He didn't know where to start.

'I gave Graham his intravenous antibiotics. He was on amoxicillin one gram; I checked this with Lorraine in the clinical room. We both checked his drug chart, the prescription was correct,' he paused.

'Go on,' Charlie urged.

He felt the detective's eyes boring in to him as he spoke. Again he hesitated feeling physically trapped but mentally exposed.

'We were being as extra vigilant as Cate, sorry, Sister Carter, had told us all to be. I checked the vial, the water for injection that it was to be drawn up in, and the vial of saline.'

'Did you draw up the antibiotic or did your colleague?'

'Lorraine did.'

'Staff Nurse Harris?'

'Yes,' he said with a tear in his eye, 'we both checked the expiry date, wrote down the batch number and checked that the seals on the vials hadn't been broken before we used them.'

'So when you checked all the vials, the antibiotic, saline and water, they were all sealed?'

'Yes,' he replied, quickly followed by, 'no.'

Charlie looked over towards Harry, then back to Tim, 'Sorry, are you saying you didn't check they were all sealed?'

'Yes and no. The antibiotic vial was sealed, definitely. The plastic vial of water too was sealed but now I think about it, Lorraine had just drawn up the saline as I went in to the room.'

'You didn't actually see her draw the saline up then?'

'No, I saw her put down a syringe as I came in to the room.'

'Do I understand that it was you who actually gave the drugs to Graham?'

'Yes I did, Lorraine was going to but she was called by Mrs Gray and I said I would give them. I thought it would be safe to do that because we had already both checked them and she could see that I was by the bed with the right patient.'

'Didn't turn out to be such a good idea did it.'

'No. Seems not.'

'Tim, this action constitutes a drug error and in this instance caused the death of your patient.'

'I checked them; I didn't mean for him to die.'

'You have just told me that you didn't actually see the saline being drawn up, it appears that Graham Stewart could have been given another drug and you were the one who gave it to him. Possibly insulin.'

'Oh God no.'

Silence. Charlie paced around the room, with his hands firmly in his pockets, waiting for Tim to respond, which he did, eventually.

'I didn't know this did I? I didn't know I was giving him something else. If I did I wouldn't have done it.' Tim could add nothing more.

'If you had followed the procedure that your ward sister has been so adamant about being implemented, you would have been one hundred percent sure what you were giving to your patient.'

'Yes.' Panic rose within him, tears welled up stinging his eyes. He had no idea which way to turn, all roads presently led to hell as he saw it.

'And you didn't?'

'No.'

'You caused the death of the patient.'

'I didn't. I didn't get the insulin. I didn't draw it up and I didn't plan this did I? My mistake was giving the drugs I admit that. Nothing else.'

'Are you sure you didn't plan this Tim?' Worth a shot to ask, Charlie could see Tim's vulnerability showing through now. Fear was a peculiar thing, often leading to confession, he waited to see how he handled his response.

'What?'

'Are you sure you didn't plan the death of Graham like you planned all the others?'

'NO, NO, NO. I didn't plan or do anything!' he yelled.

Tim shifted his gaze from the detectives and scanned

the room, anywhere except in the line of Charlie's glare.

'I am now terminating your interview,' DS Hammond paused. 'Interview terminated at 21:42.' Turning to the officer standing at the door he uttered, 'He can go! Take him back.'

'Take me back? What is going on?' Tim screeched.

'The interview is terminated. For now. You can go back to the cell for the time being.'

Tim heard further doors slam. He was trapped. Trapped in the biggest web of deceit imaginable and had no idea how to get out of it. He had no idea what was going on.

He was in utter despair, sitting squarely on the blue plastic mattress on the only bench in the cell. Home comforts definitely a thing of the past. He didn't regret a word of what he said to the detectives, they had pissed him off big time. His temporary home was dark, dank and smelt deeply musty. He tried not to think of the previous occupant. His sense of smell was giving him enough ideas about that already. Somehow he had to try to shut his mind down, to escape from this hell for even just a moment to try to regain his sanity. Thoughts of Caroline entered his head, she would be wondering where he was. Pangs of guilt emerged, slowly surfacing, he really didn't want to cause her concern. Maybe he would hold off letting her know where he was.

Maybe she wouldn't be worried at all. He wasn't too aware of the time. Maybe Caroline wouldn't even think anything was wrong. But he was banged up in a police cell, with the feeling that DS Charlie Hammond was about to make him headline news.

27

Lorraine had attempted to settle down on the mattress in the cell, it looked like she was in for a long wait before they talked to her. She was assuming that they were speaking to Tim first. All sense of time had escaped her.

Time seemed unfathomable, stripped of her watch she could only guess at the hour. Her stomach was growling, that much alone was telling her she had been there several hours. Another indicator of time, the ache in her back from the hard surface that she had tried alternately lying and sitting on. What was he saying? How she wished she knew what he was telling them. Should she tell them the truth? It was an accident though. Tim had no idea what he was giving Graham. Shit, now he was dead. As for Mrs Gray? What if they tried to pin that death on her? What if they thought she and Tim were in it together and had caused the deaths of all the other patients too? Cornered and alone, Lorraine could only wait for the sealing of her fate.

Her mind was racing backwards and forwards going over the same scenarios in her head. Most of them ended with her and Tim being sentenced to the rest of their lives in jail. Tormented by other inmates told about the crimes towards their patients.

She really couldn't bear to be shut away in this cell, the solitude was getting to her.

What if she had to spend the rest of her life in a cell? She would have no life left. What would her family think, they would be told that she had caused her patients to die; she knew they wouldn't listen to what she had to say. They were like that. Never really listened to her. Like before. They hadn't listened to her then had they. They hadn't believed her when she told them what had happened to her. She needed them then but she didn't need them now.

What Lorraine did need was Sally. A real friend beside her to listen, she knew Sally would listen to her, believe her and back her up. She could do with her right now, here beside her, comforting her, telling her it would all be alright.

What should she do? Admit to drawing up the insulin and end up in jail? Or lie about it and make out that it must have been Tim? After all it was just the two of them there. No one but her actually knew what had happened.

She had to think this out but her head was pounding. She was trying to think straight but her thoughts were merely going round in circles.

If only Sally was here she would know what to do. She would help her. She couldn't even phone her. They hadn't allowed her a phone call yet, but when they did she would call Sally.

Yes, ring Sally, she will know what to do.

The custody sergeant was opening the door to her cell. No, they couldn't want to talk to her already. She hadn't decided what she was going to say.

'Miss, get up and come with me. DS Hammond is ready for you.'

Slowly she rose and shuffled towards the opened cell door. The ache in her back prevented her straightening up to walk properly. 'How long have I been in here?' Quickly followed by, 'Where is Tim?'

The door was closed behind her and she walked past several other cells. She wondered if Tim was in one of them, wondered if they had interviewed him yet.

'Never mind him. You have enough to think about. This way.'

Lorraine was led down a small corridor to the left of the custody desk, it joined another somewhat longer, almost identical stark white corridor.

She was taken to the interview room where she instantly recognised DS Charlie Hammond as the one who had spoken at their staff meeting, the one who appeared to have the hots for Cate. Everyone else saw the way he looked at her during the meeting, except it seems Cate herself. Her thoughts were anywhere but right there in the room where they needed to be possibly in an attempt to remain sane in a totally insane situation.

The other detective was introduced as Richard Brockway, she didn't recognise him.

Charlie approached her and switched on the tape informing her who was in the room and that the interview was being taped.

Lorraine still hadn't decided what she was going to say. Panic was beginning to set in; she began to shake and couldn't stop herself. As soon as it registered in her mind that she was sitting on a chair in the interview room faced by two detectives all rational thoughts evaded her.

Charlie was transfixed on her body language. She appeared to be overreacting to her situation. Was she merely over acting, trying to divert their attention? The last thing he needed right now was a suspect faking illness to avoid their interview. He really wasn't in the mood for any delaying tactics. He couldn't be doing with the hassle of getting the on call doctor to assess her as fit for interview. Deep in his mind he knew something wasn't right. Days like today for Charlie almost always got worse and today had already been twice as long as any other day, and, twice as bad.

He paused to allow himself time to study her. She was

about 5 foot 3, shoulder length dark brown hair, and her skin was lightly tanned. She was somewhat overweight for her height, he thought. Her whole body appeared to be shaking uncontrollably now. She was working herself up into an unmanageable state.

'Lorraine, you need to calm yourself down. You need to take control of yourself otherwise this interview is going to be incredibly painstaking, for us both.'

She took time to look towards him. No direct eye contact, merely in his direction. It was as though she had heard something but wasn't too sure where the sound had come from.

'Lorraine, begin with telling us what happened with regard to drawing up the intravenous drugs for Graham would you.'

Lorraine's voice didn't seem to respond to her brain's instruction for it to speak. She was trembling from head to toe, her breathing was getting faster and she was finding it hard to catch her breath. Faster and faster the room became to spin out of control, everything was flying about around her. They were in her face. She appeared now to look right through Charlie, and was focusing on the back wall of the tiny room.

'Get away from me. I told you what he did to me but you wouldn't listen, no one would listen. Get away from me, don't hurt me. Please don't hurt me!'

She got up from the chair and before either Charlie or Richard could stop her she reached the back wall.

Lorraine was now cowering in the corner of the interview room.

'Get away from me. Don't hurt me. I told you get away.'

She began to scream, loud, piercing screams, getting louder by the second. She was flailing her arms towards Richard. 'Get away from me, don't hurt me!'

Charlie and Richard shot a glance at each other, both producing looks of utter amazement at the vision in front of them.

Charlie had seen many of his interviewees pull stunts to try to avoid questioning but never anything quite like what he was witnessing now.

He signalled to Richard to move away from her.

'No one is going to hurt you Lorraine; we just need you to answer some questions,' said the duty solicitor.

'Don't hurt me. Please don't let them hurt me,' she whimpered. Tears were streaming down her face in an almost silent reaction.

'This isn't getting us anywhere Lorraine. This little act isn't going to work with us.'

Charlie was rapidly losing patience with her. 'I am not going to play your little games. Interview terminated at 22:36. Take her back to the cell and we will resume this later.' Charlie was definitely in no mood for her nonsense, he had already had enough of that with Tim.

He desperately wanted her interview to continue but knew that she was in no state to communicate with them. His only choice was to terminate the process for the time being.

Lorraine continued to shout and scream and beg for them to go away and not to hurt her. Two officers physically dragged her back to the cells. Lorraine continued screaming out and sobbing continuously.

When she returned to her cell it was as though she felt safe. Safe, they couldn't hurt her now.

'What the hell was that all about?' Charlie said sitting in silence with Harry in his office. 'I thought she had been assessed for questioning?' He had given up all thoughts of continuing Lorraine's interview at present. She would need time to calm herself down. Time he really didn't have. He wanted this sorted out and charges brought so that they could release statements confirming that Westwood General was to remain open as the suspects had been detained in custody. *'No such luck for the moment,'* he thought.

Charlie began to tell Harry what had happened when they tried to begin the interview with Lorraine.

'What, she just started that when you two asked her questions? Has she been interviewed by police before? Has she got a record?' he looked bemused by the revelations.

'She couldn't have a record, remember all nurses have to have a clear criminal record check before they enter their training and when they apply for each new job.'

'Doesn't sound right. Let me check her out on the system. Come on you've got to admit it is a pretty unusual reaction. If they don't want to talk the usual is to keep silent not react like that.'

Harry moved to the adjacent desk to use their Police National Computer system. He typed in Lorraine Harris, 'Got her date of birth there?'

Charlie shouted it out to him reading from a copy of the booking form the custody sergeant had completed.

A few flashes of the screen and there he had it; Lorraine Harris, correct date of birth and address. Unfortunately for Detective Constable Harry Webster it was not the lucky break he was searching for. Nothing of interest was found, she was not listed as having any convictions.

'Nothing. No listed convictions. But the custody sarg would have checked this when he booked her in surely?'

'Damn it. Leave it with me for a minute will you. Looks like I need a quiet chat with local force intelligence.'

'Do you have a previous address for her?'

'Nothing on here, what about her employment criminal record check? That will have her previous five years addresses listed won't it. Give them a call will you, see what you can get hold of.'

'Already on to it boss.'

Charlie called on Pete, an intelligence officer that he had dealt with on many occasions, who covered this area. He would have access to further information about her that they didn't have. Charlie only had access to the intelligence for his own patch and that was giving him no clues to work with. Once again, Pete came up trumps for him.

Lorraine had moved away from her home area nearly five months ago, at the same time she commenced at Westwood General. She had relocated from the Midlands.

He had found one poignant entry under the name of Lorraine Harris and the date of birth Charlie had given him.

The entry was July 30th 2006. She was listed as having been the victim of crime. Something that would not have been listed on the PNC.

Lorraine had reported that she had been raped. There was a psychiatric report. It stated that she didn't take it to trial as she couldn't cope with the questioning. The mental wounds of the assault were too deep and she started shouting and screaming each time a male officer was in her presence.

'That would explain how she managed to be interviewed on ward 73 by a female detective but couldn't cope when she was interviewed at the station by him and DC Brockway,' he thought.

He returned to Harry and told him what he had gleaned.

'It's bloody great isn't it, now we have one prime suspect that we can't even get near to interview.' Charlie plonked himself back into his chair. His face expressed total despondence. He was aching for a dose of caffeine, he would have to see if Harry would go and get him some, he smiled to himself, he knew he would be only too keen to do so.

'What if we get a female officer to interview her? See if they can talk to her?' he questioned.

'Give her time to settle down and ring and see if anyone is available to do the interview would you?' he quickly responded.

'And get them to re-check the risk assessment. See that she is fit for interview before we end up getting ourselves in trouble.'

He was taking no chances. She could accuse them of putting undue pressure on her. He would encounter mountains of paperwork as a result. No, Lorraine Harris could wait, however eager he was to get this concluded, he knew he couldn't proceed quite yet.

Chalmers stepped into Charlie's office. It wasn't often he was seen down on the first floor but this whole week was turning into a week of firsts for them all.

'Charlie, we have just had a report of another death

on ward 68, again a patient who was due for discharge, tomorrow morning.'

They looked at each other startled and dumbfounded.

Charlie was the first to speak, 'How long ago?'

'About an hour.'

'But I have Tim Simpson and Lorraine Harris downstairs in custody. What the hell is going on at that bloody hospital?'

'It's either a whole gang of them working together or we have got something wrong here. We do know that Tim gave unprescribed insulin to Graham. That was the result of a drug error but it was set up either by him or by Lorraine. Surely one of them is our Fallen Angel? So how the hell have we got ourselves another body?'

'Charlie it's looking like we are going to have to close the whole place down in the morning. We just can't take the risk with patients' lives any more.'

28

'So they think they know who I am. The fools cannot get anything right. I know who I am and so do you.

They cannot prove it; they cannot prove that you have done this little one. Stay calm if they ask you any questions. Do not give them the answers. You are doing so well. They really shouldn't give away our credit to others though. We are still so very proud of you. These people must die and you are making sure that this happens. It is not fair that someone else takes the credit. You deserve it. YOU and no one else. It's ok little one; we know you did not make a mistake. We know who made the mistake. Keep up your good work. You are the chosen one. You are special which is why we choose to speak to you. More deaths then you will be free. It will make everything right.'

Oh the headaches were getting intense. Too much to handle now.

Why, oh why, wouldn't the voices go away, just for a while? Just to get rid of the headaches and the voices. No more voices please, but don't make the voices angry at me; I don't like it when they get angry at me.

*****

Cate was trying to focus on the situation at hand, six deaths on ward 73, one on ward 23 and two on 68. She sat with pencil and pad trying to piece together a jigsaw, yet the more she scribbled the less things made sense.

'The method is not the same; the other victims did not die in the same way as Mrs Gray and Graham. The death on ward 68 so far was not being linked either. Six had what appeared to be random drugs in their system. If they had the drugs inserted via their cannulas then there would have to be many nurses that did this. They died in many different wards, theatre and the recovery room. One nurse could not have been in all those places. Same for the doctors. No one doctor could have been in all those places, whoever it was is still out there, laughing at us and getting away with murder,' she thought.

It was late now, it had been such a long day but she knew that she had to stay on the ward until she was happy things had settled down, her remaining patients were safe and the paperwork completed. Ward 73 was hers, and she intended to stay at the helm.

Cate was in her office, was it hers now? She wondered. It didn't feel like it. Dr Gordon had vacated it now and she was attempting to regain command of it. She needed some time to herself, to reflect on the day's events. She knew that time was probably the one luxury she didn't have but she wasn't quite ready to face the ward and its remaining patients.

'Six unexplained deaths on the ward. No easy way to say it, and two of my trained staff are in custody, certainly no easy way to say that either. Oh God!' she thought, with an added, *'why on my ward?'*

It didn't even have to be a qualified member of staff, Vicky had proved how easy it was for a health care assistant to go to another ward and be given drugs, which only the qualified staff had access to. What if one of them had done this and somehow caused the deaths of these patients? Rachel? Joe? Heather? There were so many others.

Cate found herself again wondering about her team. She had thirty staff on ward 73. The events of the day meant that each and every one of her staff would be called down to the police station. That much she was sure of.

* * * * *

Charlie called Vicky in, he requested that she remain at the station and help him with his enquiries. Vicky was unhappy about this and pleaded with him to allow her to stay on ward 73 for the night shift she had planned there.

Vicky actually wanted to do the night shift or part of it anyway, there just had to be something that they had missed and she wanted to be the one who found it. She didn't want to leave the ward short staffed, they had her counted in their numbers for the shift; she wanted to stay on, see what she could find.

Charlie relented, this would be her last chance on the ward, and he would give her no more time than that. He knew she wouldn't dare go above him to Chalmers and question his decision; she was more astute than that. After a few hours sleep tomorrow she would be back on his team at the station, and that was where he wanted her to stay. He had his suspect in custody and that he was confident of. He just couldn't work out how she had managed to commit her crimes and get away with it for so long.

The atmosphere on the ward when Vicky arrived that night was full of tension, everyone was quiet and pensive. Vicky felt uncomfortable.

Cate had told the staff that it was likely that the ward would close and the patients would be moved to other wards in the morning. Vicky found that she was to be working with Frances. The other health care assistant, Heather, had also been brought in from one of the other wards. The only members of the ward 73 team that were on duty were Sally and Mark.

Sally really wasn't happy that she was on duty that night. Sally was adamant that she needed to go and see that Lorraine was alright. She knew her friend and she also knew how scared she would be being held in a police station. *'Shit it would scare anyone,'* she thought.

Cate wouldn't hear of Sally not doing her shift. The only way she convinced Sally to remain at work that night was to promise to ring Charlie and let Sally know if anything happened or let her know when she had been sent home.

Heather, the HCA who had been brought in from the medical admissions unit, had done several bank shifts on ward 73 so was familiar with the ward layout and routine. That helped enormously.

Mark and Sally had to trust each other with their patient care but followed the newly introduced protocol for checking the drugs and going to the patient together. They did this for the drug round too when they gave out the night time medications. They both checked them and checked the patients' name bands. They hoped that this would give their patients some form of reassurance in their nursing capabilities as well.

Heather showed Vicky where they usually went for their breaks. Vicky was going for the last break; it was almost four thirty in the morning. After the day she'd had Vicky relished the chance to have forty winks, or at least the chance to get away from everything for a while.

Heather gave Vicky the option of using the Sister's office or the store room for her break. Vicky opted for the store room, thinking that if Frances wanted to use the office or have access to any staff records then she wouldn't be in her way.

It wasn't the best of places to be sent for a break. There were no windows and the light was so bright she would have to switch it off merely to get some rest so she could think.

Piles of sealed and opened boxes of stores appeared to be quite organised in piles and on shelves, Vicky wasn't really paying attention to them. Except for the pile of oxygen masks that she moved that were at the foot of the mattress, they would surely annoy her when she settled. She had no intention of sleeping, she needed time to reflect and a quiet store room with a mattress was ideal, it reminded her of the night shifts she had worked many years ago.

As she switched the light off she turned to lie down on the mattress. She knocked her head against a box, something heavy came tumbling out on to her makeshift bed. She quickly switched the light back on and saw the answer.

'Oh shit, bloody hell!' she exclaimed out loud.

She immediately jumped up from her proposed solace.

Vicky now had the answer to how the murderer had committed their crime!

Vicky exited the store room and immediately went to

tell Frances that she was leaving the ward for ten minutes, saying that she'd had a message to ring her husband. She assumed that Frances wasn't aware of who she was and wasn't going to worry her even more tonight by letting on, not just yet anyway. Vicky had a feeling that she was about to find out anyway.

Vicky knew that she had to let them know where she was going, so they knew she wasn't there if they needed to call her and wouldn't worry where she was. Each and every staff movement was being taken very seriously and she had to be seen to comply with their newly set rules.

Vicky exited the ward, flew past her uniformed colleague on the door without questioning and moved swiftly along the corridor.

She went through the only exit open at night, the back door of the A & E department so she could get outside.

Quickly she took out her mobile phone from her pocket and dialled Charlie's cell number. She knew he would wake to the sound of her call or in fact he may not even have got any rest yet. If he was thinking about this case as he did all the others. Charlie was like a dog with a bone not letting go until it was solved.

Charlie immediately answered. 'Vicky, what you got?' he asked sleepily.

'Look I know how it was done. I know Charlie, can you get down here?'

'Oh shit, thank goodness, do you know who?'

'No, I don't know who but I have a good idea how we can find out who it is, that is if they are still doing it. In case there is someone else helping Tim or Lorraine, you never know.'

'Right what do you need?'

'Have you still gone those mini cameras?'

'Recorders, yes, have six here at home, kept them in case we needed them again.'

'Right, how quickly can you get here? I'm outside A&E.'

'About five minutes, I'm dressing as we speak.'

'Ok, bring them down and I'll wait out here for you and fill you in.'

'I'm on my way.'

'We've nearly got them Charlie, I know it. We've bloody nearly got the sick little bastard and I don't think it's the ones you got in the cells.'

Charlie already had two of ward 73's staff nurses in his custody; he was beginning to wonder how many more he would have by the morning. Vicky must be on to something to call him out like this. He wished he could get this concluded and fast.

Vicky was waiting as she had said outside the main entrance of the general hospital.

She had, whilst waiting for Charlie to arrive, contacted the nurse co-ordinator who was on duty that night. She too was aware who Vicky was. She'd been informed that night when her colleagues had changed over shift. Just in case she needed her help.

Kiera arrived just as Charlie's car drew up. 'Charlie, this is Sister Kiera Hadden, the senior nurse and hospital co-ordinator on duty tonight. I need both your help here. I need to set up the recorders in the store rooms of some of the wards. Starting with 73, I can easily sort that myself. I am going to need you Kiera to sort out the other wards, choose three at random would you. We will start by putting them in the store rooms. Take it from there in the morning but I need this doing now.'

'What have you found Vicky?' asked Charlie.

Vicky explained to Charlie and Kiera what had happened when she went on her break, about being sent to use the store room.

'I was using the store room for my break; they had put a mattress in there for me so that I could get comfy. Now, there is everything and anything kept in there from oxygen masks, dressings, bandages, tubing and guess what IV FLUIDS.'

Kiera looked shocked. 'The staff are sleeping in the store rooms on their breaks? They are not meant to sleep at all whilst on duty!'

Vicky continued, 'What if our suspect has been spending their break in the store rooms? They would have had access to the stock boxes of IV fluids: in a room that had the door locked whilst they were on their break. They would have been alone with these boxes of fluid for an hour and a half without being disturbed. If our Fallen Angel had this access then maybe they would have been able to add drugs to the bags of fluid. That would explain how these patients could have been getting the unprescribed drugs. It's the best theory I can come up with anyway.'

'Hell,' said Kiera.

'Hell,' said Charlie. 'In that case let's get this bastard and hope that they are still doing this so that we can stop them. It's about time we got hold of some proof around here.'

'The other wards borrow bags or whole boxes of fluid from each other all the time. That way the bags move from ward to ward easily. The nurses aren't moving Charlie. The fluid bags are!'

'But that would mean that whoever is doing this would have to have the drugs,' said Kiera.

'Yes, I showed how easily that could be done by going to several wards to borrow drugs. I wasn't challenged by any member of staff when I asked to borrow several different drugs for IV use.'

'Oh no,' Kiera added.

Kiera and Charlie took five of the recorders, Kiera telling staff on duty she needed access to the store rooms, saying they needed to check stock of fluids. They couldn't trust anyone to know what they were actually doing. Gossip would spread through the hospital and their suspect would get to hear of it no doubt.

Vicky had returned to the ward half an hour after she left for her break and she went back to the store room. The others would just assume that she was going back to her break.

She set up a camera in one of the corners, mostly hidden by boxes at one side and some oxygen masks to the other.

Charlie decided that he would go home and await any calls from the station. He didn't think it likely that they would see anything on the tapes overnight. Vicky assured him that she would ring him any time if she had anything.

Charlie rang the station to inform them how many of the remote cameras they had installed at Westwood. He notified the remote monitoring unit that six cameras were in place and that he needed them to set up the tracking monitors at the station. They were now monitoring the store rooms of Westwood General. Vicky was confident that it would only be a matter of time before their Fallen Angel was caught. Charlie wished he had her optimism.

Cops were now watching six monitors simultaneously. Whoever entered any of the store rooms would now be on camera, watched live down at the station. If something was going on they would know about it now.

It was Sergeant Andy Campbell's turn to watch the monitors. He was alternating two hour stints with some of his colleagues. So far only two of the six store rooms had been used by staff taking their breaks. He had seen several members of staff go into the stores and take out supplies. Nothing unusual. He had also watched as Heather, the health care assistant on ward 73 entered the room and settled herself down on the mattress where she slept for thirty minutes, before waking. It was then he spotted what he was looking for.

29

Charlie and Chalmers walked purposefully on to ward 73.

'Where is Sally Mears?' bellowed Chalmers at a bemused Heather.

'Sally? She's gone out for a fag; she'll only be a few minutes.'

'Where has she gone for her fag? We need to find her,' Chalmers bellowed.

'Out the main entrance, it's the only entrance open at night; you probably passed her as you came in.'

Charlie and Chalmers headed though the main hospital corridor and straight out the main doors of the Accident and Emergency department. There was Sally standing having her fag chatting to a couple of their colleagues, as if nothing out of the ordinary had or indeed would happen.

Two coppers who had been relieved from their duties for a break were chatting to her and laughing with her.

Chalmers and DS Hammond approached them calmly and stood, one either side of her.

'Sally Mears?' boomed Detective Sergeant Hammond.

'Yes, hi. You are here late, well, early really,' she was smiling through her obvious tiredness.

'Sally Mears,' Charlie said as he put a hand firmly on her forearm, 'you are under arrest for the suspected murders of six patients at Westwood General Hospital between 01/04/08 and 13/04/08. You do not have to say anything, but it may harm your defence if you do not mention when questioned something which you later rely on in court. Anything you do say may be given in evidence.'

Sally tried to shake off Charlie's hand, which was now becoming a firm grasp.

'What the hell? ME? Oh come on guys you are having a laugh. You have to be kidding.'

The two coppers she had been chatting to couldn't believe what had just happened. A normal looking qualified nurse who was taking a fag break from her shift.

'Come on Sally, it's over now,' stated Charlie.

'It's not me.'

'We can continue this at the station.'

'IT'S NOT ME!' shouted Sally 'IT'S NOT ME!'

'Come on lass, don't you think we've heard that before?'

Chalmers had produced his handcuffs and was securing Sally's wrists as she protested.

Two of the porters had come out for a fag and were waved back by the uniformed guys. Sally looked at them and shouted towards them, 'Tell them it's not me, they think I killed them, TELL them, you know me Ted, TELL THEM!'

Ted wasn't able to get anywhere near to Sally. By the time he heard what she was saying she was being ushered into the police vehicle that had just drawn up beside them.

* * * * *

Vicky was left to inform the hospital managers that any patient who had an intravenous infusion running must have it taken down and their fluids stopped immediately. Any patients who needed to have drips would have to wait to have them until nearby hospitals had sent some of their stock for them to use. Under no circumstances was any patient at Westwood General to be given bags of fluid in stock there. All fluids on the ward were to be gathered up and left by the staff at the ward entrance door. They would be collected by the uniformed officers there. All these bags of fluid would be taken and kept as possible evidence.

Vicky wanted to be able to tell the staff what they had uncovered but this just wasn't the procedure, 'bloody procedures,' she mumbled to herself as she sat in the staff room with the list of suspected deaths in front of her.

It frustrated her that they could only pin the deaths on ward 73 on Sally at the moment, they still didn't have enough evidence to prove that tampered fluid bags had been used on the other wards. For now they just had to hope that she would stop the 'cry of innocence', and come clean to them all.

30

Sally was still protesting her innocence as DS Charlie Hammond presented her at the custody desk. He was so tired and it was beginning to show on his face.

This case had begun to drag him down, but thanks to Vicky he could actually see the light at the end of what seemed to be a long dreary tunnel.

Sally was asked all her personal details, fingerprinted and given a blue paper suit to change into. A female officer accompanied her to a small toilet area where she was told to change out of her uniform and put on the paper suit. The contents of her uniform pockets remained where they were; her cigarettes too. The officer would not let her keep them.

She was advised that she was going to be put in a cell until such time they were ready to interview her. She was absolutely horrified. What the hell did they think of her? She was in a police station, in her uniform. For goodness sake! The criminals in there would be laughing at her and falsely identifying her as the killer at Westwood General. She hoped that no one had seen her at the desk when she came in.

Somehow, she had to get out of there before this sick joke of theirs went any further. Unfortunately she had no idea how. Not yet anyway. She knew that given time she would come up with something. She always did. They just hadn't realised yet who they were dealing with.

Charlie now had three members of ward 73's team in custody and what seemed to be an ever growing list of patient deaths, nine dead patients, so far only six that seemed to be linked. He wanted to be able to charge Sally with all nine deaths but knew he couldn't until the post mortems were in and any possible link revealed to him. *'Some bloody case,'* he thought yawning broadly.

Very unceremoniously Sally was taken to a cell. The custody sergeant didn't waste any time in banging the cell door shut and leaving her in total solitude. She found herself completely alone, feeling that she still didn't understand why they had taken her here. She understood what they had said to her, but didn't understand why they thought she was the one they were looking for. Her cell was barren. The atmosphere smelt of isolation, the air was putrid. No way could she stay in here for long. She just had to get out and quick.

Charlie had a quiet word with the custody sergeant. They had made their decisions regarding Tim and Lorraine. Tim was to be released, the issues with him were professional, not criminal. He had possibly committed a drug error and although this had had devastating consequences they were certain it was not premeditated murder. If further issues came to light after talking with Sally or receiving forensic test results then they could always speak to him again.

Lorraine was granted bail. She had been seen by the psychiatric on call doctor prior to leaving the cells. They had to be sure that she was safe to be bailed and go home. At least they had a reason for her reaction, but Charlie was still unsure of her involvement, especially as she was the murderer's flatmate, though for now he didn't have enough evidence to hold her.

Charlie had to refuel before he started any questioning so he practically crawled into the canteen, firstly ordering a caffeine fix before a huge breakfast.

Sally was led out of the cell that she had spent the past hour in, to an interview room. She was ushered to sit at the far chair and someone she hadn't seen before sat down beside her.

Turning to the bleached blonde beside her Sally thought

she would begin her own interrogation, 'Who the hell are you then?'

'If I were you young lady, I would certainly change your attitude towards me.'

Sally pulled a face, she looked totally disgruntled. 'And?'

'I am Julie Pearson, the duty solicitor. I have been allocated to represent you.'

'Represent me? What for? I don't need anyone to represent me. These idiots have lifted me and brought me here under false pretences. As soon as I tell them that I have nothing to do with the deaths on our ward I will be going home. So I really don't need you.'

'Are you refusing representation?'

'Of course I am. I don't need a solicitor. Didn't you listen to what I just said?'

'Sally, if you change your mind at any point you can ask them to stop the interview and request legal representation. You will be allocated whoever is the duty solicitor.'

'Thanks but you don't realise that I am not like the others that you get in here. I haven't committed a crime. I don't know why you have brought me in here. I will explain that I don't know anything and I will be out of here soon.'

Julie slowly got up from her seat, gestured with her hand to Charlie that she was ready to leave and exited the room.

Throughout Sally's brief conversation with Julie Pearson, Charlie had remained silent, as had DC Trent. They certainly couldn't force her to accept legal representation, even though he knew that she really did need her services. Sally just didn't know this yet.

She was however, about to find this out.

DS Charlie Hammond introduced himself formally and advised Sally that they were going to record the interview.

Sally watched him unwrap two new audio tapes and load them into the recorder.

'Tape 'A' is the master tape and we will require it to be signed by you and the officers present. Tape 'B' will be used to produce a transcript of the tape. The tapes are numbered and logged in a register for security purposes,' he stated.

'Right, get on with the questions then so I can get out of here,' Sally hastily retorted.

'All in good time Ms Mears, there are procedures to be followed. Present in the room are: myself Detective Sergeant Charlie Hammond, Detective Constable Vicky Trent and Sally Mears. Can you please confirm your name for the tape.' He looked at Sally, she appeared unconcerned by her predicament. She was sitting back in her chair like she was about to chat with friends not undergo a police interrogation.

She merely nodded her head in agreement.

'Ms Mears, please provide a verbal reply. The tape is not very proficient at picking up non verbal responses,' the recurrent sarcasm in his voice was audible.

'Yes, just record it, and then get me out of here,' she demanded.

'I suggest that you have a change of attitude Ms Mears, otherwise this interview is going to take forever. I have all the time in the world to spend here with you, but I am sure you want to get this over with as soon as possible. So let's start again shall we? Can you confirm your full name for the tape?'

'Sally Ann Mears,' she sighed and made a 'huffing' sound. God they were idiots, but maybe if she answered their questions she could just get herself out of there, like he said.

'Please confirm your date of birth and your home address for the tape.'

'Would these stupid questions never cease,' she thought, but gave him his answer anyway.

'Finally I need you to confirm that there are no others in the room except you, myself, and DC Trent.' Charlie turned toward Vicky, 'Turn on the video would you.'

Sally watched as Vicky turned on the television in front of them.

'You brought me here to watch telly? What are you lot on?'

'Ms Mears, just watch the tape.' Charlie was in no mood for smartarse replies tonight. If she wanted to play games, she had certainly picked the wrong guy, and indeed the wrong time to do this.

The images on the screen were showing her the store room on the ward, she instantly recognised that. Sally just couldn't understand why they were doing this. What good was this going to do?

'I have been in to this store room a million times, why would I want to watch a video of it?' Sally asked.

DS Hammond merely repeated his request to her to watch it.

Sally was very quickly reduced to silence. There in black and white was an image of her taking in a mattress and making up a bed. She gasped, what would they think, she was sleeping on duty, all be it on her break! She would be in trouble now!

'Most of us sleep in there on our break, is that what I am here for?'

No one answered her. She then watched as the footage showed her sitting on the mattress and look up at the boxes around her. She then proceeded to take out several handfuls of items from the pockets of her uniform.

'What's going on?' she asked them.

No reply was given to her. DS Hammond and DC Trent continued to focus on her reactions and expressions whilst she watched the tape. Sally appeared to be puzzled at what she saw and became unsettled in her chair, fidgeting and tapping her feet on the floor.

Sally's image was then seen arranging what was now clearly visible as different glass vials of clear drugs on the mattress. She then got several boxes from the shelves and took out a variety of syringes and needles before getting a box of intravenous fluid and taking out the entire contents.

Now surrounded by bags of fluid, needles, syringes and drugs, she was then seen assembling the needles and syringes and drawing up the drugs at random.

What happened next appeared to stun even Sally herself.

She took the bag of fluid, still in its outer safety packaging and turned it over to the reverse. She then inserted the needle through the outer plastic packaging in to the drug insertion bung in the fluid bag. She was then seen to push the plunger on the syringe adding the drug to the fluid.

She held up the bag to examine it and appeared pleased with the outcome. She was smiling. The video showed her repeating this process twelve times until the entire contents of the fluid box had been injected with what appeared to be random drugs.

She was then seen to be placing the bags of fluid back in to the box and returning it to the shelf as though nothing had happened. She put the used syringe into the paper covering she had taken it from and the needle back in to its covering sheath. These items and the rubbish were then put in to her uniform pocket before she was seen to settle on the mattress and appear to go to sleep.

'Oh come on, that does look like me, but it can't be me, I didn't do that, I think I would remember doing something like this, don't you?'

'That's the question we were hoping that you would be answering for us Sally,' answered Charlie.

'What, you can't think it was me?'

'How daft do I look Sally, you have just watched the video, the same as I have. That is definitely you in that store room adding drugs to the fluids. So tell us then, where did you get the drugs from Sally?'

'What do you mean, I have no idea, I didn't have any drugs.'

'You can't deny that the person in the video is you, you are seen to be doctoring the bags of fluid with random medications, have you nothing to say in your defence?'

'In my defence?'

'Yes, Ms Mears.'

'No idea what you are on about.'

Charlie got up from his chair across from Sally; he walked about the room for a moment or two. 'Ms Mears, you can either talk yourself round in circles or we can get on with this interview. The choice is yours. Either way you will face further questioning about your part in the deaths of six patients at Westwood General. We can either do this now or later. It makes no difference to me.'

'I don't have anything to tell you. That isn't me in the video, it may look like me but it isn't me is it,' she said, then paused and added, 'six?' in a surreal tone.

Charlie was in no mood for her games.

'I can see that we are not going to get anywhere tonight.' Waving at PC Jackson, he signalled towards Sally, 'take her back to the cell.'

'Sally, maybe some time spent in the cells will help you remember, I will interview you again later.'

'Can I go home then?'

'You are going nowhere except back to your cell, probably for a very long time.'

'I'm not going to any cell. I am not a criminal, I was in the middle of my shift, and I have to get back to my patients. You guys really aren't real.'

'Ms Mears, it is you who are sadly deluded.' He turned once again and signalled to PC Jackson, who was waiting outside the interview room. 'Take her out of here.'

He wasn't going to give her any more of his time. Experience had taught him that even a few hours alone in a barren cell gave the incentive most people needed to want to talk. Before long she would be asking to speak to him.

Sally was taken back to her cell, and she began to realise how Lorraine and Tim must have felt. She wondered what had happened to both of them. Were they showing them videos of them too? Where were they? Was anyone looking after her flat if she wasn't there, like she had when Lorraine was in the cell.

Alone in the cell Sally found it cold. The cell itself was stark, containing only a bench with a very thin mattress on it. The door to the cell was or used to be navy blue. It had faded in the years since it had been painted she thought. In the middle of the door was what she thought to be an opening. Maybe they would speak to her through it, she really didn't know.

Sally had never even been inside a police station before let alone been locked up inside a cell. She was more frightened than she knew she could be. She sat on the bench and drew her knees up to her body. Curling in to herself she began to weep. The tears just wouldn't stop.

How on earth had she got here? What was going on in this place?

She had a headache too, both sides of her temples ached and she felt as though her head was going to explode.

* * * * *

Charlie had rung Cate to let her know that Sally was under arrest and detained at the police station. She was utterly horrified. 'But you have only just released Tim and Lorraine, why Sally now?'

He went on to briefly explain he had evidence of her

crime.

It was seven-thirty am when Cate was woken by the sound of Charlie's phone call.

She showered and got ready to go into the ward. She needed to be there to help Frances to organise the transfer of patients to other wards. A day off just wasn't on the agenda for her until all this had been sorted out.

Charlie had explained that he'd had to close down her ward until matters were concluded with Sally and further forensic examination of the ward had taken place.

This somewhat upset him, he empathised with her at the prospect of losing all that she had worked for during her career. One sick individual had spoilt it for everyone. He knew it would take Cate a long time to recover from this experience. The forensics couldn't move in until all the patients had been moved out to other wards.

She allowed herself a few moments to think before she left the house and prepared for battle at work. She turned on the television and located the news channel.

Would this never end, were all her so called trusted staff in on it? She felt they had taken away all her professional credibility. She felt responsible for Sally and her actions, after all she was the one who had interviewed and appointed her. Not once had she had cause to distrust her or question her professional abilities. How had she managed to miss something so huge? She wondered if she would ever know the answer to that.

The morning's news report was booming loud and clear, it stated that someone had been taken in for questioning in connection with the recent deaths at Westwood General Hospital, and was helping the police with their enquiries. Charlie hadn't told her that news of Sally's arrest was going to be national news before she even got to work.

She flicked from one channel to another, some reports stating that it was a member of staff that was helping the police with their enquiries. No name was available as yet; it wouldn't take the press too long to find that one out.

The transfer was organised and co-ordinated by Frances, posthaste. As Cate arrived for work she was in time to see the last patients being taken to alternative wards by the porters. Not a soul was left, other than a particularly shattered looking hospital co-ordinator.

She looked around her ward, her domain for nearly three years now, taken away from her. She felt cheated, sick to the stomach with worry about how everyone would perceive her. Would she be seen as responsible too, she wondered? Would they all think that she must have known what was happening? Could she have stopped it happening in the first place? She was sure she couldn't have stopped Sally. She wavered on this point, were there signs that she had missed with her? She sat down at her now deserted nurse's station and trawled through thoughts of Sally and her working life with her on the ward. Cate could recall no instances that concerned her, she had never had to call Sally in to her office to reprimand her or pull her up on her clinical practice. Yet she was responsible for all these patients dying. She just couldn't get her head around the events of the past few weeks and knew it would take her many years to do so.

31

The voices were back. Would she never get rid of them?

'You have let us down. You have let yourself down.'

The voices always came with the intense headaches.

'They think they have their Fallen Angel. You must not let them take you. We can tell you how to get out of this. We are there for you as you have been for us. You have done well. You got rid of those people that we told you to. If they don't find all the fluids there will be many more whilst you are here. HA!! Fallen Angel maybe, but we are no match for them. We have a plan for you. Keep quiet and we will get you out of here. We want to get you out so listen hard and follow what we say. You have shown us that you can follow us. Follow what we tell you and we will get you out of here to safety. Listen dear angel. Listen.'

* * * * *

Sally was awoken by the sound of the flap in the cell door opening. It was an outwards opening flap that could only be opened from the outside via a spring bolt. Through it she could hear an unfamiliar voice. 'Morning love, here you go.'

A red plastic tray was passed through to her containing toast and a paper cup of what looked like tea, but tasted like dish water.

She really could do with a fag. Not like she could just light one up, the bastards had taken them away from her when she was brought in last night.

She thought about shouting out but instead decided to bang on the flap and see if she could attract their attention. That's what they all do to get them to take notice she thought, just as she caught sight of a button on the wall she could press to get their attention.

* * * * *

Cate met up with Charlie the next morning in her office, she was going through the paperwork from the past few days when he appeared at her door.

'To what do I owe this visit? I thought you would be down at the station dealing with Sally? Surely you don't need more from me?'

'I do Cate. Actually I do need more from you.'

She was waiting for some wild passionate declaration or

invite. It wasn't to come. She was obviously misreading him. Again.

'Cate I need your professional opinion. How easy would it be for Sally to have done this? I realise now how easy it would be to obtain the drugs from different sources but would it go unnoticed when she added the drugs to the fluid?'

'It's not something that I have tried Charlie, but if you come to the clinical room with me then I can try it and we can see can't we. I am still trying to come to terms with Sally being the 'one'. She never gave me cause to doubt her or her clinical practice.'

'That's the thing with crime.' Cate looked towards him with a quizzical look on her face. 'Criminals often look and appear the same as you and I; they don't come with a tag for ease of identification! My job would be so much easier if they did!'

He was actually managing to lighten the atmosphere between them in what was the most unusual of circumstances, Cate gave a small giggle.

'I realise that but she, well, she was so typical, normal, I mean. Whatever normal is!'

'They all are Cate.'

'What I can't understand is how she managed to hide her illness for so long; she must have been in such internal turmoil.'

Charlie shook his head, 'That's your field, not mine,' he smiled directly at her, 'not something I will lose sleep over. Hand that one over to the professionals. Most of the criminals I deal with are canny and claim innocence, this time though, she really didn't seem to be aware of what she was doing, in fact she seemed totally unmindful of her crime, it was as though something I said didn't ring right to her?'

'I don't know which is worse.'

'If one indeed is worse,' he added.

'Yes. I feel for her though.'

'She could have sought help, being a professional surely she would have realised the possibility of a psychiatric condition that she needed treatment for?'

'Well, you would think so. But the way I understand it schizophrenia is so hard to diagnose and the person can be drawn into a surreal reality and believe what the voices are saying and is compelled to listen, however distressing this may be for them.'

Leading the way through the now empty ward the two of them reached the clinical room.

Cate got one 500 ml bag of fluid, a needle, syringe and a plastic vial of saline. She proceeded to draw up the 5 mls of saline in to the syringe.

She did not remove the bag of fluid from its protective plastic covering. She turned the bag over to the reverse side and smoothed out the plastic outer covering taut to the additive bung on the inner bag.

She inserted the needle into the bung with as much ease as she would have if the plastic outer covering were not there. She depressed the plunger of the syringe and added the saline from the syringe to the bag.

She held the bag up to see if she could actually see the needle mark on the outer packet. If she really looked for it then yes she could see a tiny needle mark. She had never even thought of looking for a needle mark in this place before.

Turning to Charlie she tore off the outer packaging and examined the additive bung. The mark of the needle was barely visible to the naked eye. She thought she might just be able to see it purely because she was looking for it.

'Shit Charlie, that is so dangerous. It really isn't something that any of us would have thought of. We just trust that the bags of fluid are secure because the outer packaging is intact. We all check that the bag is labelled with the fluid name we are wanting and check the date to ensure that it has not expired, but not once in all the years I have been nursing has it ever crossed my mind that the fluid inside may not be what it is labelled as, or indeed that someone would have doctored the bag with fatal medication. That is so sick if I hadn't seen your video evidence I just would not have believed it. As most of the intravenous drugs we use are colourless, almost any drug we have in the cupboard could be added in the way I have just shown you and no one would know about it. If this is what has been happening then it is something that the manufacturers of the fluid will have to look at because there really is no way to tell if something has been added like this.'

She paused for a moment, 'Fluids are a common item that is 'borrowed' from one ward to another too, any member of staff requesting a bag of fluid or indeed a whole box could relocate it from one ward to another quite easily. Without question, a doctored bag of lethal fluids then arrives on a ward with fatal consequences. There would be no link to any member of staff at all, like with Sally.'

'Quite the budding detective Sister Carter,' Charlie said with a smile. 'How about lunch?'

'What?'

'Lunch.'

'Now?'

'Yes Cate, I'm sure they can spare you now there are no patients here. We don't even know when the ward is re-opening do we. So, how about we go for some lunch?'

'As long as we ban all conversation about dead patients and bags of fluid count me in. I can't get my head around all this at the moment,' she said flashing another of her real unforced smiles across at him.

'It's a deal Cate.' Charlie was smiling now and finding Cate receptive to raising a smile too. Maybe they had a chance to discover each other now their work stresses were lifted?

32

Lorraine didn't know which way to turn when they let her out of the police station. DS Hammond had spoken to her and explained that she was bailed to return in a week.

'Can I ring someone to come and pick me up?' she enquired.

The custody sergeant didn't look up as he replied, 'Phone is in reception. Ask to use it on your way out.'

'What about Tim? Is he still here?'

'He was released earlier.'

'Oh. Ok.'

He wasn't going to be entering into a full conversation with her, she realised that. She wasn't on ward 73 discussing a patient with a uniformed officer. This was no professional liaison.

Things were totally different now, she was, in their eyes, just another one who had been banged up in the cells, bailed to return, she thought.

She was escorted through one door to find herself at the main reception.

'Can I ring someone to come and pick me up? I have no money with me though.'

'Give me the number and I will make the call for you.'

'I want to ring Sally Mears, my flat mate,' she rattled off her home number.

At the mention of the name 'Sally Mears' the desk sergeant pulled a face.

'Why are you looking at me like that?'

'Like what?'

'You pulled a face when I said I wanted to ring my flat mate.'

'I don't think there is any point ringing her.'

'Why?'

'You haven't heard?'

'Haven't heard what? I have been in your cells, how would I get to hear anything?'

'Sally Mears is under arrest.'

Lorraine gasped. They had her as well! 'But she wasn't on duty when the two patients died.'

'I can't tell you more than I already have. She is under arrest pending further enquiries. You would be better off getting yourself a taxi home.'

Lorraine wasn't listening to him. Why on earth had they

taken Sally in? None of it was anything to do with her.

'Call me a taxi. I have enough money at home to pay them.'

She wandered out of the building and sat on the bottom step of the entrance way. She felt almost trance like. Things had just not been real for the past day or two. She could hardly remember the events on the ward with Tim that led her to be arrested. As for Sally being arrested too, that was absurd. She needed to talk to her, needed to explain what had happened to her. She couldn't deal with all this on her own, she felt as though she was falling apart at the seams. Life was out of control. Sally would know what to do; she would cheer her up and get things back to normal. Only she couldn't could she, the bastards had got her in the cells too hadn't they.

She was busy staring into space when her taxi drew up in front of her. She heard the horn of the car and jumped up in surprise. She must have looked a total mess, she hadn't showered in days and was wearing an old set of clothes that they had given her.

The taxi ride was short; their flat was less than ten minutes' drive from the police station. She felt terrible having left Sally in there but she hadn't known until they had let her out. If she had known before she would have tried to find her, somehow she would have managed, she was sure of that.

The taxi dropped her off outside their flat. 'I need to go in and get you some money, I won't be a moment.'

The driver looked at her disdainfully; he had heard that one from his customers many a time. Again he would take a chance and wait. If she didn't come out he would go in after her and claim his money.

It took Lorraine two minutes to return with her fare. Again he looked at her in surprise. It wasn't often that happened, they usually got dropped off at a random flat, made it look like they were going in and nipped out the back way, after their free taxi ride.

He was thankful for the lack of hassle, he had only just started his shift and it was going to be a long shift as it was, without chasing his fares round the streets for the sake of a few quid.

Lorraine now had her purse with her, thinking that she needed to sit down with a cup of tea to ponder her next move, she walked towards the newsagent at the top of the street. It was a few hundred yards, but she really needed some milk and perhaps a newspaper. As she turned the street corner the shop was in front of her, entering she was immediately dumbstruck by the newspaper stand. There it was in bold black print 'Fallen Angel Caught'.

Caught? She wasn't caught, she was out on bail. What was going on? They never accused her of being the Fallen

Angel. Damned newspapers getting the story wrong, she thought. She picked up a pint of milk from the fridge, and copies of the Daily Mirror and Express. She would read two versions of the story and read between the lines. Just to see what they were reporting.

As she approached the counter to pay, she felt uncomfortable. The guy serving was about forty, unshaven, and looking at her in a manner that unnerved her. She couldn't pinpoint what it was that made her feel so uncomfortable and knotty inside.

She paid her money and made a hasty retreat to the flat. She didn't look behind her all the way home. She needed the sanctuary of home, the solace and the peace to think about what on earth was going on around her.

Arriving home she dropped the papers on the sofa and hastily went to make herself a cup of tea. Everything looked the same as it did when she left for work the other day. Nothing was any further out of place than it usually was! Sally had left the washing up from her tea when she left for the night shift, but that really was nothing out of the ordinary. There were several letters sitting on the doormat, two days had passed since anyone had been there to pick the mail up. She would investigate the post later.

Right now she needed her cup of tea. She sank into the tranquiliity and comfort of the sofa. After her tea she would shower and return to the realms of humanity.

She picked up the first of her newspapers and studied the front page. 'Fallen Angel Caught'. As she read the article there was a mention of 'Sally Mears'. She found herself speaking out loud to herself, 'Sally, what the hell are they talking about Sally for?'

She continued to read the article. It seemed to accuse Sally of being the Fallen Angel; she had been arrested on suspicion of the murder of six patients!

She threw the newspaper on the floor; it was like holding hot coals. She couldn't bear to hold it. They must have got the wires crossed, she thought. Reporting what they wanted to instead of the real story. She leant over and picked up the second paper from the coffee table. She again studied the front page. Again they had named Sally as the 'Killer Nurse'. *'What was going on?'* she thought. Her mind was racing, thoughts and emotions running amok, confusing the reality of what she was reading.

She would have to ring one of the others at work to find out what really was happening. Would any of them talk to her, she wondered? After all, she was arrested on the ward in connection with two deaths on her shift wasn't she.

The only person she could think to ring who would know what was really going on was Cate. Lorraine dialled the number for ward 73. It was unusual that Cate didn't answer it immediately. If she was in her office, she would have been the nearest person to answer. Lorraine swiftly remembered that the detective was in her office. That would explain why she wasn't answering. She wondered if he would still be there. *'It was two days since she and Tim had been taken off the ward, anything could have happened since,'* she thought.

Why wasn't anyone answering the phone? She hung up, no point hanging on, maybe they were busy. In desperation she searched the flat for her sheet of staff phone numbers. She knew Sally kept the list somewhere, in case they needed to get hold of each other to swap shifts or something when they were off duty.

She found it in the top drawer of the kitchen cabinet. That was where Sally used to put all sorts of papers that she didn't want to lose.

Lorraine dialled Cate's mobile number. It rang and she received an immediate answer.

'Hello?'

'Cate, it's Lorraine.'

'Um, hello Lorraine, where are you?' she questioned.

'Home. Do you know what is going on with Sally? I keep hearing all sorts of rumours, the papers are full of lies and I just don't know what is going on. She isn't here at the flat either. The cops told me she was at the station but wouldn't tell me anything. What is going on?'

'Calm down Lorraine, catch your breath.'

'Cate just tell me what is happening. I can't handle all

this uncertainty. It's been hell in the cells you know and I come home to all these lies. I can't work out what is going on'.

'Lorraine, getting all het up isn't going to help. Sally is under arrest.'

'Oh come on Cate, what are you doing about it huh? Have you gone there and tried to talk to them? Have you told them that they have got the wrong person?'

'No.'

'Why the hell not? She needs you to help her!'

'Lorraine, you don't know the full story here. They have evidence against her.'

'What bloody evidence? They can't have. She hasn't done anything.'

'Lorraine I am in no mood for this right now. She is their suspect and they have evidence that shows she is the person responsible for the patient deaths. I suggest you get on and sort your own issues out regarding your situation, rather than worrying about her. You are still suspended. The hospital will make a full enquiry as I expect will the police. The Nursing and Midwifery Council have also been notified and your registration will, I assume, be suspended too, until the investigations are completed.'

For once Lorraine was silent.

'Lorraine, are you still there?'

A 'Yes' slipped meekly out.

'Are you alright?'

Another meek 'Yes' followed by, 'No, not really.'

'Have you got anyone that you can talk to?'

'No.'

'What about your friends or family?'

'Sally is under arrest.'

'Yes.'

'She can't talk to me then?'

'No Lorraine she can't.'

'Then I have no one. I won't be here long anyway. Bye Cate.'

'Do you want me to stop by for a while? Lorraine, are you still there?'

Cate received no further reply from Lorraine, the line went dead. She redialled several times but got no answer.

She was beginning to get concerned. She knew where her flat was; maybe she should pay her a visit. Despite what she might have done Cate liked her and she really did need someone to talk to and help her through things. Gathering herself together Cate decided her only option was to go and see her and see if she could be of any help.

Entering the block of flats Cate found the door to number three open, she found that unusual. Why would Lorraine have left it open? Maybe she had decided to visit one of her neighbours? Maybe Cate was worrying unnecessarily. She pushed the door so that it was fully open and called out for Lorraine. No answer. She entered and continued to call out her name. She could hear the television on and edged herself into the flat cautiously. As she popped her head around the lounge door she could see Lorraine lying on the sofa. Thank goodness, she was alright, she must have fallen asleep with the exhaustion of the last few days.

Cate was about to turn round and leave when she noticed several silver wrappers on the floor. On closer inspection she identified them as medication strips. She picked them up, five in total, a variety of different medications. The strips were empty. She noticed a few pills lying as if dropped on the carpet.

Reality struck her. 'Oh hell!' she exclaimed. 'What have you done?' She looked up at Lorraine's face, she was a deathly white, she wasn't breathing. Cate reached for her mobile and dialled 999.

Simultaneously she attempted to tilt Lorraine's head back and check for an airway. No breathing, no pulse, she gave one sharp thump to her chest. Nothing. Not a stir from Lorraine. She examined the medication packets. Valium, paracetamol, ferrous sulphate, brufen. Well the girl certainly wasn't messing about here she thought.

As she was attempting to commence cardiac massage she heard the familiar tones of the ambulance nearing. It seemed like an eternity before they reached the flat and took over from her.

Lorraine's limp body was taken off to the hospital, she was covered in tubes and drips. Suddenly all Cate's energy drained from her and she collapsed on to the nearby armchair and sobbed. She cried and cried, disregarding her surroundings. She didn't surface until she felt a soft hand rest on her shoulder. She looked up and there he was. Detective Sergeant Charlie Hammond. He bent down to her level, and without a word gave her a hug.

He asked one of the uniformed officers to take Cate home. She was in no fit state to drive and Charlie insisted that she be taken home. He had two uniformed officers with him, having all come in the one car, one of them could be spared to get her out of there. It was no place for her at the moment. Forensics were on their way and would be turning Lorraine's flat into a major crime scene within seconds of their arrival. Charlie had to remove Cate before they arrived. He may need her to be fingerprinted later, depending on what the forensics found; after all she was the one who had found her. He decided not to bother her with this; if this proved necessary then he would put it to her later.

33

Sally was lying on the thin blue mattress that was her only sanctuary and comfort in the cell she was beginning to feel she would never get away from.

She began to shout out, calling for the voices to go away. She didn't stop shouting even when the sergeant on duty came and spoke to her through her little vent in the door.

She just kept shouting at the voices to leave her alone, what they had done to her, why had they made her do this, she just wasn't making any sense. Well, not to Sergeant Ray Morton who was hearing her shouting that is.

Nothing seemed to get through to her, she didn't seem to be hearing what Ray was saying to her, he tried raising his voice but it was as if she couldn't even see him there.

He called for the desk sergeant to attend who also didn't think her reaction was 'normal'.

Fred, the desk sergeant, rang Charlie's extension. It was Vicky who answered. 'I think you better come on down here and take a look at this Angel of yours, seems like she's completely lost it here, nothing we can do with her.'

Vicky immediately left her desk and took the stairs one flight down to the block where the cells were. She passed through several sets of key pad locked doors, each with a different code, on her way down.

As she approached the cell block she could hear shouting in what to her sounded like two or maybe three different voices.

'What on earth is going on here?'

'Told you Vic, it's your Angel, looks like she's doing a good job of losing the plot here.'

Looking through the vent, Vicky saw Sally curled up in the foetal position on the mattress, which she had on the floor. The voices coming from her didn't sound like her, and she appeared to be arguing with them about something they wanted her to do. She couldn't quite make her out. Vicky noticed that Sally hadn't even seen her at the door. She was looking right through her.

'Open the door for me would you?'

'Hey Vic, you sure? Could be nasty.'

'As I said.'

As Vicky entered the cell she received no response from Sally at all. She just didn't see that she was there with her. Even touching her gently on the shoulder and speaking to her provoked no response.

'Bleep the on call psychiatrist will you, we need them down here like now, this one needs to get out of here.'

Vicky left the cell and used the phone at the sergeant's desk to ring Charlie.

For once Charlie was having lunch, not his usual bag of chips but at Levi's on the high street with Harry Webster. He hadn't told Vicky where he was going, she presumed he was still at the hospital. Apologising to Harry, he reached for his ringing phone.

'Charlie, listen, just to let you know Sally has gone in to some sort of trance, shouting at what she is calling voices. I've got the psychiatrist on call on the way now. Definitely doesn't look like she will be ready for any more questions today that's for sure,' Vicky said on the phone to Charlie.

'Thanks, just what we need, all this and no prospect of a quick trial. I don't think the hospital is going to be very happy with us. I'll come by when I get back in, see where you are at with her, and stay with her will you Vicky?'

'Of course, see you later.'

'What's going on?' Harry asked

'Sally is playing up down at the station. Vicky has called the psych's in to see her before we bring her down again for further questioning.'

Harry looked at him in amazement. He couldn't even think of a sensible reply so decided on silence.

* * * * *

Joanne Hall, the on call psychiatric registrar appeared approximately half an hour later at the custody suite.

She was of average height, with dark wavy hair, deep brown thoughtful eyes and always well presented. She and Vicky had met on several occasions at the station before and in some respects Vicky was glad it was her who was on call today. She had a mutual respect and knew she would do the best for Sally. Vicky knew Sally was ill and that she wouldn't be staying at the station, she needed proper psychiatric care. But, as per protocol, she had to get her seen by the psychiatric team for assessment before any decisions could be made.

Vicky briefed Joanne about why Sally was there and about her recent change in behaviour. She went in to speak with her and achieved the same response that Vicky and Ray had.

None.

It was as though she didn't see them at all. She looked right through them, shouting out as if talking to someone else.

Sally remained curled up hugging her knees to her body calling out sounding like she was arguing with someone. The voices were all coming from her.

'Vicky, there are some types of psychiatric illness where

the sufferer hears voices. These voices can be triggered by any number of things. They can cause intense headaches and total confusion for the individual concerned. Some remember what the voices say to them but many of them do not have any recollection of hearing voices at all. If she has been hearing voices that she thought were telling her to harm her patients then this would have been very real to her. She would have felt a compulsion to follow what the voices were saying to her. If she is asked about something they had told her to do she may not remember at all. The voices can somehow be separated from the reality of everyday life.'

'Oh my goodness. You mean she may really have no idea what she has done? Yet she may have caused the deaths of so many innocent patients?'

'That's exactly what I am saying, it's only a provisional diagnosis at the moment, and I'll need to speak with her when she comes out of this, but I have a pretty good idea that this is what has happened to her. She probably has suffered some form of trauma or abuse in her younger life that she hasn't had counselling for so hasn't allowed herself to deal with. The result is this is the way her mind has found to deal with it itself.'

'Bloody hell. How do these people manage to get in to the caring professions then? Surely they would be picked up during the selection process, occupational health etc?'

'No, not necessarily. If the condition is dormant then

the person will not be displaying any symptoms and there wouldn't have been any diagnosis made in her early years if she didn't seek help, no one would have been aware of it.'

'So there was no way she could have been stopped. No way to tell what she would end up doing?'

'You got it.'

'Shit,' was her simple answer.

'Let's get some transport and an escort sorted out and I'll see her again in the psychiatric unit later on.'

Vicky asked Ray to organise a car to take Sally to the unit at the General Hospital. How ironic was that, Sally ending up in the psychiatric unit in the hospital where she was working less than twenty-four hours ago.

Joanne informed Vicky that Sally would not be fit for any interviews in the foreseeable future. She could not give her any indication of when she would be returned to their custody so they could continue their investigations.

She was certainly not mentally stable at present and would need stabilising on medication before being able to answer any questions. If she was right about the voices she knew she would be of no help to them and would have no recollection of events in the last week.

The voices would have been like a separate entity for her, nothing to do with Sally, but someone else.

Sally was taken handcuffed to the Pendall Wing of Westwood Hospital, the psychiatric unit within its grounds.

She would not be released from handcuffs until she was safely deposited in the secure unit.

Charlie feared he wouldn't ever get a prosecution as it looked likely that Sally would be at the psychiatric unit for some time before they would be declaring her fit for further police questioning or a court appearance.

She didn't appear to have any comprehension about her transfer or leaving her cell. She was taken to a small bedroom that was simply furnished, with a single bed and a built-in wardrobe. There were no loose items of furniture other than the bed. There was a small window opposite the bed but it was reinforced with bars across it.

She was given a nightdress and helped to change into it.

She was left with nothing but the hospital nightdress she stood up in.

* * * * *

The story of the Fallen Angel had somehow reached the front pages of all the daily newspapers. Up until now some of the papers had carried it on their front page but never the whole page. Today was the exception. Today was a total media explosion.

Chalmers was raging as he read the papers on the news stand on his way into work. How on earth had they got hold of the story so quickly, he dearly hoped that one of his force hadn't leaked the story, for their sake if nothing else. All hell would break loose if he found out it was one of them.

The story even carried the by-line of 'Psycho nurse' - now that definitely wasn't released for general consumption. As he thought about it, Chalmers realised it could equally be one of the patients from ward 73 who leaked the story. There were plenty of witnesses on the ward when the deaths of Graham Stewart and Mrs Gray occurred. No one on the ward would have missed the commotion of two cardiac arrests. Maybe a member of staff had succumbed to the financial incentives of the newspapers? The offer of a few hundred quid would loosen anyone's lips, especially if they were on a low salary. He knew this only too well. The leaking of stories and indeed falsehoods was the bane of their investigations. If news of an arrest or maybe a crime that was yet to be solved reached the public the story changed tenfold before the truth came out. Often their court cases were biased, and on occasion cases lost due to public persuasion in the wrong direction. He hated the weight of public opinion when they really didn't know the facts.

It worried him that the public would slate them for allowing the hospital to remain open whilst the Fallen Angel continued to claim victims. They were not in possession of the facts, but he knew that wouldn't be seen as salient. They saw what they wanted to see.

34

Sally was trying hard to focus on the voices, but she just couldn't hear them today, in fact she hadn't heard from them for a while. She wasn't too sure how long it had been, but she was missing them and feeling insecure as a consequence.

The voices didn't usually stay away from her for long, and certainly wouldn't stay cross with her, but she did really miss them. She felt alone without them. They always told her what to do and how to do it. She never questioned them, she knew better than that, too fearful to cross them.

Generally the outcome of listening to the voices was positive for her, even though in this instance they had somehow landed her in a police cell then a psychiatric unit. She knew if she listened for long enough and deciphered which of the voices to take heed of, when they returned, she would surely be told how to get herself out of this predicament, she knew now why she had done what she did. She knew that the voices she heard were right all along and would get her to safety as long as she listened to them and followed their instructions. But right now, they were not there to tell her what it was that they wanted of her.

As for everything else that she heard people around her talking about, she really had no idea what they meant. She heard the news report about the Fallen Angel, and she heard her name. Things just weren't clear to her yet. The voices would surely tell her what was going on. Everything was too confusing at the moment. She had to wait for the clouding in her head to disperse.

If the voices didn't get her out of here, then Marie would. She would be home soon, everything would be alright then and back to normal.

She was forced to attend therapy sessions in the unit. She really couldn't be bothered with answering their questions, primarily because they kept going on, asking her why she would want to kill someone. Why would she plot to murder someone that was placed in her care? She really had no idea what they were on about and they were beginning to bore her.

Why did they want to question her about her life as a nurse? Her home life? Her sex life? The cheek of them!

The particular therapist she had to see today really bored her.

Jessica Reid, thirties, dyed blonde shoulder length hair with dark tips. At least Sally found amusement in studying her hair and dress sense! Jessica seemed to dress ten years behind the times. Sally had never been too fashion conscious but this girl really needed some help!

Sally wondered if she could sit in silence when the questions began, maybe then she would get taken back to her room and her suffering would end. The constant chatter irritated her; it didn't allow her space in her head to listen to the voices. She needed to listen for them and they were obstructing this process.

Sally sat in the corner of the therapy room, pondering her fate. She was sprawled out across two huge floor cushions. The room was designed for relaxation, comfy sofa, bean bags, cushions, all in pastel colours.

She felt she should take advantage of the opportunity to chill out, after all once she got back to work and her usual shift pattern, her relaxation time would be greatly curtailed.

As she scanned the room she realised there was no ornaments, no books and no real furniture. It wasn't something that she had picked up on before, the bloody drugs they were giving her seemed to frazzle her mind and lower her awareness to her surroundings. Maybe they were wearing off a little, now that would be good.

As Jessica entered the 'comfy room' as they called it, Sally didn't even acknowledge her arrival. She just couldn't be bothered with her today; she had better things to do, like listen out for the voices. She didn't want them to think she was blanking them out, that would really displease them.

'Hi Sally.' Jessica sounded bouncy and cheerful and Sally wasn't in the mood for it.

'What's up?'

'How are you feeling today?'

'Ok.'

'I thought we could begin today by you telling me about your family.'

'No.'

'No what Sally?'

'No, I won't talk about them.'

'Does this subject trouble you Sally?'

'No, I won't talk about them.'

'What is bothering you? Can you tell me about your childhood maybe?'

Silence.

'Sally?' She had turned to face the wall, totally blanking Jessica.

Jessica took a deep breath, 'This is going to be a struggle today if you don't give me a little leeway Sally. If something is bothering you, how about we have a little chat and I can help you with any problems you have.'

The patronising tone in Jessica's voice stuck in Sally's

throat as she heard the words directed at her.

'And how about you just fuck off and leave me alone.' Sally was becoming infuriated by this little upstart now.

'How about you afford me some respect so we can get some issues sorted out Sally?'

'How about you go away and think up how you can stop being so bloody patronising. If you work out the answer to that then maybe I will talk to you.' Sally signalled the end of their interaction by curling up on the floor.

Realising she was not going to get anywhere with Sally, Jessica turned and left the room. She just about managed to say 'Bye' on her way out. She knew attempting to continue any form of conversation with Sally today was going to be fruitless. *'Give her some space,'* she thought, *'and go back and try again later.'*

'Damned psychiatric nurses, always thinking they can get you to tell them what they want to hear. That bitch just picked the wrong person to piss off,' muttered Sally, just as Jessica was out of earshot.

Three hours later Jessica returned to see how Sally was faring. She had not moved from the cushions on the floor, in the corner of the 'comfy room'. Several members of staff had checked on her, peeping around the door, trying to remain unseen doing so. They had failed in their attempts; Sally had spotted their shadows on the wall. She chuckled each time one of them appeared, thinking they were getting one over on her. No way, she thought. I am one step ahead of you all. The longer they remained ignorant of this fact, the sooner she would be able to get herself out of there, and as far away from them as possible.

Jessica this time sat down beside Sally on the cushions. Sally didn't move. Jessica took this as a sign to stay as Sally didn't change her position or turn her back on her.

'Are you ready to talk to me Sally?'

'Not really, I am tired today, but you can stay for a bit if you really need to.'

'That's great.'

'Not really.'

'Oh it is Sally; maybe you can start telling me about your life?'

'What about it?'

'Well, you choose, what part of your life do you want to tell me about?'

'Don't know, my life isn't very interesting.'

'Oh, I think it is Sally, try me anyway.'

'I am a nurse.'

'I think I know that Sally, don't I. Did you enjoy nursing?'

'I do enjoy it. Why did you say *did*?'

'Sorry, I didn't realise. You know you won't be going back to nursing?'

'Of course I will, it is my career, I love my job!'

'Why don't we talk about something else, tell me about your childhood.'

'No.'

'Is there something about your childhood that worried you?'

Sally turned to face the wall, totally blanking Jessica.

'Sally?'

'Go away.'

'Sally, you can talk to me you know. If there something you need to tell me.'

Sally turned sharply towards her, 'I said no.'

'I heard you. It sounds to me like there is something bothering you. I am asking if you need my help?'

'No.'

'Did something bad happen when you were a child Sally?'

Again no response.

'I asked you if something bad happened to you when you were a child. Can you tell me about it?'

There was no verbal reply given. She was curling herself up on the cushions, almost in a foetal position, rocking herself back and forth.

For a moment Jessica watched her. She was unsure of her next move but realised it certainly wasn't going to be verbal.

She reached out towards Sally's arm, to put a reassuring hand on her, just as she did so, Sally let out a loud cry. Jessica withdrew her hand in fright. She wasn't expecting that!

Sally began shouting, crying out and continued rocking back and forth. Her cries were getting louder. Two members of staff appeared at the doorway. Jessica was almost relieved at the sight of them.

Both had quizzical looks on their face. 'I didn't even get to talk with her, not really, she just started all this.'

'Ok,' answered the taller of the two male nurses. 'Let's get her back to her room.' The three of them dragged her to her feet and frogmarched her to her room. Sally continued crying out, incoherent words, seemingly unaware of what was happening to her.

'Go and get her prescription chart and see if she is due a dose of valium.'

'Right.' Jessica went for the chart.

Returning with two five milligram tablets and a blue plastic tumbler of water, Jessica found that Sally was lying on her bed, still curled in the foetal position.

She put the medication in her mouth, and immediately put the tumbler of water to her mouth, giving her no choice but to take some. One of the nurses appeared and gently stroked her throat, Sally seemed unaware of this. She automatically swallowed. The medication had been taken.

'She should calm down a bit now, what happened in there Jess?'

'No idea really. I asked her to tell me about her work

or her family. Then I asked her about her childhood. She just seemed to freak out. Wouldn't answer me and started rocking then screaming out.'

'Better give the doctor a ring, get someone to come and review her. See what they can do for her, shame really, she seemed to be doing so well.'

* * * * *

The voices were strong today; Sally was hearing them loud and clear. They were telling her to get out of the psychiatric unit. Or was it her inner voice that she was hearing? It was definitely the voices that had told her to get the cash and a new passport, she could not deny that. At least she was glad she listened to something they said to her, even if at the time she didn't know why she was doing it, that day seemed months ago.

Sally just wouldn't believe that she could have done what they were telling her. She remembered the video they had shown her, but couldn't understand why she was in it. Why did they say that it was her that murdered the patients? She was a nurse, she looked after them. It was all so confusing.

The voices seemed to know all about it. When they spoke to her they already knew. They were praising her for her work. She didn't understand. None of it made sense yet.

She was beginning to take notice of her surroundings

and the people around her.

'Perhaps the medication was being reduced,' she thought. Something was certainly making it easier to hear the voices.

She certainly wasn't going to let on to them that she was watching them. They were already trying to blame her for the murder of several patients. What would they come up with next? She certainly wasn't going to hang about to find out. The voices had told her what to do. She had to follow what they said. She didn't want any more trouble.

Sally began to watch the staff. She found that they were creatures of habit. They always took their breaks in the same little staff room, located at the end of the main dining room. As a patient in the unit Sally didn't have access to this area but she could see it through a half glass panelled door. *'It wouldn't be real glass,'* she thought, *'not with so many nutters in here.'*

She hadn't paid much attention to her fellow residents whilst in there. She had no idea how long she had been there, her hair could do with a cut though, which gave her an indication that she may have been there weeks rather than days.

The other patients seemed to mope about; they weren't interested in talking to her unless they wanted to borrow a fag. She ignored them all, they had nothing she wanted and she wasn't giving her fags away to anyone.

She began to watch the staff as they came in and out of the key pad door. This was the main entrance and exit of the unit. She had found no other external doors but assumed that there must be more the other side of the half glass door that led to the staff room. She wasn't interested in looking there; she had plenty to occupy her, sneaking around in the main areas. She had found a great vantage point, watching from behind the lounge door when they didn't realise anyone was about.

For a unit where the staff were meant to know the whereabouts of their patients at all times, she was decidedly unimpressed. Maybe it was because the main door had a key pad lock on it that they assumed there were no exit points and no escape routes for them. She would just have to prove them wrong and love every minute of doing so.

After watching many of them going out the door she finally knew the key code. This hadn't been hard to achieve. Four digits, top right, middle, middle left and 0, she wasn't sure of the other numbers but the 0 stood out.

She repeated this every time she saw one of them open the door, 'top right, middle, middle left and 0.' Some of the nurses had even asked her what she was repeating, it was actually written down on her chart, she couldn't believe they were so stupid.

With this information firmly lodged in her mind Sally

tried the code a few times before planning her escape.

The staff always took a supper break after the patients had finished their supper in the evening. Once they were all safely out of the dining room, it was assumed that they would either be in the lounge area or their bedrooms. The bedrooms were locked during the day and they were allowed no access at all. She had often witnessed some of the others kicking up a fuss when they weren't allowed to their rooms. She saw one young girl repeatedly kicking at her bedroom door one day in utter frustration of not being able to get in. Rules were rules, was the only answer she got as she was marched back to the communal areas.

It did seem reasonable to Sally that the rooms were locked. A pang of professionalism hit her, if they were in the rooms then they couldn't be seen by the staff. Someone could harm themselves or have a seizure and no one would be aware of it.

The handover for shift change was held in the main staff office that was positioned almost next to the main entrance door. She could not go anywhere near there at this time, they would see her approach it. At the start of the night shift, two of the staff did the medication round. Most of the patients were ushered into their rooms for this ritual. Once safely in there very few came back into the communal areas. After medications were finished any remaining patients who were in the television lounge were persuaded to go to their rooms to settle down for the night. It seemed to Sally that they had one cushy night duty. All the patients in their rooms, no one wandering about the unit to bother them. They were meant to check on them hourly. Some were on more frequent checks if they were deemed to be a risk, either to themselves or to others.

She had watched them do their checks one night. Hiding in the bathroom, she monitored their movements and studied their routine as if her life depended upon it. To her, it did.

Their routine seemed to vary depending who was in charge of the night shift. One particular male nurse, Tommy, gave the impression he wanted an easy night at work. The staff would give out the medications and have everyone in their rooms by ten o'clock. They would come round and check them at midnight, after eating their supper in the patients' dining room. He would then not send any of the staff to do further checks until six am. That gave them six hours break from their patients. Sally knew why. Having sneaked out of her room one night, she found that all four members of the night staff, including Tommy, who was meant to be in charge of the unit, were asleep, sprawled out on the cushions in the 'comfy room'.

Ideal, she thought, bloody damned ideal.

She watched Tommy and his three sidekicks perform

their ritual of midnight checks, regular as clockwork, pacing about checking the unit and their patients. Hearing them pass her door, she waited a moment then opened it slightly. From her vantage point she could see them checking the rooms further along the corridor. Ten rooms to a corridor, two identical parallel corridors.

Not once did any of them turn to look behind them. They appeared content with the head count; all their patients were in their rooms, most of them asleep she assumed. Closing her door slowly to ensure the click shut was as silent as possible she waited until she heard them pass by her room on their way back to the 'comfy room'. They definitely were creatures of habit. Sure enough, when she dared to exit her room a few minutes later all four of them were sprawled out, chilling. If she wasn't so concerned with her escape she would have thought about ringing the local health authority. They really were taking the piss, sleeping on duty. *'After all, anything could happen couldn't it,'* she thought. Like I could venture out the front door. Totally unnoticed. She stopped herself from laughing out loud at her thoughts. It would serve the lazy bastards right and drop them in the proverbial. Tomorrow morning there would be total pandemonium, and she would be the cause of it all!

Sally returned swiftly and silently to her room, which was only about twenty foot away from the gaggle of staff. If she waited a while she was sure that they would all be asleep. She would give them half an hour. She didn't have a watch; they had taken that away from her along with all the other personal items she'd had with her on her arrival. She was getting a good judge of time, without her watch. There was a clock in the corridor, almost outside the 'comfy room'. She could check that before sneaking a look to ensure they were sleeping.

She misjudged her timing by five minutes. *'Not bad,'* she thought. It was twenty-five past midnight. She peaked through the gap in the open door. Sure enough, four sleeping staff members sprawled out where she usually ended up spending her day.

This was her one and only chance. If they caught her trying the lock then she would surely be marched back to her room and watched all night. They wouldn't leave her alone for a minute.

As she approached the door, she could hear snoring. She had no idea which member of staff it was, she didn't care either. If the other three weren't woken by that sound then she had a good chance of escape. It bode well for her.

She raised one very shaky hand to the key pad. *'Mind over matter,'* she thought. This is my chance; the nerves have to be controlled. I have to get out or the voices will be angry with me and not help me again. She hastily keyed in the four digits, top right, middle, middle left and 0, and turned the handle.

She was surprised that it opened. Goodness knows why this surprised her, it just seemed too easy. She drew the door towards her, widening the gap for her escape. She slid through the widest gap that she dared open and gently pushed it to. She held the latch so that it wouldn't click loudly and alert them and gently released it as the door once again fit snugly in its frame.

The cold midnight air hit her as it breezed around her soothingly. It seemed so long that she had experienced the great outdoors and the natural elements. She savoured the initial experience as though she had not felt it before, time had taught her to forget how wonderful the sense of freedom was. She allowed herself only moments to enjoy it. There was so much to be done she couldn't waste a moment. With no baggage and her new-found freedom she was off. Turning her back on Westwood General for good.

Sally was pleased that she took the time to listen to the voices. It was the posh lady who explained it all to her. She liked to listen to her. She was the one who gave praise. She also seemed for once to be very organised. Sally had listened and acted on the instructions of the posh lady. Three months ago she really didn't understand why she had to do what she was instructed to do but now she saw the whole picture. She appreciated it now but knew she had to act quickly and was confident the instructions could be followed easily. She knew her way round the hospital site well; even in the dark this posed no problem for her. Sally made her way to the garden that lay between the car park and the oncology unit. It was a beautiful garden maintained for the patients to enjoy and relax in. She headed for the main seating area where there were three benches, each one carrying a dedication for someone's departed loved one. It was the middle one that she was most interested in; she knelt in front of it and inspected the ground beneath it. It didn't look as though it had been disturbed. That pleased her immensely.

She began scrabbling with her hands at the earth, pushing it away, and digging down three or four inches. She had taken a chance and it had paid off. She loosened more of the earth until she felt a little plastic package beneath her fingers. She pulled at it to free it completely from its hiding place. Shaking off the excess dirt she checked the contents. Yes, it was all there, cash in sterling and euros, her passport and house keys. She was free again.

* * * * *

Charlie wasted no time in gaining entrance through Sally's front door. He bashed through it with one sharp kick, not for one moment stopping to allow Jackson the chance to gain entry.

'Police!' shouted PC Jackson. Goodness knows what he

was expecting as a response, if any.

They had been advised of Sally's disappearance from the psychiatric unit at six-thirty am. The staff couldn't confirm the time that she actually left the unit. They also appeared to have 'lost' the signing sheets that documented their hourly checks to each patient's bedroom. Not one of them could come up with an adequate explanation of how she could have exited the building. Chalmers had sent two detectives down there post haste to find out exactly what had happened there that night. So far he was totally pissed off with their answers and poor attempts at explaining themselves, '*Another damned investigation into clinical practices at Westwood General,* ' he thought.

Entering the hallway Charlie spotted a familiar figure through an open doorway. He couldn't quite believe the vision in front of him, Sally was sitting almost catatonic on the rug in the lounge, surrounded by dozens of newspaper cuttings, all strewn about the floor, yet appearing not to focus on anything in particular. What on earth was she doing back here? If he'd had any inkling she would have come back home he would have tried here hours ago.

'Sally,' he said, 'shall we get you back?'

'Tell me what is going on?' she said back at him, quickly followed by, 'Who the fuck are you? I have just got home to this, where is my sister?'

Charlie lent down towards Sally, put her hands behind her back and allowed PC Jackson to cuff her.

'No point trying to be a smartarse Sally.'

'I'm not Sally!'

'Right, anything you say. You are still coming with us though.'

'Fuck off, get out of here.' She began to struggle with PC Jackson as he tried to get her to stand up. She tried to hit out at him.

'You can add assault of a police officer to the charges if you want. I am perfectly open to that one Ms Mears, believe me.'

'Charges? What fucking charges?' she paused and looked straight at him before continuing, 'I will scream the place down if you come any nearer to me.' She opened her mouth to mimic the intention to scream, showing her commitment to her threat.

'Get her out of here!' Charlie was sick of her childish antics. He wasn't going to take it from her.

As threatened she began to scream, 'Call the cops, call the fucking cops,' over and over again the same three or four words were all they heard screamed at them.

Again PC Jackson attempted to get her to her feet, without success.

Glancing towards the clippings Charlie saw that they

were all reports on the Fallen Angel and the patient deaths, all thrown about over the rug.

'What was she doing? Why take the trouble to escape the unit to return home?' he thought.

'Planning on going somewhere?' Charlie queried as he saw a rucksack perched on the sofa.

'Get your hands off me!' she managed before continuing her screaming rant.

It took both PC Jackson and DS Hammond to get Sally back on to her feet.

They hadn't brought anyone from the psychiatric unit with them to her flat. It was the last place they thought they would find her. They would deal with her themselves and deposit her back to psychiatric care themselves. The sooner she was back there, the sooner she could get treatment so that they could re-arrest her, get her to court and achieve their much wanted conviction.

Sally did not attempt to respond to either of them, she was trance like, after her initial outburst towards them. She was not even appearing to see that they were there.

As they bundled Sally into the back of the patrol car Charlie rang John, the on call for psychiatry, letting him know they had found her. He confirmed that she should be taken to the secure psychiatric wing at Passmore General

Hospital, John would meet them there with a standby team ready for their arrival. They couldn't risk any more smart moves by her trying to make another escape. This one was a certain danger to the public and maybe to herself. She needed twenty-four hour watch, whether it be police watch or in the psych unit. Charlie was beyond caring. She was going to be watched by someone, even if he had to stay with her himself. He wasn't risking losing her again. He needed this conviction badly.

They would take no chances of her escaping again. It wasn't exactly far for them, Passmore was four miles south of the city and would take them less than ten minutes if the roads were clear. No way was Charlie waiting for John to send a car and member of staff for her.

John really wasn't happy them taking Sally without him or one of their staff with her, she couldn't vouch for her state of mind or how she would react.

Charlie assured her that she was cuffed and they would bring her in themselves.

Dragging her along the hallway Sally started shouting, 'Where is Sally?'

Sally finally decided to speak to them properly when she was in the back of Charlie's car. She was through continuing to protest her innocence. It appeared that she had no recollection of the voices and her recent episode of shouting. She mentioned nothing about it. She was reacting as if nothing out of the ordinary had happened.

She raised her voice and looked directly at Charlie, 'IT'S NOT ME. IT'S NOT ME THAT YOU WANT!'

He didn't dignify her with a reply. She continued in her protestations.

'It's not me; it's not me that you want. Why won't you listen to me? You are kidnapping me. What the hell do you think you are doing you thick bastards?'

She was shouting and screaming at them, trying to struggle with the handcuffs, to no avail. The only thing she was going to achieve was abrasions to the skin around her wrists.

* * * * *

She woke to find herself in a strange room. Where was she? She didn't want to be in these unfamiliar surroundings.

What the hell was she wearing? She looked down at her attire. She appeared to be wearing someone else's nightdress. Nothing else, just someone else's nightdress. She didn't want to be wearing it. Where were her clothes? Where the hell was she? It was all too confusing for her.

Suddenly the door opened and a kind looking nurse walked in, 'Here you go sweetheart,' she said handing her a glass of water and a tablet.

'What is it?'

'Just something to calm your nerves and settle you down so you can think literally.'

'Where is Sally? Where is my sister?'

'Don't worry pet, she'll be back in no time, now take your tablet for me. It will help.'

She seemed so confused, nothing was familiar, she didn't fit in. Why had they brought her here? She'd had such fun during her travels, and now they had spoilt her memories, she tried to remember, but couldn't. They were even taking her memories away, she felt nothing, her soul wasn't right.

She remained catatonic for two months. She was medicated heavily; she found it hard to think at all and had almost given up being able to think for herself again. She would rarely come out of her room and was never seen to be talking with any of the other residents in the unit. The solitude was her only friend.

She wouldn't have any interaction with staff or other patients, she sat on her own, didn't read, didn't watch television and refused to eat. She didn't give the staff any hassle, but certainly wasn't making any progress either.

The psychiatric registrar had commenced a changed regime of drug therapy for her. The change in medications was beginning to work for her. She was supervised taking her drugs to ensure she took them and didn't hide them under her tongue to spit out later. Most of their patients tried that at some stage, they were acutely aware of that one.

When she did start speaking she began protesting she wasn't Sally.

'Why do you ignorant bastards keep calling me Sally? If it's Sally you want then go and get her. Stop pissing me off and let me get on with my life. Goodness knows how long you bastards have had me locked up in here.'

'Come on Sally; let's get you back to your room.'

'Standard bloody reply.'

'What?' queried the nurse.

'That's all you kidnapping bastards keep saying to me. Back to your room Sally, have some pills Sally, get some rest Sally, and talk to us Sally. I am not bloody Sally, how many times do I have to tell you? What's up with you, you stupid idiots? I am Marie!'

'You can be whoever you want to be Sally. Is it Marie who is talking to you today then?'

With that, she was escorted back to her room and 'encouraged' to take her medication.

* * * * *

Cate had visited Sally shortly after she had escaped. She thought seeing Sally would bring closure and she would finally believe that it really was one of her trusted staff that had done this.

Unable to converse with her, Cate didn't manage to lay things to rest, there was something not right, something she wasn't expecting, she knew that nothing Sally could say would justify having killed at least six patients, but this didn't seem to be the same Sally that she had once known! Sally hadn't even recognised her, she just looked straight through her.

The staff told Cate that it was the medication that changed her. This didn't convince Cate. She insisted that Sally wasn't like this when she visited her before she escaped. Sally had looked right at her then although not spoken to her. This time she was different, totally not herself, but maybe they were right; maybe it was just the medication.

* * * * *

Charlie put a coffee down on the table in front of her. 'You need to stop beating yourself up over this Cate,' he said as he took her hand.

'She is just not the same; it is like she has given up trying,' she said. 'What if she didn't do it? What if she just loaded the syringes but never actually did it?'

'Cate, the evidence all throws her way, and if she won't talk to us, what can we do?'

Cate shook her head and squeezed his hand more. It had been almost two months since Sally was re-arrested and, he was right, the evidence was against her, but Cate just couldn't shift the uneasy feeling that it wasn't her, it wasn't the Sally she knew anyway.

'Are you still free for dinner tonight?' he asked, breaking her train of thought.

'Yes,' she smiled broadly. 'Are you cooking or me?' she said with a hearty sigh, as despite all the heartache over the past months, she had actually found her soul mate and he had found his new best friend. Cate knew that she would never replace his wife, she didn't want that, she just knew that they were together and that was a good enough reason to get up every day.

35

Charlie decided that two months sedation and therapy was far longer than he had intended to wait before he had Sally Mears in custody and he wanted to do something about it. If not for the sake of the investigation, then for Cate's sake, so much depended on putting this case to rest.

He arrived, unannounced, as was his style, at the Passmore General Hospital, Psychiatric Unit. He found Joanne in the office along with several other members of the team there.

'DS Hammond, how are you?'

'Doing well and yourself?'

'Fine thank you, what brings you to see us then, Sally Mears?'

'Any idea when she will be fit for transfer to the cells? I have to get this case closed for many reasons!'

'It's not going to be yet Charlie, no way is she ready yet, she refuses to talk to anyone. Keeps saying she isn't Sally and that she is Marie.'

'Part of her psychiatric problems? Some sort of split personality?'

'Well, that is one way of putting it but with her I think that things are much more complicated.'

'That's what Cate says.'

'Within psychiatry we refer to hearing voices as having 'auditory hallucinations', and this is often classified as a symptom of schizophrenia. Having said that, she doesn't seem to be hearing voices, just keeps asking for us to find Sally. Bit beyond me I am afraid detective.'

Charlie sat and pondered for a minute or two.

'Do you mean that Marie and Sally are one?'

'Well, Marie could be the other voice. Sometimes they give the voices names to identify them.'

'Right,' he replied, 'can I see her for a minute?'

'Of course, but I am not sure how she will treat you!'

The only words Sally graced Charlie with were the ones he was glaringly familiar with. 'I am not Sally. Why won't you listen to me?' she said before starting to sob.

Charlie looked at her, and wondered if what Cate actually saw was another person. 'I'm listening,' he said.

'I can prove it to you,' she sniffed.

'How can you prove it to me Sally that you are not Sally, go on, I am giving you a real chance here, one chance though!'

'Take my fucking prints,' she begged, she looked like a woman scorned, angry to the point of explosion.

Charlie didn't quite know how to react, he just kept recalling the words of Cate, *'she just seems so different, she doesn't even have the same look anymore.'*

Charlie decided to send PC Jackson to follow this lead and get Sally's fingerprints. Maybe if he pandered to her just this once he would be able to gain her confidence and finally get his conviction. He thought it was worth a shot, seeing that nothing else he tried seemed to work with her.

Her prints were taken directly to Charlie at his request. He wanted to submit them himself, as if she was lying, he would know she was aware enough to be interviewed by them and face trial.

Charlie opened the envelope that had been brought up to him. He scanned her dabs into his computer. The beauty of this system was that he could look up the dabs they had on record for her when she was first brought into the station and with ease compare the two sets.

'Damn!' Followed swiftly by, 'Hell almighty... What the bloody hell is going on here?'

To his horror, they were not the same. Nothing about the two sets of prints was the same.

Charlie was going to have to admit that they had indeed made a mistake and got Marie and not Sally. This could mean a whole new case in itself if Marie chose to file a complaint.

He called Cate, 'You were right!'

Cate fell silent.

'Cate?'

'Does she know?'

'Not yet.'

'Thank you,' she said.

'No thank you, it just means that it is far from over.'

Officers who searched Sally and Lorraine's flat found a passport in the name of Marie Ann Mears. It stated the same date of birth as their very own Sally Ann Mears. They also found Marie's birth certificate, contained within a small wallet in her travel bag.

Further investigations established that Sally and Marie were actually listed as having two different passport numbers. Officers had found tickets to prove that Marie had been travelling and could not have been involved in the murders on the wards. This was vital evidence as the person in their video tape could only have been Sally.

The passport they found at the flat was certified to be genuine and was in Marie's name and date of birth. Sure enough it was found that she was born in London and had a twin sister, Sally Ann. Unfortunately for Charlie and Chalmers her story checked out.

Sally Ann Mears was also listed as having a current passport. He hoped to goodness that she hadn't used it recently.

'Where the hell had she got to, and how?' Charlie said to Chambers, things were getting too much for him now; this case had gone from the sublime to the ridiculous. He had his collar in the cells once, now it appeared she had disappeared in to thin air, replaced by her twin who had no part in the crime at all but had been treated like a second class citizen for the past months.

'*How much worse could it be?*' he thought.

* * * * *

'Sally used to write to me abut you.'

'She did?' Cate questioned Marie as they sat in the hospital canteen drinking coffee.

'This is much nicer than the stuff they have been giving me,' Marie said, 'but then again I have been drugged up most of the time so it is hardly surprising that it all tasted the same!'

'I am sorry,' Cate said.

'Sorry for what? You helped me, you knew!'

'But I should have made my point clearer.'

'Stop it, it is all fine, the best thing we can all do now is try and get on with a new life.'

Cate nodded.

'And hope that she stays away,' Marie whispered into her drink. Cate noticed a single tear fall down her cheek. At that point she felt helpless.

* * * * *

Sally was sitting on a warm and inviting beach; taking in what she felt was some well-deserved sunshine. 'Those sneaky bastards at the psychiatric unit kept me there against my will, I told you I would get out. Didn't I?' she said looking across the ocean. She didn't feel alone as she had her voices to keep her company, she was tired from fighting them and had settled down to the fact that they were there and that was that.

The posh lady had told her that she deserved a break and was to enjoy herself; they would not be making any demands on her whilst she rested. Sally did feel guilty about not being able to be at home when Marie got back from her travels though. She actually had no idea what had been going on since she had been away.

She was wishing she could see her Marie; she missed her so much and was hoping that she would work out what had happened to her and believe what she told her about the voices.

They had never spoken about the voices but Sally

believed Marie would know what she was talking about once she explained. She wondered if they had both suffered at the hand of their father when they were little. Sally had always assumed that it was just her. The posh lady told her that Marie would understand and that she was to talk to her about it.

Maybe this was the right time to tell her; maybe if she understood the voices too, she would be able to tell the police that it wasn't her that harmed those people. Yet something didn't make sense to her at all, the number six that the detective kept saying she had to face up to.

'Why does it keep repeating itself again and again?' she thought, 'six, six, six,' she muttered. She just couldn't work it out, but it kept on bugging her. *'There must be a reason,'* she thought, as she packed her bits up and headed back to the hostel where she had been staying.

She picked up the Pembrokeshire Echo from the store she regularly visited.

'Bit cold out there today missus?' said the shop keeper, he, Bill, had become a familiar face in her life of late.

'A little, but a good surf I guess, if you surf,' she said feigning interest.

'Hello Lorraine,' a young girl said as she picked up some sweets from the counter.

'She is away with the fairies today if you ask me young'un.'

Bill laughed.

'Me?' Sally said.

'I said hello Lorraine, and you ignored me,' Jess said.

'Oh, Jess I'm sorry, fairies, absolutely!' she said with a smile before putting her money down on the counter. On her way out she turned and took a double look at Jess, 'Six,' she said.

'Six.' Bill answered.

'She had seven, she ate one when I was standing there,' Sally's tone was quite anxious.

'Always let her have a little penny sweet while she chooses,' he laughed, 'luckily they are only a penny, otherwise I'd be pretty skint now, let all the little blighters get away with one sweet!'

At that moment it dawned on her why six deaths didn't make sense. Suddenly she felt a warmth of satisfaction tingle through her body and she smiled broadly as she shut the shop door behind her.

36

Senior Nurse Manager Cate Hammond, was waiting for the third candidate of the morning. She and her two colleagues were conducting interviews for the post of Staff Nurse within their day surgery unit. Cate had commenced her new post six months after leaving Westwood General. She had relocated several hundred miles away and now lived in an idyllic stone cottage, five minutes' walk from the sea front with her two beloved cats and her new husband.

The strain of events in her previous post at Westwood General had led her to take time out from the profession to evaluate her career and indeed her life. She had, after much deliberation, decided to remain in the nursing profession, after all she realised none of it was her fault, she couldn't have prevented Sally Mears from killing her patients.

Yet, through all the upheaval and heartache, she had also found a friend in Marie. She liked her; she had actually liked and respected her sister for the time she knew her. Cate would often stare at Marie, thinking that if Sally were her sister, she wouldn't turn her back on her either.

Cate would often approach the subject with Charlie, usually to a cold answer of, 'maybe she is ill, maybe she couldn't help it, but she is still a murderer *on-the-loose...*'

Once a copper, always a copper she would think.

Cate and her two colleagues were sitting adjacent to each other at a small table; their next interview wasn't for half an hour. She suddenly caught a glimpse of Marie out of the window and decided that it was a good cue to take some fresh air.

'Hey,' she called to her as she swung through the double doors.

'Came out for a fag!' Marie stated holding it up.

'You should give them up.'

'I know but the little gits make me smoke!' she smirked. Marie had moved down to Pembrokeshire to work as a nursery nurse in the school adjacent to the hospital Cate now worked in. She had moved about a month before Cate and Charlie did. She and Sally had grown up there. It was shortly after their mother had died when they were four that their father decided to move.

Cate had visited Marie on a couple of occasions, previous to Charlie making one visit, liking it and deciding to stay.

Just then, Cate was called by a staff nurse, 'Sister, there is an urgent phone call for you!'

'Best take it, probably Charlie not knowing what to do with his lunch I left him to heat up,' she laughed.

She left Marie sat on the bench in the sun, but when she returned Cate's face said a million words.

'Sally!' Marie said immediately, the panic grew inside her, 'I had a feeling things weren't right.'

'Oh, Marie, I am sorry if I scared you,' she said sitting with her. 'It's Lorraine.'

'Who?'

'Lorraine... she was a staff nurse on duty the night the two patients died. Police had arrested her and Tim on suspicion of murder before all the evidence stacked up against Sally.'

'She's confessed?' Marie asked.

'She tried to kill herself you know,' Cate paused, 'she was as white as a sheet, she said she couldn't cope with it. I didn't know what she meant then.' Cate fell silent and started to cry. 'I saved her.'

'What happened to her?' Marie asked rather confused.

'She had counselling and went back to work in Westwood General.'

'So she's confessed?' Marie shook Cate, 'Answer me, is my sister innocent?'

'She's dead!' Cate sobbed.

* * * * *

The car journey to Westwood General was made in silence. Charlie had asked for a police patrol to drive them down as he was still lead investigator on the case. He had made sure he was not taken off the case until it was finally closed.

As they approached the main entrance Marie broke her silence and started to sob.

'She was a good girl; she was always a good girl!'

Cate held her close, 'Sometimes, things happen and we cannot control them.'

'He didn't touch me, it was always Sally.'

Cate looked for a long moment at her.

'Our dad!'

'Enough said,' Cate thought as she held her tighter.

As they walked through the corridors, the reality of what had happened in the place suddenly became very apparent to Cate. She was finding it hard to breathe and thought of the times that had happened to Charlie because of the memories of his wife.

'In there Sir,' a uniform at the entrance of ward 73 said. He pointed them in the direction of the Sister's office, Cate's old office.

There was a body, which had been covered up by white sheets on the floor near the door.

Marie gasped and her legs gave way from under her. Charlie grabbed her and sat her on a chair in the corridor.

'You have to pull yourself together, for Sally's sake,' he said looking at her with compassion she hadn't seen before.

Cate sat with her while Charlie walked back to the body, 'Cause of death?' they overheard him ask.

'OD, insulin!' the doctor announced, 'instant death by all accounts,' he added.

'Marie,' Charlie said turning to her, 'are you ready?'

Marie took a deep breath and stood, falling slightly to the side, where Cate took her weight. They looked at each other momentarily and proceeded to follow Charlie.

Marie stood in the room just feet away from her sister with tears dropping from her eyes.

'I'm sorry, I'm so sorry,' she sobbed, 'I should have helped more, should have looked after you more. What have I done?' she screamed.

Cate pulled up a chair and sat Marie opposite Sally who just stared at her sister.

'They said six!'

Marie blinked back her tears as Sally spoke.

'I didn't harm six!' she said, as she started to rock back and forth. 'Lorraine tried to frame me for a murder I didn't do,' she said with a snigger and looked at Cate, 'it is six now! I made it six... not them."

Silence fell amongst them, Marie felt completely helpless.

'I didn't mean to harm anyone; they said it would just make the noise go away!' Sally added reaching for her sister's hand.

'Who said it Sally?' Marie said entwining her fingers with hers trying to keep her voice steady through the tears that broke almost every word. She couldn't bear seeing her beautiful, childlike sister looking so vulnerable. She had witnessed it for so many years when they were just children. She had promised her that she would look after her, but now she realised she hadn't, it wasn't just Sally who was a murderer, in hindsight it was also her.

ABOUT THE AUTHOR

Maggie Wilson, a trained nurse and midwife, was brought up in the beautiful countryside of Berkshire. She has 26 years experience in Nursing and Midwifery, and has used her extensive career to draw on experiences in many clinical environments within her fiction writing.

Maggie says: 'The legacy of having made my mark in the world and leaving something behind is hugely inspiring to me. For my grandchildren to pick up my books in years to come will be a unique and exciting gift to have left for them.' She continues, 'I've come to realise that truth really is stranger than fiction and that sometimes, with great effort and personal discipline, dreams really can come true!'

WWW.MAGGIEWILSONBOOKS.CO.UK

Follow for up-to-date news on
Maggie Wilson, also find us on Facebook.

INSIDE
OUT

Sandra Russell has cause to report an assault. Having little memory of events leading up to her allegation, she fears no one will believe her.

DC Vicky Trent stumbles across a second woman with cause to report a similar incident –

There seems to be little evidence to support their claims, with the exception of the one thing that they have in common - they have recently been treated in the A&E department of Chesterwood General Hospital.

Was Detective Sergeant Hammond about to relive the nightmare of a previous case at Westwood General?

He can afford to take no chances where patient safety is concerned.

Hot on the trail of the erroneous Dr Matt Robinson - DS Hammond races against time whilst encountering further victims with their own brand of allegations.

And where exactly is the illusive Dr Sam Hughes?

AUGUST 2011